Silver Heights

J.L. Cole

Black Rose Writing | Texas

First printing

This is a work of fiction. Names, characters, businesses, places, events, and incidents are either the products of the author's imagination or used in a fictitious manner. Any resemblance to actual persons, living or dead, or actual events is purely coincidental.

ISBN: 978-1-68433-508-4
PUBLISHED BY BLACK ROSE WRITING
www.blackrosewriting.com

Printed in the United States of America
Suggested Retail Price (SRP) $18.95

Silver Heights is printed in Calluna

*As a planet-friendly publisher, Black Rose Writing does its best to eliminate unnecessary waste to reduce paper usage and energy costs, while never compromising the reading experience. As a result, the final word count vs. page count may not meet common expectations.

To my Dad, for showing me what hard work looks like
and always pushing me to pursue my dreams.

And to my Mom, for inspiring me and being the
kind of person I want to be.

Silver Heights

PART ONE

CHAPTER ONE: RAYNA

January 1995

If things hadn't changed, Rayna Parker probably would've wound up dead by thirty.

That might be a little dramatic. She perhaps would've been depressed, possibly knocked up, maybe homeless, but for sure miserable. Those were the not-so-bad options. The very worst-case, but probably the most-likely scenario, was that Rayna would've ended up exactly like her mother.

The direction of her life took a drastic turn on the day Rayna found herself in a church, wearing a too-small green dress, waiting for a wedding to begin on a hot July afternoon. Despite the setting, it was not a religious revelation that changed the course of her life. It was when her eyes swept across the room and settled on a young man with a broad chest that strained against a blue button-up shirt.

She supposed, thinking back, the real moment of change came a little before that when she agreed to go with her college friend, Chloe Miller, to visit her family ranch. They made the six-hour trip in Chloe's barely held together Dodge Neon, which had no air conditioning and the musty smell of dust mixed with old food radiating off the seats. The last two hours of the drive had been down a straight road with only a static-filled AM radio station for distraction. The farther north they travelled the more spaced out the towns got until it was mainly just rows of fields, dotted now and then with a scattered herd of cattle. Rayna had enjoyed the drive with the wide-open scenery casting out in either direction. There was so much space, so much room to breathe. It was like as the sky opened up and the buildings were replaced by field after field of green grass with blue above, a weight slipped further and further off her shoulders. She couldn't remember the last time she had felt so light.

Just as the water tower of Silver Heights came into view, they turned off on to a gravel road. The floorboards rumbled beneath her feet as dust swirled around them. They drove for almost twenty minutes before Chloe announced that they had finally arrived. Lilac bushes lined the ditches on either side of the approach, their branches supporting shriveled brown clusters of flowers, a shadow of the former beauty they had been just a month ago. Behind them, tall pine trees had stretched upwards casting the long driveway into shade. Two old Ford trucks were parked outside a modest-sized house with a big porch leading up to the front door. Just beyond the house she could glimpse the top of a barn. Rayna had liked it immediately–it had brought to mind the acreage where she used to visit her grandma years ago.

The next day Rayna found herself among strangers, waiting for the wedding of a cousin of the Millers to start ("She's a third cousin," Chloe had said with an eye roll. "Everyone's related out here."). Rayna shifted self-consciously and tried to tug the borrowed dress of Chloe's higher to cover her cleavage. While Rayna and Chloe were of similar height, the rest of their features were opposite. Whereas Rayna was curvy and curly, her friend was slender with long, flowing hair that Rayna could never have achieved no matter how hard she tried.

While Chloe chatted non-stop to those around them, Rayna nonchalantly surveyed the room. She let the murmuring voices wash over her until they blended into one sound of unintelligible chatter, rising and falling like the tide, punctured now and then by a sharp peal of laughter. Her eyes wandered over the people crowded in the little room, drifting from one person to the next. Near the front, an elderly lady sat wearing a blue dress suit and a matching hat fit for the Queen. She was talking loudly with a group of ladies who surround her like planets hovering around the sun. An exuberant outfit for an exuberant person. Rayna watched her for a little, wondering what it was like to be bold enough to wear whatever she wanted just because she damn well felt like it. It must feel so freeing.

Her gaze drifted away and then stopped on *him*, the man in the blue shirt. He was tall, she could tell that even as he sat leaning back, casually chatting with someone behind him. He had short brown hair that looked naturally tousled, and a bit of chest hair peeking over top his collar. He turned and his eyes locked with hers, sending a thrill through her.

"Who is that?" Rayna whispered to Chloe, discreetly nodding in his direction.

"On the end? That's my brother, Ethan. Why? You think he's good looking?"

Rayna made a non-committal sound and forced herself to look away. It wasn't until the reception in the community hall across town that Chloe finally introduced them.

Chloe led Rayna through the crowd to the table where Ethan was about to sit down. "Ethan!" she squealed, standing on her tiptoes to give him a hug.

"Hey Chlo," Ethan said. "Finally decided to come visit us, eh?"

"I thought I would grace you with my presence," Chloe grinned. She turned and gestured to Rayna. "This is Rayna, my friend from Lethbridge."

"Nice to meet you, Rayna," Ethan gave her a crooked smile and extended his hand. "It's good to know there are people out there who can put up with my sister."

"It's really the other way around," Rayna said, enjoying the feel of his big, warm hand around hers.

Real man's hands, Rayna thought. They were rough and calloused, going well with his muscular arms. It was obvious he spent most his time doing manual labour; his skin had that natural sun-kissed look city dwellers tried hard to duplicate with lotions and tanning beds. Chloe and her brother shared the same deep blue eyes, and the same coloured hair, but that was where the similarities ended. Chloe reminded Rayna of a sparrow; small and energetic, flitting from one thing to a next in a storm of constant chatter. Ethan came across more like a large tree; towering a good foot over them both with his strong, solid body.

They sat down and were soon joined by Ethan's friend Daniel. Chloe gave him a hug and introduced him as her honorary brother.

"Nice to meet you," said Daniel, sitting next to Ethan. "Chloe doesn't bring friends home very often. Actually, she doesn't come home at all now."

"I have a busy life," Chloe said, unashamed.

"Yes, we've all heard how important you are now." A voice in the form of a red-haired man said plunking down next to Chloe. "We're all so honoured you've taken the time to come today."

Chloe narrowed her eyes at him, "What are you doing here?"

"I'm here supporting our lovely friends, who are getting married." He leaned across Chloe to Rayna. "Hi, I'm Craig, Chloe's ex-boyfriend who she secretly still loves. She's probably told you about me."

Chloe pushed him back in his seat. "Actually, I haven't mentioned you once."

"That hurts," Craig said. "Ethan, tell your sister to be nice to me."

"You're on your own, I'm afraid," Ethan leaned back with an easy smile. "She doesn't listen to anyone, stubborn as a mule."

Chloe frowned. "You're supposed to be on my side. Besides, you all should be extra nice to me. I brought home a cute girl who you aren't related to, must be a nice change."

Daniel shook his head mockingly, "A couple years in the city and suddenly you're making in-bred jokes? Too good for Silver Heights now?"

"Don't worry, I'll get the city-slicker out of her." Craig put his arm around Chloe, who promptly pushed it off.

Rayna grinned at the exchange while sipping from her water glass. She could feel Ethan's leg pressed slightly against hers under the table, and a nervous energy pulsated through her. She tried to stop looking at him but couldn't help herself. Oh, he was very good looking. He had a bit of a gentle giant thing going, with his laid-back country boy grin. She had a very pleasant vision of that blue button-up shirt slowly sliding off his arms and dropping to the floor, his hands grazing her shoulders as he slid her dress off...

"Can I get you a drink?" he asked, startling her out of her daydream.

Rayna's cheeks flushed. "Sure."

"I'll get you one," Craig said to Chloe. "Don't worry, I know what you like."

"I guess I'll get my own." Daniel sighed, getting up after them.

As soon as they left Chloe turned to Rayna with her eyebrows raised.

"What?" Rayna said.

"My brother?"

"What about him?"

"You have that look in your eye," said Chloe.

"What look?"

"The look like you like what you see."

Rayna snorted, "So?"

"I'm just saying," Chloe said. "Don't break his heart, okay?"

"Oh, stop. We just met."

"I know him, and he likes what he sees too."

"How do you know?"

"Because he hasn't stopped staring at you."

Rayna felt rather pleased at that. "What's with you and Craig?"

"Nothing," Chloe said. "We've been friends since we were born. We dated a bit in high school. End of story."

"He still likes you."

She shook her head. "Not going to happen. If we stayed together, we probably would be married by now, all my high school friends are. I can't think of anything worse– twenty-one, married and stuck here? No thanks."

"So, Rayna," Daniel said after they got back with the drinks. "You go to college with Chloe?"

"Yes, but a different program. I'm studying business," she answered. She ignored the pang of panic she felt whenever she told people that. There was only one more year until she graduated, and it was looking more and more likely that all she would leave with was a massive student debt and a degree that she had no idea what to do with. What she wanted to do was be a writer. Not a journalist though, she didn't have a passion for current events like Chloe did, who was in the Broadcast Journalism program. Rayna wanted to write novels, which everyone knew was next to impossible to make a living doing. She definitely did not have enough money to go the starving artist route, she couldn't even afford to move out of her parents' place, so she picked business in hopes it would lead to some sort of lucrative career path. So far all it was leading to was stress.

"Rayna and I met waitressing," Chloe chipped in.

"I can't even picture you waitressing," Craig said.

"I hate it, I'm always getting in trouble."

"Do you live in Lethbridge?" Daniel asked, ignoring the other two.

"I do, but I was born in Saskatoon. We moved around a lot."

Daniel opened his mouth to ask something else, but Ethan cut him off, "How long are you out for?"

"A month," said Rayna.

Chloe sighed. "Will you two please stop interrogating her?"

"Our poor little Chloe can't stand it if the conversation isn't about her for more than two seconds," Daniel grinned. Before Chloe could respond, the MC got up to start the program. As soon as the dance started, Craig pulled Chloe laughing on to the dance floor.

Daniel leaned over. "Would you-"

"Like to dance?" Ethan finished, cutting him off.

Rayna bit her lip to keep from laughing. "I don't know how to do that type of dancing," she said.

"Two-step? It's easy, I'll show you." Ethan took her hand and led her onto the floor. She saw Daniel smile ruefully after them.

"Just follow my feet," Ethan instructed. "It's quick, quick, slow, slow."

Rayna clumsily tried to get the music to match her feet as Ethan led her. He pressed her close to avoid bumping into someone on the crowded dance floor. She would never forget how she felt in his arms that night. His scent of fresh air and hay mixed with cologne washed over her, making her dizzy as they swayed to a George Strait song. His hand rested gently on her hip as she tilted her head up to look at him. She was close enough to feel the heat radiating off his skin. If she stood on her tiptoes, their lips would have almost touched. She watched his gaze drop to her mouth and knew he was thinking the same thing.

Rayna fell hard and fast for him after that. They spent most the following nights staying up late in the back of his truck, talking and looking at the many stars that were always prominently on display in Silver Heights, their hands intertwined and her heart thumping against her chest. They went horseback riding through the pastures, with the open sky overhead and the lonesome grass hills stretching for miles, unencumbered by houses, roads or street lamps.

It was damn romantic was what it was. Their first kiss had been leaning against the barn for heaven's sake, like a scene straight out of one of the western romance novels Rayna loved to read. Him pressing her against the wood, his hand in her hair and on her hip, sliding tentatively down to graze her backside. It had been the first of many fun and passionate make-outs all over the ranch. No sex though, which she thought a little odd at first, but then she decided it was charming. Sex was how her other relationships had usually started, but this one felt different. This one was different.

Not that Chloe believed her. As they started on the long trip back to Lethbridge after the month was up, Chloe was uncharacteristically silent behind the wheel. She leaned forward with exaggerated concentration as she peered at the empty road.

Rayna finally had enough and turned the radio down. "What's up?" she asked.

"What?"

"What's wrong?"

"Nothing." Chloe continued to stare straight ahead.

"Come on Chlo, is it me and Ethan? Is it too weird for you?"

Chloe looked at her, "You want to do this?"

"I want you to stop being mad at me."

"I'm not mad."

"Right."

"It's just... he's my brother. I don't want him to get hurt. It's been a while since he had a relationship."

"He told me about his ex." Rayna tried not to sound defensive. She knew Ethan had dated his high school sweetheart, Mila, until they were twenty-one when it ended. She also knew he hadn't really been with anyone since then, but she supposed maybe there weren't that many options in Silver Heights.

"You guys are pretty different, I just don't know if it's a good idea."

"What do you mean?"

"Come on Rayna, you've dated how many guys this past year? Two? Three? And you break up with them for no reason."

"Derek broke up with me," Rayna reminded her.

"Yeah, because you never called him, or initiated anything, or even really liked him."

"That's not true."

Except it had been. Her last boyfriend, who'd ended things a few months before Rayna met Ethan, had been nice enough. The sex had been decent and he made her laugh, but he had been a little too pushy. He had an annoying habit of pestering her about how they were never at her place, and how he had yet to meet her parents after being together for five months. Was she not committed to him? Did she not feel the same? She believed his exact words were she was 'closed off and wouldn't let him in.' It was the usual complaint, which led to the demise of many of her relationships.

"Look Rayna, I just want what's best for both of you. Ethan's like my parents, dedicated church-goers who will probably never live anywhere other than Silver Heights. Just make sure you're on the same page."

"We're just getting to know each other, Chlo." Rayna said, irritated. Why couldn't Chloe just let her be happy? When was the last time she had felt like this? Not in a while, maybe not ever. Besides, it wasn't like anything needed to be set in stone right away. They were young, they were having fun.

Except eight months later, after several long-distance phone calls and one dramatic surprise visit leading to a spontaneous proposal, here she was. Clad in white, standing in the back room of a church she had never been in before, waiting to walk down the aisle.

So, perhaps Chloe had a reason to lecture her after all.

Rayna paced back and forth around the room, white lace swishing around her legs. She was doing her best not to panic for two very important reasons. One, she did not necessarily trust her new deodorant brand, and she had a feeling sweat stains and body odour would not contribute to her bridal beauty. And two, she didn't want Chloe noticing how close to freaking out she was, because she was pretty sure her one and only bridesmaid would encourage her to leave Ethan at the altar if given half a chance.

"Where is he?" Rayna said for the umpteenth time. It didn't help to ask, but it at least broke the uncomfortable silence.

Chloe looked up from her position slouched against the wall. "I'm sure he will be here soon."

Rayna wasn't. Just once she needed her father to show up and be there for her. It wasn't too much to ask. She hadn't expected him or her mom to be at her high school graduation, or her basketball games or school concerts... but she needed them here today, if only for appearances' sake. She spun and continued her pacing, the silvery veil pinned to the dark mass of curls on her head swishing around her arms. "Can you go look for him? Please?" she said over her shoulder.

Chloe sighed and pushed herself up. Rayna watched her leave and relaxed a bit when the door closed. The last thing she needed was Chloe's sullen presence right now. It seemed like all they did was argue lately-Rayna was surprised she had even agreed to be in the wedding party. The night Rayna told Chloe she was engaged to her brother hadn't been great, but Chloe had truly lost it when Rayna told her the wedding would be in two months.

"Two months? What about graduation? What about moving to Calgary with me? What will you even *do* out there?" Chloe had fired the questions like a machine gun.

Rayna opened her mouth then shut it. She would say 'be happy,' but Chloe wouldn't understand. Chloe didn't get Rayna's world. She was one of those effortlessly happy people, all giddy and talkative and full of potential. Rayna wasn't like that, not even close.

She slid a sweaty hand down the side of her dress, trying to smooth the lacy fabric clinging to her hips. She could hear the murmuring voices of the guests in the sanctuary and the soft tones of recorded instrumental music serenading them. There weren't many people in attendance, and those who had come were mostly Ethan's guests.

That was okay though, Rayna didn't need a big wedding. She would have been happy signing papers at the courthouse, or better yet, eloping in Vegas. But it was clear Ethan's family would've revolted. They could barely hide their disapproval as it was. A church wedding was non-negotiable, as Ethan's mom Carol had declared with her arms folded over her chest and her eyes practically spitting fire. It didn't really matter to Rayna, the result would be the same anyway. At the end of the day she would be Mrs. Ethan Miller, a married woman.

Married.

The realization sent jolts of panic across her gut. *Calm down, Rayna,* she scolded herself. It was normal to be nervous on your wedding day. She thought it must be, although she didn't know many people her age who were married. It wasn't like twenty-one was an unheard-of age to get married. She was old enough to vote and drink in any country now. She wasn't a child, yet she kind of still felt like one. The person she was presenting to the world today looked grown-up, even pretty, but that wasn't her. It was a stranger playing dress up.

Rayna tried to steady herself as she waited for Chloe to come back. She had no idea what time it was, but they must be getting close to starting.

Where the hell was her dad? What on earth was taking so long? Maybe Chloe couldn't find him. Maybe he had left. Maybe they both had.

Or maybe Chloe was trying to kidnap Ethan and drag him from the church. Rayna wouldn't put it past her.

She waved ridiculous image from her head. Despite what Chloe might think (what probably everyone at this wedding was thinking), this was a good decision. She was not making a mistake.

She wasn't.

Rayna shook her head. It was no use second guessing–she was in the church wearing the dress. This was happening.

Pushing her thoughts aside, she stared at the door, waiting for it to open and for Chloe to enter. She debated peeking outside and flagging someone down to go find her, but just as she was about to lurch across the room the door opened and Chloe slipped in with Rayna's father in tow.

"Found him," Chloe said, a little breathless. She looked pretty with her hair pinned up and her cheeks the same rosy pink as her bridesmaid dress. "They're going to start soon."

"Okay," Rayna said, her voice higher than normal.

"You okay?"

Rayna nodded. "A little nervous."

"You look beautiful," Chloe said, which Rayna assumed was the closest she would get to saying anything supportive. There was a slight lull as the instrumental music faded away and a new track started up. Chloe whirled and moved past Rayna's dad and opened the door slightly.

"That's the entrance music, they must be seating my grandparents." She threw a glance at the silent man standing beside her, then back at Rayna. "I'll give you two a minute?"

Rayna was about to say no, but Chloe slipped out and gently shut the door. She shifted, feeling even more self-conscious as she looked at her father across the room. The man before her was her own blood, yet so much still a stranger. He looked older than his forty-three years. What was left of his hair had thinned and turned grey, deep lines furrowed his brow and his once-muscular frame had turned slack with a slight pouch for a belly. He looked like a man life had thrown its worst at. In some ways it had.

He spoke first, breaking the silence. "You look nice."

"Thanks." She moved to stand next to him by the door, the lace swishing around her legs.

"Are you sure you want to do this?"

Rayna looked at him, surprised.

"It's no small thing, what you're about to do. If you want, we can leave right now."

Rayna blinked, emotion rushing into her chest. "I... I know."

But did she? A year ago, she didn't even know Ethan existed. Now she was pledging herself to him and changing everything in her life. A minute a go she was going to graduate university and attempt to make her own way. Now she was on the verge of committing herself to a man and to a life completely different from the one she was used to. Well, that was the idea, wasn't it?

"I know," she said more firmly. "I want this."

Chloe opened the door, "It's time, see you up there." Then she disappeared.

Rayna took her dad's arm and let him lead her out. They walked down the hallway and passed through the doors into the sanctuary. The guests scattered around the pews all stood. Rayna could see her mom in the front aisle, staring stonily at her. She looked away and focused straight ahead, where Ethan stood on the steps of the stage waiting for her. His hands folded in front of him and a big, confident grin on his face.

Rayna took a breath and started towards him.

CHAPTER TWO: ETHAN

When Ethan was a boy, he had almost died. It had been stupid really, his own fault. His dad had gotten the bright idea to try and raise some pigs, more for fun than anything. As if they didn't have enough work to do with their four-hundred head of cattle and two-thousand acres of grain land. Ethan had sat on the fence and watched his dad unload the pigs from the trailer-they were great big, ugly things. Clumps of mud and dung clung to their bristly hair as they snorted and squealed an unearthly high-pitched sound. And the *smell*, it was like a mixture of garbage and sewer. Ethan remembered thinking if Wilber had smelled this bad, then the spider would have definitely been less inclined to save him. There were five of them altogether; all sows, and they must have weighed over five-hundred pounds each.

Dad had come up to Ethan and leaned against the fence, watching them. "Now don't go into the pen okay? Pigs can be dangerous if you mess with them."

Ethan nodded, but immediately the thrill of danger coursed through him. Surely, they weren't that dangerous. They were just pigs, he was pretty fast... he bet he could outrun them no problem. As soon as his dad had turned and walked away, Ethan quickly eased himself down the wood fence on the side of the pigs. He eyed them shuffling around and snorting, but they didn't seem to pay him much mind. As quick as he could, he darted across the pen and leaped onto the other side, triumphant. Nothing had happened. They didn't even notice him. Feeling slightly disappointed, Ethan climbed down and picked up a piece of mud that had hardened in the sun.

"Hey, stupid." He threw it at the nearest pig, who snorted and skirted away. Ethan ventured out a little farther from the fence and bent to pick up another one. Suddenly, there was a loud squeal behind him. Ethan looked up in time to see one of the biggest pigs barreling straight for him. He turned to run, but he slipped in the mud and the pig bore down and hit him hard, knocking him flat on his back. Terrible pain shot through his leg. He screamed as he looked down and saw she had bitten him and was throwing her head back and forth. Ethan writhed and twisted, trying to get away. His dad suddenly appeared and yelled at the pig, hitting her in the face until she let go. He grabbed Ethan and ran for the fence, hauling them both over.

Death by pig would have been a sorry way to go. But some people in this world had met their end this way, as his dad told him later during a furious lecture. As luck would have it, Ethan only had a minor incident. There wasn't any serious damage done, although he did have a permanent scar on his leg now. When his dad asked him why he'd deliberately disobeyed him and put himself in danger, Ethan had looked up tearfully from the hospital bed where the doctor was putting in stitches and said he didn't know. But Ethan had known–it was the thrill of danger that made him want to jump off the fence and harass an animal that was more than triple his weight. The intoxicating feeling of not knowing how it would turn out, that anything could happen.

Ethan got that same feeling the day his mother warned him against Rayna.

It happened on the day he ended up proposing. Not that he'd planned to do so when he woke up that morning. He hadn't even planned on going to see Rayna that day.

It had still been dark out when Ethan got up and wrapped himself in layers of clothes before heading out to his truck. He wished he had thought to start it earlier to let it warm up. That winter had been one of the worst ones he could remember. Every morning he and his dad had to spread straw out for the cows to bed down in and snow plow a trail in the field so they could actually walk. After feeding they spent a good chunk of time breaking up the ice in the dugout for the cows to be able to drink. The poor buggers looked miserable every morning with their ice-crusted backs all hunched together, wind and snow swirling around them.

On those kinds of days, Ethan often wondered how the Aboriginals had survived way back in the day on this unforgiving land without the use of modern inventions to keep them warm and fed. He couldn't imagine how much harder life was then. He supposed they spent most of their time around a fire waiting for spring, which sometimes didn't bother to come until almost May. More than once Ethan wished he lived somewhere warmer. But then on the still days, when the blanket of snow first covered the ground, sparkling and winking in the sunlight, and the trees stood tall, with their branches straining to support their new white burden, Ethan's love for the land rekindled. Then when spring finally came and the new calves began to drop, the winter months just made him appreciate it all the more.

It was a part of him, as it was a part of the generations before him, since Great-Grandpa Thomas had brought his family over from Ireland to start a new life for himself. Apparently, Thomas Miller had walked for eight days until he'd come upon Silver Heights. He'd stopped here because it had the biggest, healthiest trees. Most others took the small-treed land and least amount of bush, because it had been easier to clear and settle on. Great-Granddad Thomas had done the exact opposite, and it turned out that the land he'd chosen was the best for farming and cattle.

As Ethan did most mornings, he went over to his parents' place for a cup of coffee before he and his dad set out for the day. Ethan fought a yawn as he backed out of his driveway, the snow crunching beneath the tires. As was the case for most nights back then, Ethan had been up till almost three in the morning talking on the phone with Rayna. He was basically living on coffee and the long-distance bills were killing him, but it was worth it to hear her voice. At that point, Ethan had gone down to Lethbridge twice to see her, crashing on a sofa at Chloe's place when he did.

It was only a short drive over to where his parents lived, a few miles down the road in what they called the Big House, but he could barely feel his fingers by the time he arrived. He parked in front of the house and turned the truck off. The short walk to the porch left him breathless. The cold seeped into him, freezing the air in his lungs. He shrugged off his coat and work coveralls and hung them on the peg inside the door next to his father's things and walked down the hall. Both his parents were already up, he could hear their muffled voices coming from the kitchen. They looked up as he walked in and immediately stopped talking– he got the feeling they had just been discussing something to do with him.

"Morning," Ethan said, sitting across from his dad in the place he had always sat growing up.

"Morning. How was your night?" His mom passed him a mug full of coffee and he cradled it in his hands, warming them.

"Good. Going to be another cold one today."

His dad grunted in agreement as he fiddled with his coffee cup.

An awkward silence had fallen and Ethan eyed them suspiciously. "What? What's going on?"

His dad ran his hand over his bald head and glanced helplessly at Ethan's mom. "Well son. It's just that, your mom and I feel…" He trailed away and looked miserably at his cup.

"Oh, for goodness' sake." His mom turned to him. "Your father and I feel you're getting a bit too serious about that girl."

"What? With Ray?"

Mom nodded. "I know you have been seeing her for a few months now, but we just don't think it's a good idea."

"And why is that?"

"Did you know she doesn't attend church?"

"How do you know?"

"Chloe told me when they were out. She tried to use it as an excuse not to come. She said it would make Rayna uncomfortable. Also, it's obvious her home life isn't great, what with the way she talked and dressed when she was here."

"Why does any of that matter?"

"The person you marry needs to at least believe in the same things you do. You may not realize it now, but if you marry someone so different from yourself, it will be a very long road."

"Ah Mom. This is too much this early in the morning," Ethan said, forcing his voice to sound light.

"You need to know exactly who you are involved with before you get too invested. That's all I'm saying," his mom had said. "Did you even meet her parents when you were down there?"

"No, she said they were on holiday."

He hadn't added that both times he had gone down there she had an excuse for why they never went to her place. He didn't think on it much though, she would introduce him when she was ready. Although, he would think given they had been together for six months now that she would be ready enough.

He forced the thought from his head. "Anyway, I didn't think you were the type to judge someone based on their upbringing."

"The rules are different when it's the person your son could wind up marrying. I'm sure she is a lovely girl... I'm not saying she isn't, but I don't know if she is right for you. What about Mila? You two were so good together."

"Please stop bringing her up."

"I'm just saying, you will be twenty-six this year, you don't want to waste time. Most of your friends are getting married, you can't tell me you're not thinking of it."

Ethan had looked at his dad for help, but he kept his eyes firmly on his coffee mug. "Geez, Mom."

"Don't 'geez, Mom' me. This is serious."

"Sorry. We need to go, it's getting light out." Ethan stood. "I appreciate your concern, but you don't know Rayna like I do."

"I don't think you're thinking clearly about this. She..."

"All right Carol, enough," Dad said, standing as well. "We need to get going and you've said your piece."

His mom pursed her lips, biting back whatever it was she was going to say as they headed for the door.

Ethan had tried not to let his mom's words get to him. Yes, he and Rayna were different, but he liked that about her. It at least made things interesting. His mom had always been a worrier, but she needed to learn when to take a step back. It was this same controlling behavior that caused her and Chloe to nearly tear each other's heads off whenever his sister came home.

Rayna just needed to come out again and spend time with his mom. They needed to get to know one another better, and then his mom would come around. She better anyway, because Ethan wasn't planning on ending things. He was planning on sticking around as long as Rayna would have him.

It had been a while since Ethan had been with anyone. After the disastrous Mila saga, he hadn't wanted to dive into anything new. He had his work on the ranch to keep him busy, so he didn't spend much time thinking about it. Then Rayna came. He felt a warm pleasure just thinking of her, with her dark, spiraling curls that grazed her shoulders and her eyes like little pools of chocolate with golden flakes scattered throughout. Her voice, which was deep for a girl, vibrated through him to his very core when she laughed. She had a way of looking at him that made him want to wrap his arms around her, pull her to his chest and keep her safe. And a way of kissing him that made him want to do a whole lot of other things.

He spent most of the day thinking of her and thinking about what his mom had said. By that afternoon the urge to see her had become almost unbearable. He decided he would drive up to surprise her that night and ask point-blank if he could meet her parents to get that worry out of the way. With this plan in mind, Ethan had called Dan to see if he could cover for him with chores and then he hit the road, hoping to get there before midnight.

So really, it ended up being his mom's fault that he went up there that night. She'd planted thoughts of marriage and meeting parents and Rayna in his head like a weed, which had rapidly grown. He hadn't proposed because his mom told him Rayna wasn't right for him. Of course not. It had nothing to do with his mom or that reckless feeling, like he was leaping off a ledge into dangerous territory. One thing had simply led to another, and that evening he'd called to tell his shocked parents he and Rayna were getting married.

She came towards him now, looking stunningly beautiful in her white wedding gown. Ethan watched her come closer, barely able to keep still. In a few moments she would be his.

His wife.

He stepped forward to take her hand from her dad, ready to jump off the edge and see what happened.

CHAPTER THREE: RAYNA

"I'm so glad that's done." Rayna kicked off her shoes and reclined back on the hotel bed.

Ethan chuckled as he loosened his tie and rummaged through his overnight bag. "It wasn't that bad, was it?"

"Between our mothers scowling at us all night and my side of the family sneaking in alcohol..." Rayna shook her head.

Ethan's mom, her new *mother-in-law*, had insisted there shouldn't be any alcohol at her son's wedding. That of course did not sit well with Rayna's parents and their few friends, who not-so-stealthily kept sneaking drinks in and got spectacularly plastered at the back before the speeches even began. This did not go unnoticed–Rayna was sure Ethan's mom had now confirmed her worst fears that her son had hitched himself to a bad apple. It didn't matter that Rayna had only drank water the entire night; the appalled look on Carol's face as she watched Rayna's mom drunkenly sway to "YMCA" said it all. To be fair, Rayna had been pretty mortified as well watching her mother's eccentric dancing. Her father, of course, had been nowhere to be found at that point. But Rayna's embarrassment was an old one, familiar to her in every way. It was just another humiliating moment in a lifetime of memories, and a clear confirmation that moving as far away as possible was in everyone's best interest.

"I'm just glad it's over," Rayna said again.

Ethan straightened, holding a bottle of champagne and two plastic wineglasses. He sat on the edge of the bed. "Probably not the wedding you imagined for yourself, eh?" He popped the cork and poured her a glass.

Rayna sat up and took the offered drink. "I don't know what I imagined." She took a sip, enjoying the bubbles fizzing on her tongue and sliding down her throat. "This is nice."

"So," Ethan said fiddling with his glass.

"What?"

He shifted on the bed, clearly uncomfortable. "We never really... talked about this part."

"Talked about what?"

"About... um... sex. Our past and stuff." His face was turning a delicate shade of red as he stared down at his hands.

"Oh, like how many people we've...?"

"So, you have then? I mean, I kind of figured. Not that it's obvious, I just know you're not religious or anything..." He trailed off helplessly.

Rayna's eyebrows rose. "Are you asking if I'm a virgin?"

Was he expecting her to be? Was that still a thing?

"Cause I'm not," she added flatly.

She had been fifteen the first time, still a child in so many ways. She had been at a party when a boy named Chase took an interest in her. Rayna could still remember how electric she'd felt next to him with his arm against hers. Suddenly he'd moved towards her and pressed his mouth firmly on hers. Rayna had pulled back in surprise.

Chase had smiled and said, "Have you ever been kissed before?"

Rayna had shook her head no.

"You should be, you should be kissed every day with lips like yours." Then he bent and kissed her again. He had moved so slowly and sweetly, Rayna had melted into him. Then he kept going, feeling her body with his hands, pushing her down on the couch and easing himself on top of her.

Rayna had got home at almost two in the morning, but her parents hadn't waited up for her–they probably hadn't even noticed she had gone out. She went up to her room and sat on her bed for a long time, hugging her knees to her chest.

Since then there had been others. Sometimes it was great, sometimes it wasn't. She never imagined one day she would have to sit and discuss it all with her husband on her wedding night. She looked at the man beside her now and felt a shimmer of shame.

"I was young the first time," she said, then went on quickly, needing to explain. "We never talked about it, my mom and me. About saving it for someone special or whatever. I had to figure stuff out on my own."

Ethan put his hand on hers, stopping her. "It's okay, I don't need details or anything."

"I take it you've only been with Mila?"

Probably, she thought a little bitterly. Of course, he would be better than her in this area too. Rayna had seen a picture of Mila in Ethan's photo album of them together at graduation. She was tall, blond and drop dead gorgeous. The image of him with her made Rayna feel a little sick. He probably thought he was downgrading.

"Well..."

"What? More?" Rayna looked at him surprised. "It's okay, I just didn't know you would do casual. Chloe gave me a huge lecture about how you didn't do that."

Actually, it would be better this way, at least they would be a little more even.

"No, it's not that."

Then it dawned on her. The reason they always stopped when things got heated and why he was so awkward talking about it now. She had figured he'd wanted to take things slow and she had been fine with that. Then they were engaged and planning the wedding, so it seemed to make sense to just keep waiting, but suddenly it was a little clearer.

"Are you... I mean, have you ever been with someone?" Rayna asked.

"No, this will be a first." He shot her a nervous grin. "We did talk about it growing up. At length. Basically, in my teens I thought the fires of Hell would consume me if I looked at a girl wrong."

"Really?" Rayna couldn't keep the shock out of her voice. She didn't think she knew anyone over twenty-five who hadn't done it yet–she barely knew anyone her own. "But Chloe..."

"Please don't tell me anything about my sister's sex life," Ethan said quickly.

"Sorry. It's just, I didn't realize. But, weren't you and Mila together for like, five years?"

"Six. We were kids when we started dating."

Rayna thought about this. "So, was just sex off limits? Or was everything? All the bases?"

"I guess you could say anything not PG."

"How could you date someone for years and not... you know."

Especially someone who looked like Mila.

"Cold showers." He huffed a laugh.

"Oh."

"Anyway, I didn't want you to... well, to think I know what I'm doing." He was dangerously close to crushing the plastic cup in his hand.

Rayna's heart squeezed in her chest. *I really do love him.* The thought released something inside her she hadn't realized she was holding on to, like she'd been waiting all day for a confirmation that she wasn't a complete idiot for getting married. *I love him.* She leaned in and kissed him.

When they paused for breath, she whispered against his lips, "Let's change that."

He grinned and took their cups and set them on the nightstand.

"Just one sec, okay? Actually, can you unzip me?" Rayna stood and turned so her back was to him. Ethan moved behind her and ran his hands across her shoulders and down her back. She shivered at his touch. He unlaced her dress, then kissed her neck lightly.

"One sec," she whispered, clutching her dress to her. She grabbed her overnight bag and hurried to the bathroom. Rayna quickly shimmied out of the dress and let it fall heavily to the floor. She put on the white lacy lingerie outfit she had carefully selected a few days ago and strategically positioned her breasts for the best cleavage. Then she took the pins out of her hair and did her best to smooth down her curls with water from the tap.

Rayna stared at herself in the mirror, turning this way and that. She may not be a virgin, but she was still nervous. This was the start of everything; of their lives together and being a married couple. She took one more shaky breath and turned to leave the bathroom. She paused as she opened the door and saw the scene before her. Ethan had placed candles all around the room and turned the lights off, casting them in a dim glow. He waited, leaning against the headboard with his shirt slightly unbuttoned and his hair a little tousled. She had to say, her husband was incredibly sexy.

Thinking those words sent tremors through her, *my husband.*

He sat up straighter when he saw her. "Wow," he said, his eyes travelling down her body.

She smiled as tears unexpectedly filled her eyes.

"Everything okay?" He moved towards her.

"It's fine. It's just..." She laughed, wiping her face. "It's just this is really nice."

Ethan sat on the edge of the bed and pulled her gently to him. "You look amazing," he whispered.

Rayna bent and gave him a lingering kiss. They moved backwards onto the bed, her hands sliding down and unbuttoning his shirt. He shrugged out of it and pushed it to the floor. She ran her fingers through the soft curls of his chest hair, enjoying the feeling of it against her palms.

Ethan reached down and slowly pulled the lingerie up over her head, his eyes fastening on her freed breasts rising and falling with each breath. He brought his hands up and cupped them, gently rubbing his thumb over her. She moaned against his lips and tilted her head back as he kissed her throat. His hand sneaked around her waist and gently he eased her down so she lay on her back and he hovered over top. He continued to kiss her neck, moving ever so slowly down to her chest, and lavished attention on her soft curves. She squirmed underneath him, arching her back and digging her hands into his hair.

He took his time, kissing and caressing her with his tongue until she was ready to burst. He moved back up to her mouth, kissing her hard. His hand travelled down her body until he reached her lacy undergarment, then he pulled them off so she was completely bare.

He paused as he looked at her. "You're so beautiful," he murmured.

Lightly, he ran his hand down her stomach and stopped, hovering below her belly button, barely touching her there. She smiled and took his hand, gently moving it down to help him explore. His breath came out in ragged bursts, and she felt him tremble. She undid the button of his pants and pushed them down. He paused, helping her take them off. Rayna laid back and moved until she could feel him against her. He breathed harshly as she slid her hand down and touched him. Gently, she guided him to her. Ethan gasped as he entered, and she wrapped her legs around him, pulling him deeper still. His chest shuddered as he gripped the headboard and rocked hard back and forth, moving fast. He groaned then collapsed on her. They laid still, their breath moving as one, their bodies hot and sticky with each other's sweat.

He pushed himself up on one hand and looked down at her. "I love you, Rayna."

"I love you too." She ran her fingers through his hair and smiled. "That was pretty good, you know."

"Yeah?"

"Yeah."

"Next time, I'll get more than a 'pretty good.'" He grinned.

She laughed. "You know what I mean."

He looked at her, suddenly serious. "We're going to be good, me and you."

"I know." She said it so quietly she wasn't sure he heard.

CHAPTER FOUR: CAROL

Carol told him not to marry her.

She knew the moment she saw that girl exactly what kind of person she was. Not that it had mattered then, Carol wasn't the type to judge. No, it only began to matter when her fool of a son decided he wanted to date her.

Then it mattered.

Quite a bit.

It was last summer when Chloe came barging into the house with Rayna in tow. Carol had been looking forward to Chloe's visit for weeks. She didn't come home much these days. It had been a fight to get her to agree to come for as long as a month, so Carol had accepted the condition that Chloe would bring a friend.

Carol had been putting the finishing touches on a hamburger soup for supper when she heard the front door open and slam shut, followed by Chloe's voice hollering that she was home.

"In the kitchen." Carol answered, excitedly untying the apron from around her waist.

Chloe came bounding in wearing ridiculously short shorts, of course, but Carol was determined to keep a friendly air and didn't point it out. "Ah, the prodigal daughter returns." Carol had said and gave her a hug.

"Ha, ha." Chloe rolled her eyes (a gestured Carol despised) then turned to the girl behind her. "Mom, this is Rayna."

The girl smiled at her. She had her dark hair pulled up in a bun and was wearing cut-off jean shorts with a low-cut tank top, which showed off the perspiration winking on her generous chest.

"Nice to meet you," Rayna said.

"Yes." Carol gave her a tight smile.

Rayna turned to Chloe. "I'll go get the rest of the shit out of the car." She pulled the tank top away from her stomach. "It's hot as hell outside."

A foul mouth too. This was who her daughter was keeping company with in Lethbridge. Terrific. She probably had a tattoo on her lower back as well.

It didn't even occur to Carol that Ethan would be the least bit interested in this girl with a sailor's mouth and exposed breasts. Why would it? Ethan had always been sensible. She supposed now, looking back at the situation, she could see how a summer fling would have developed. He was a single twenty-five-year-old male, and Rayna was new, young and pretty.

Fine.

A summer fling.

Carol could handle that. Then fall came and then winter and still they were in a relationship. It was around then that Carol realized she needed to wake Ethan out of his daydream. It wasn't a practical relationship. Ethan needed someone sturdy, someone capable of supporting him on the ranch. So, she had a talk with Ethan and what does the boy do? He drives down to Lethbridge that night and proposes. Not only that, he informed her the wedding would be as soon as they could book a place. Then, when she pressed to know why exactly they were rushing things, he wouldn't give her a straight answer. *They just wanted to*, like that was a good enough reason to bind yourself to someone for life. Were her children trying to drive her mad? She expected nothing less from Chloe, who had always been difficult, but Ethan? What happened to the head the good Lord had placed on his shoulders? He barely knew this girl.

"You can't control their decisions, Carol." Her husband Jim helpfully said as she ranted to him.

"I know that." Carol had snapped. "But I can *help*, can't I? I'm their mother, I'm not going to bite my tongue while they act like idiots."

Jim had shrugged, about as useful as he always was when it came to this sort of thing. He had never been one for dealing with conflict.

It wasn't just the obvious fact that Rayna had different moral standards than Ethan. It was more than that. Carol had grown up in Silver Heights; she had been born and raised on a farm a few miles west of where she lived now. She knew this place, knew the challenges of the lifestyle they lived. The unpredictable and long working hours could take their toll on the best of them, but especially on a farmer's wife. It was double-duty being married to a man who ranched. Not only were you expected to help on the busy days–

chasing cattle, running combines and fixing fences–but you were also in charge of making sure the house didn't fall to disrepair and that everyone's bellies were full. Then just as you lay down to relax, guaranteed a helpful neighbour would call to let you know you had cows out wandering down the road.

Carol never felt it was unfair. Her husband was a hard worker and she did all she could to support him, but this life wasn't meant for just any woman. No, it certainly was not. Did this little city-slicker think she could just waltz in and everything would be hunky-dory? She had no idea what she had agreed to when she'd decided to follow Ethan out here. This place wasn't for the tender-footed. It wasn't for the lazy, and seeing as how Rayna and Chloe both slept in till almost ten every day they had been out this summer, Carol was fairly certain Rayna hadn't a clue about real life out here.

So, it had been with both their interests at heart when she had tried to talk to Ethan. Now look at the mess they were in. It would not end well, that much Carol knew.

Carol's phone rang, scattering her thoughts. She picked up the receiver and twisted the cord in her hand. "Hello?"

"Hi Carol, how are you? It's Margie calling."

Annoyance rose within her. Margie was an elderly lady from church who loved to be in the middle of other people's business. Oh, how she nearly exploded with glee when she heard about Ethan's quick marriage. She probably was calling to try and get more gossip to report to the ladies in her Bible study. "Hi, Margie. I'm fine thanks, how are you?"

"Oh good. That boy of yours back from the honeymoon yet?"

Uh huh, just as Carol suspected.

"He got home yesterday."

"Will they be at church this Sunday? A couple of us old gals got them a little something for the wedding."

"Well, that's nice..."

"It's a quilt. Beautiful pattern, Janet got us the material."

"Very nice Margie, I'm sure they will love it."

"We wanted to come to the wedding, but it was a little short notice, you know."

Fish all you want, I'm not giving you a thing, Carol thought, tightening her grip on the phone.

"Uh huh. I got to go Margie, I'll see you Sunday." It was always best to keep these conversations as brief as possible.

"So, they will be there? Ethan and his wife? His wife goes to church, right? She only came once when she was out we noticed," Margie pressed.

"Of course she does. I'll see you." Carol hung up and stared at the phone, thinking. Perhaps she needed to go pay her daughter-in-law a little visit. Just to make sure they were on the same page.

Yes, that would be a good idea. She needed to let Rayna know exactly what was expected of her out here. Time for the honeymoon to be over and reality to set in. She couldn't say she didn't warn them.

CHAPTER FIVE: RAYNA

Rayna took a few steps back and squinted at the picture she had just hung. She had been going non-stop for the past two hours, unpacking and arranging the few things she'd brought from Lethbridge. As well as putting away the overwhelming number of wedding presents someone had moved into the house while they were away on their honeymoon. The community had all got them gifts, even though hardly any of them had made it to the wedding. At the moment, Rayna was trying to decide where to hang all the pictures and wall decor she had slowly accumulated over the years. Next to her book collection and writing journals, her wall art was one of her most prized possessions. She had just hung one of her favourite pictures above the kitchen sink. It was a painting of a line of colourful birds perched on a tree branch. Their heads were tilted in different directions and their feathers were slightly ruffled, as if they had just landed and were filling the sky with their happy chirping.

Rayna felt a rush of pleasure looking around her new home. *Home*, that's what this place really was. It wasn't just a house; it was a home. It wasn't anything fancy, but it was a decent size. There was a master bedroom with an en-suite, two extra bedrooms and a bathroom on the main floor. The living room had enough space for two couches facing one another and a coffee table in between, with a fireplace in the corner. Carpet covered the floor in the living room and in the bedrooms, but hardwood claimed the kitchen and hallways. The walls were painted a light eggshell blue, which Rayna found she quite liked. While Ethan had done a good job keeping it clean, it was obvious he was a bachelor. He had no décor of his own besides a few mounted deer antlers, and there seemed to be a permanent smell of bacon, like it had seeped into the walls.

Rayna loved it. This was a place she would spend years, not picking up and moving, but *staying*. Putting down roots, raising babies, having friends over and growing old. It was almost overwhelming. All her life she had been used to being unsettled, but now for the first time she could pack away her suitcases and let them collect dust.

This morning she had awakened to a racket of deep squawks and shrill chirping as some enthusiastic birds had exchanged their morning greetings outside her bedroom window. For a heartbeat she hadn't remember where she was. The unfamiliar sounds seemed so foreign to the roar of traffic punctured by sirens that she was used to. Sunlight poured through the gaps in the blinds, causing strips of light to fall across the bedding where she laid snug under a quilted blanket. Ethan had long since gotten up and started the day, so she had just laid there for a moment longer with the sleepy warmth that surrounded her and enjoyed the unfamiliar feeling of sheer happiness.

Rayna smiled to herself and bent to pick up a box with a new toaster in it when she heard something behind her. She turned around and her heart slammed in her throat.

"Fuck!" Rayna's hand fluttered to her chest.

Carol had suddenly appeared and was shrugging off her jacket. She frowned at Rayna. "Watch your language."

"Sorry." Rayna looked around her. Ethan wasn't with her.

Great.

This was the first time she was totally alone with her new mother-in-law. "You scared me. I didn't hear you come in."

"Yes, well, I thought I would come by and see how you were settling in." Carol looked around with her lips pressed together in a tight line. "I don't think that picture belongs in the kitchen, do you?" She pointed to the one Rayna had just hung.

"I like it there."

"It would look better in the living room." She sat at the table and looked at Rayna expectantly. Rayna noticed for the first time how her mother-in-law bore a striking resemblance to her daughter. They shared the same light brown hair, high cheekbones and slender frame. Whereas Chloe wore her hair long, her mother kept hers cut above the shoulder and pulled back in a ponytail.

"Um... would you like something to drink?" Rayna asked.

"No, thank you. I want to have a bit of a chat though. Have a seat."

I'll stand, thank you. The thought came pettishly to mind and Rayna immediately chided herself. There was no need for her to be childish and rude. Just because Rayna sensed from the beginning that Carol didn't like her, didn't mean it was true. Yes, she had been difficult about the whole fast wedding thing, but to be fair, having her only son meet and marry in less time than it took for a pregnant woman to grow another human being had to have been hard. Rayna thought charitably that she should at least give her the benefit of the doubt.

Rayna pulled out a chair and sat down stiffly, then forced her shoulders to relax. "What can I do for you, Mrs. Miller?"

"To start, you can call me Carol, since you're a 'Mrs. Miller' now. I would say you can call me Mom, but I think that would make us both uncomfortable."

Her tone had a slight aggressive edge to it that made any good intentions Rayna had melt away. "Yes, I think so."

"Right, well, we didn't get much of a chance to talk before the wedding. It did happen very quickly. Ethan assures me you're not pregnant."

"Not that I'm aware of," Rayna answered dryly.

Carol shot her a look. "I do think you two moved way too fast, but there's nothing to be done about it now."

"Is there something I can do for you, Carol?" Rayna knew she sounded rude, but she decided she didn't care.

"I want to talk to you about church," said Carol.

"What about it?"

"Church is very important to this family. To Ethan. I understand you don't usually attend and I hope you won't cause a problem over it."

"I think this is something Ethan and I can talk about, but I don't have an issue with church." Rayna hadn't really given it much thought, but the time she'd went she hadn't minded it.

"But do you have faith?" Carol pressed. "It's important you and Ethan..."

"That's a little personal," Rayna cut in. *And none of your damn business,* her tone implied. She wasn't about to dive into a heart-to-heart conversation with this woman.

"It's not personal. It's a simple, straightforward question."

"Why does it matter?"

"Why does it matter? Because it affects everything! I don't want my grandkids growing up without Christian values."

"Well, as you said, nothing can be done about it now."

There was a tense silence as they stared at one another. Rayna could feel a very clear line being drawn between them, and she waited to see if Carol would cross it.

"Well," Carol said finally, getting to her feet. "I'll see you at church on Sunday then. We'll be having lunch at our place after. Ethan always comes."

"I'll talk to him and see if we will," Rayna said. "We'll let you know."

Carol paused by the doorway, "I know what this is, you and Ethan. He saw a sweet little girl in need and being the kind of guy he is, he wanted to save you. He doesn't see you for who you really are. But I do. You think you're on some adventure marrying a rancher and moving out here. You think you won, getting my son to marry you. It won't be long before you both realize what I already know. That this was a mistake. I don't believe in divorce, but if it comes to that, I hope you have the good sense not to have children first."

With that she turned and left.

Rayna was too stunned to say anything. She sat frozen until the front door slammed shut. "Well, up yours too," she said into the silence.

Rayna stood and picked up the toaster. She stared, lost in thought, at her warped reflection in the shiny stainless-steel exterior. The thing was, Carol had just effectively voiced everything Rayna was trying hard not to think about. What if Ethan had only married her because of some misguided sense of duty? Rayna didn't know why Carol felt she needed saving—maybe because she came across as someone who was lost, which was sort of true. But Carol couldn't possibly know how right she was, unless Ethan had told her something...

No, Rayna told herself firmly. Ethan wouldn't have said anything, and he didn't save her. She didn't need saving. She could have taken care of things on her own. She had it handled before he came along. She'd had a plan in place. Get educated, get a good job, get out. That was the plan. Marrying Ethan just... accelerated it a bit.

And yet. He sort of did save her. Rayna remembered the relief she had that night when he proposed and those words crossed his lips, 'Come with me and leave all this.' He'd even paid off her student loan. Is that how he viewed their marriage? Like he was her saviour?

To hell with that. Rayna would not go through life feeling like she owed her husband anything. And okay, maybe it did feel like an adventure, but what the hell was wrong with that?

And maybe we will wake up one day and realize it was a mistake.

No.

Carol was wrong about that. Rayna refused to let her poison this. Deciding to take a break, Rayna set the toaster back in the box and grabbed a bottle of wine from the fridge. She poured herself a generous amount and took a few gulps. Usually, she was very careful about drinking, and it was only three in the afternoon, but just because she was sure Carol wouldn't approve, Rayna poured herself a second glass.

****

That night Rayna lay in bed beside Ethan, feeling exhausted. It had taken several hours to put everything away, and then she had to scramble to make supper, which ended up getting cold before Ethan finally came in from working. She understood he needed to work– he had explained how they were getting ready for the busy season coming up and there was a lot to do– but he could have at least called her to let her know he would be late. He wasn't the bloody king of the universe. Rayna had other things to do besides make a supper that wasn't even going to get eaten.

No, stop it, Rayna, she told herself firmly. *You're overthinking things because of Carol.* She knew she was. It wasn't Ethan's fault; it was his mother's. Still, it would help a little if Ethan acknowledged she was in a bad mood, but as of yet he seemed not to notice anything was off. It made her even more annoyed.

Ethan sighed gratefully as his head hit the pillow. He rolled over and put his arm across Rayna and kissed her on the cheek. She fought the urge to wipe it off as a child would.

"I had a delightful visit with your mother today," she said, unable to hold it in any longer. Originally, Rayna planned not to complain to him, she didn't want to be *that* wife. But, well, he was annoying her too.

"Oh?" Ethan said, nuzzling against her neck.

Rayna subtly moved away from him. "Yes. Is she always going to pop by unannounced and not bother to even knock?"

"Probably."

"That's not okay, Ethan."

Ethan sighed and pushed himself up. Resting his head on his hand, he looked down at her. "She means well, Ray, just give it some time."

"She doesn't think I'm good enough for you."

"That's not true, she's just protective." He ran his hand lightly over her shoulders and despite her anger she shivered at his touch. "Can we not talk about my mom right now?"

"What do you want to talk about then?"

Ethan grinned. "I don't really want to talk about anything. I only just started having sex, you know."

He leaned down to kiss her, but Rayna put her hand up stopping him. "Do you feel like you saved me?"

Ethan flopped down and rubbed his hand over his face. "What?"

"Why did you marry me?" It was her turn to roll over and lean above him.

"Because I love you, Rayna. I want to spend the rest of my life with you, and because I was a twenty-six-year-old virgin and horny."

Rayna swatted him. "I'm serious."

"So am I!"

"You want to go to church, right?" Rayna said.

"Yes, I like to go."

"Do we have to go to your mom's after?"

Ethan sighed. "We don't have to, but I would like to. Ray, I work with my parents, which means we will see them a lot. It would be best for everyone if you could try with them."

"I'm not the problem," Rayna said hotly.

"Okay, okay." He waited a heartbeat then said, "Are you finished?"

"Fine." Rayna plopped back down.

There was a slight pause then he said tentatively, "Can we have sex now?"

Rayna snorted a laugh. He took it as the sign to go ahead and enthusiastically turned to her for a kiss. A few moments later, Ethan was sound asleep with his leg overtop of Rayna's. She lay on her back, listening to his steady breaths, and stared into the darkness.

Carol was wrong. She knew nothing about her or about them. It wasn't a mistake. She had made the right decision. Rayna closed her eyes, willing sleep to come. The thought drifted across her mind before she could stop it; *didn't I?*

CHAPTER SIX: RAYNA

Rayna was six years old when she first started keeping secrets.

She discovered that lying came hand in hand with keeping secrets, so she became a liar that day too.

She had observed the other children's parents who had come to the kindergarten tea were sitting proudly at the tables with their child between them. They smiled and laughed; the dads looking proudly at the various crafts presented before them, their moms kissing their cheeks affectionately. Rayna had stood uncertainly a little ways away from the group, eyeing the doorway. She knew her parents would not be coming, having seen the letter from the teacher left unopened on the counter that morning. Rayna had moved it onto the couch, hoping her mom would take notice of it there, but apparently, she hadn't, or if she had she didn't care.

The teacher, Ms. Davis, came over and bent down in front of Rayna and asked, "Are your parents coming today, Rayna?"

Rayna immediately answered, "They're sick." The lie slid so smoothly off her tongue she almost surprised herself.

"That's okay, you can sit with me." Ms. Davis took her by the hand and gently led her to an empty table. Rayna saw Ms. Davis exchange some knowing looks with the other adults and she squirmed with shame. It wasn't the first time she was the only kid without parents there, and it wouldn't be the last.

Throughout her school years, lying only became easier, and her secrets stayed hidden. It wasn't hard to keep up since Rayna changed schools every couple of years. She developed a little story to tell her friends if they ever asked. She said her dad wasn't around because he worked with the government. She thought it sounded like an important and busy job. Her dad actually worked for an engineering company, but that seemed boring to Rayna and she wasn't really sure what he did. She told the other kids her mom was sick with cancer or something, so it was easier to go to their house instead of hers. That's why her mom was never at the school concerts or the field trips.

It never occurred to her to ask her parents to come to anything–she'd developed an understanding early on that wasn't something they did. And she never, ever asked friends to come over. It was too risky. She never knew what she would find when she opened the door and walked into the house. Sometimes, her mom would be flying around the kitchen preparing supper and humming to herself. On those days, Rayna would sit at the table with her homework and happily chat about her day and taste whatever it was her mom was cooking.

Other days, Rayna would walk in and her mom would be lying on the couch with an empty wine glass dangling from her hand as she stared vacantly ahead. Some days were even worse. Some days, Rayna found her mom laying as still as a statue on the floor, vomit by her mouth, and she would try to wipe it and wake her up. Other times, her mom's moods swung unpredictably and Rayna did her best to remain unseen. Her mom liked to talk to her when she was in one of these moods. She liked to complain to Rayna about different things; her job, her life, Rayna's dad...and her favourite, Rayna herself. These days were more common than not.

When Rayna came home from school and saw her mom with an empty wine bottle and a second already on the go, she tried to tiptoe to her bedroom, but she wasn't fast enough.

Her mom had raised her head from the couch and peered blurry-eyed at her. "Rayna? Is that you? Come in here," she called, her words slurred and heavy like she had cotton in her mouth.

Rayna shuffled in with her head bent, "Yes, Mom?"

"Sit up, I hate when you slouch."

Rayna straightened her shoulders.

"How am I raising such a messy child?" Mom said. "Your hair is a mess."

"Sorry." Rayna did her best to tame her hair, but she had been born with wild, springing curls and had trouble keeping them in order.

"Sorry? God, my fucking life. How did I end up here, with such a messy child?" Mom sighed and narrowed her eyes at Rayna, the next insult already on her lips. Rayna stayed stock-still, letting her mom's words wash over her as she went on and on.

When her dad got home, he took one look at the situation and his face twisted. "Christ, Alice, leave the girl alone."

Mom sprang off the couch and followed him into the kitchen, "Where the fuck do you think you're going? Don't walk away from me."

"Calm down, you're acting like a crazy bitch."

A smashing sound indicated the first missed blow of some plate or cup or whatever it was her mom aimed at her father's head. Their voices rose as their fight escalated. Half the time they didn't even know what they were fighting about; all they knew was they wanted to tear into each other.

Rayna would take the opportunity of being left temporarily alone to slide into her favourite hiding spot, the space between the couch and the wall. She kept certain things back there; a few toys, a couple books and most importantly, her notebook. There she would sit crouched, blocking out the roar of their voices as she determinedly entered her own worlds. She would flip open her notebook and continue with whatever story she was working on, then when she couldn't think of what else to write she would use her toys to act out what she had written. When finally, the door slammed, signaling the exit of her father, she would peer around the top of the couch to make sure the coast was clear, then quietly as she could she would make her way to the fridge to see what she could find for supper.

Sometimes, her dad wouldn't come back for days and Rayna wasn't sure if he was ever going to. He always did though. He would show up smelling of something strong that made Rayna wrinkle her nose. He would ruffle her hair as she sat eating cereal, as if nothing had happened. It was a game of pretend that they all liked to play. They pretended Mom didn't always smell like wine and Dad didn't smell like bourbon. Rayna would pretend not to hear the fights and her parents would pretend, sometimes, that she wasn't there at all.

The very best times were when Rayna got to visit her grandma's little acreage. Rayna usually got to go for a weekend once a month when they lived close enough, and then for most of the summer holidays. Her grandma would greet her on the front porch with a bone-crushing hug and Rayna would feel a weight slip off her shoulders and sail away with the car that had dropped her off. She spent most of her days playing in the woods while Grandma worked in her garden. Rayna would help collect eggs from the hens and feed Grandma's old horse, Huck, oats from a bucket. They usually always had soup for lunch; her grandma could make the most creative, delicious soups.

She and Grandma were quite similar, Grandma said so herself, much to Rayna's delight. They both had very curly hair, Grandma's even used to be dark like Rayna's was. They also both liked to be outside, and they were both writers. Grandma had a whole shelf in her living room of books she had written. Rayna would stare at them and gently run her fingers down their spines. One day she would have her own shelf with her books on them.

She told her grandma this, and she smiled at her. "Of course you will! They will be the best books ever. Now read me one of your new stories, I want to hear what my little writer has been working on."

And Rayna would. She never shared her stories with her parents, or with anyone else really. But her grandma was different, she understood that stories were little bits of yourself and you didn't just go throwing them around.

At night she would curl up in her bed and her grandma would read her a chapter from whatever book they had picked out together. Just as Rayna started to fall asleep, her grandma would lean over, kiss her forehead and whisper, "I love you, little bug." Rayna would feel herself completely relax for the first time since her last visit.

There was no place Rayna loved more than the little blue farmhouse. It always smelled good, a mixture of fresh baking and a flowery scent that clung to her grandma's skin. Every inch of the walls was covered with memories and trinkets. It couldn't be more different from Rayna's own house, which had bare walls and very little décor. Rayna could spend hours walking slowly along, studying Grandma's things–it was like a personalized museum.

There were pictures of Rayna's mom in various stages of youth, signs with funny little sayings on them such as "Experience Wildlife, Have Children," and images of her grandpa, who never smiled because he didn't like showing his crooked teeth. Sometimes her grandma would point to a picture and tell Rayna some funny story linked with it. Her favourite was one that hung above the kitchen sink; it was a black-and-white picture of Grandma and a few others taken probably when they were in their late twenties. They were all sitting in the living room; her grandma was in a housecoat while everyone else was dressed formally. She told Rayna how her grandpa had a fancy work event that evening, which she had refused to go to (they had a fight that day about something, she couldn't remember what). He had come home after, very intoxicated, at three in the morning with a few friends. They woke her grandma up and made her come take a picture with them. Even though she had just gotten out of bed, she looked lovely with her dark curls swept behind her shoulders and her round lips fighting between a frown and a smile.

Rayna loved to sit and study the photograph and try to imagine the moments before and after the camera's button was clicked. Her grandfather, who looked very handsome in the picture with his arm casually around Grandma's shoulders, would die in a car accident only a year after the photo was taken. Grandma would raise her daughter by herself and never marry again. Rayna would peer hard at their faces, wondering what they thought life had in store for them at that moment. They probably never would have guessed their futures.

Rayna was eleven years old the last time saw her grandma. Mom had come this time and was sitting in the living room with Grandma while Rayna laid flat on her stomach in the hallway. She had been absorbed in the game she was playing with her dolls when the voices of her grandma and her mom became louder, shattering the world she had been in.

"You are both out of control." Grandma was saying. "You need to get your life in order."

"Don't pretend like you know anything that goes on in my life." Mom had spat. "You have no idea."

"I know that you can barely take care of yourself, much less Rayna," Grandma said. "And until you get back on your feet, she should stay here with me."

Rayna's heart had leapt in her chest at those words. *Yes, please say yes,* she silently pleaded with her mom.

"You want to steal my daughter from me now?" Mom's voice was full of rage. "How dare you. You have some nerve."

"You're a drunk Alice, you need help. You and Greg both need..."

Rayna could hear the slap from where she was in the hallway. She scrambled to her feet and hurried into the living room. Grandma was clutching her cheek, a shocked look on her face.

Mom turned and saw Rayna standing there. "We're leaving." She grabbed Rayna by the arm and hauled her towards the door.

"I don't want to go, I want to stay with Grandma." Rayna had tried to stop, she grabbed the walls as she passed, but her mom kept dragging her forward. "Grandma! Grandma!"

Grandma came, her eyes red. "Stop Alice. Just wait, please."

"Stay out of my life!" Mom had yelled. They were outside now, Rayna was screaming and crying as she got shoved into the car. Grandma came around beside her and opened the door.

Rayna threw herself into Grandma's arms. "I want to stay with you."

"Shh... baby girl, it's okay," Grandma said, stroking her hair. Mom came around and pulled her mom off Rayna and slammed the door shut. Rayna had sobbed into her hands, listening to the rise of voices outside. Mom finally got in the driver's seat and started the car.

Rayna had pressed her face to the window and watched her grandma standing in the driveway until she faded from view. "I hate you," Rayna whispered to her mom.

Her mom heard though and slammed on the brakes. She turned around in her seat and smacked Rayna hard in the face. Rayna was too stunned to move. Her face scorched with her mother's imprint. Without a word, her mom turned back and continued to drive. The next day, Rayna had come home from school and a moving van was outside their house. She never saw the farmhouse again until she was fifteen, when she and her mom went to clean it out after Grandma had passed. The doctors said she died from a heart attack. Rayna knew better. She had died from a broken heart.

The house seemed a little smaller than Rayna had remembered it being when she returned to clean it out after four years away, but other than that it looked exactly the same. She half-expected her grandma to come meet them on the front porch when they pulled up. Despite knowing she wouldn't, Rayna had stared at the door in anticipation when she got out of the car, and a crushing weight of disappointment engulfed her when she did not appear. She walked in numbly as the familiar scent surrounded her. The kitchen looked as if her grandma had just walked out of the room; a tea cup was sitting on the table with still a sip left, cookies were saran-wrapped on a plate and in the fridge there was a pot of leftover soup. On the fridge were pictures of Rayna until she was eleven years old, like she had been frozen in time. Rayna had wandered through the house, lightly running her hands over her grandma's things. She went into the living room to find her mom mercilessly tearing things off the walls and stuffing them into cardboard boxes.

"Are you going to help me or what?" Mom had said over her shoulder. "Look at all this junk."

Rayna stood still, watching. "What are you going to do with it all?"

"Donate most of it, throw out the rest," Mom said. "Put personal pictures in this box, no one will want those."

Rayna's voice trembled, "How can you be like that? How can you not want to keep anything?"

"I don't like clutter," Mom answered. "Get going please Rayna, I don't want to be here all day."

A wave of fury vibrated through her. She turned her back on her mom and started carefully removing things from the wall. She pulled off a sign that said 'Fill a House with Love and it becomes a Home.' Rayna stared at it, the feeling of loss so great it threatened to overwhelm her. This was the place she had felt most loved; the place that had been her home. After today, she wasn't likely ever coming back. Rayna breathed in great gulps of air, fighting down her emotions until she'd stuffed them deep inside her. She placed the sign in the donation box, then went over to the bookshelf and picked three of the books her grandma had written. She put them carefully in her backpack by the door and then went back to the living room to help pack up the rest of her memories.

Rayna hadn't thought about the farmhouse in a long time, not until she took a trip out to Silver Heights last year. The countryside had been such a strong mirror of the little acreage that it made her heart ache. When she arrived back home after her month away visiting Chloe's hometown it had been quite late, she opened the door and let herself into the house.

"Rayna? Is that you?" Her mom had called. Rayna's heart immediately dropped. She could hear the drink in her mom's voice.

"Hey, Mom." Rayna had said, going into the kitchen where her mom sat slumped in the chair, her hair a mess and her wineglass, as ever, inches from her hand.

"Come sit," her mom demanded.

"No, Mom, I'm going to unpack."

"Sit with me, just for a bit." Her mom went to pat the chair next to her but missed and almost fell over.

Rayna sat on the edge of the seat. "Where's Dad?"

"Out, of course. God, I hate him sometimes." She poured more wine. "I really fucked up, you know? Don't marry young, Rayna."

"Okay, Mom."

"I mean it. Such a fuckin' mess. I could have been happy. God, I hate work."

Rayna sat stiffly in her chair as her mom rambled on and on, one topic leading to the next, each linked by how miserable life was. This was Rayna's role, to sit and to listen to all the shit her mom needed to get out.

Finally, when her mom was swaying more than talking, Rayna stood up and helped her to her feet.

"Let's go to bed." Rayna led her mom down the hallway. She helped her go to the washroom, then she got her to bed and made sure she was on her side. Rayna stared down at her mom lying in the semi-darkness, her mumbling talk making no sense.

"I met someone," Rayna said quietly.

"Oh?" Her mom raised a groggy head.

"He's a rancher."

Her mom flopped back down and rolled over. "I wonder how long this one will last."

Rayna didn't answer. She backed out of the room and went to the kitchen and cleaned up the mess, then went up to her bedroom and sat on her bed. Nothing had changed while she was away. Of course, Rayna hadn't expected it to, but it felt like she had lived a different life the past few weeks and it was a little shocking being back. She had forgotten this was what her real life was, not out riding horses on a beautiful ranch in the country.

As the days turned into weeks, Rayna found herself thinking almost obsessively about the quiet little town in the middle of nowhere. In her mind the colours of the sky and the land were brighter than they had been, the air a little clearer and the smell a little fresher. At night she dreamt about a farmhouse which looked a lot like her grandma's old place. Coming out of the door to greet her was a boy with laughing blue eyes and large, strong hands. She dreamt of a life full of love and purpose. One so very different from all she had known so far.

CHAPTER SEVEN: ETHAN

The Silver Heights Baptist Church was as familiar to the twelve-hundred community members as their own houses were. The modest-sized white building stood proudly near the center of town. Its stain-glass windows filled the wide sanctuary with a colourful array of light, and a large solemn cross was used as a backdrop behind the handmade wooden pulpit.

Ethan had sat in the same wooden pew his entire life. As a kid he used to lie on his back and watch the ceiling fans swirl in a steady circle while the elderly pastor's words rumbled overhead. Pastor Eric had been the pastor at Silver Heights for many years. He had been retired for a while now, and a younger man named Pastor Tom had taken his place. For the more youthful congregates, this change had been extremely welcome. They approved of his exuberant sermons and how he passionately exclaimed his points every Sunday, pacing the stage like a lion as he eyed the pews like he was issuing a challenge. The significant number of elderly parishioners in the church, however, often complained about his brashness as they adjusted their hearing aids and exchanged barely concealed eye rolls when he slammed his fist down yet again.

Ethan liked Pastor Tom and his wife, Angie, who had become good friends over the years, and he enjoyed church. He liked going every Sunday and visiting with his neighbours and friends as they exchanged news and talked about crops and the cattle market. He enjoyed the one time a week when he had an excuse to take most of the day off and make the half-hour trip into town.

But today he was nervous.

Today would be the first time he and Rayna went as a married couple, and while he knew folks around here meant well, they could also be a little overbearing. It started almost as soon as they walked in. People rushed over to shake their hands and throw their names at Rayna with excited voices. A few of the ladies went right in for a hug, which Rayna awkwardly returned while shooting Ethan a panicked look over their shoulders. Margie, the leader of the pack of elderly ladies, came over and proudly pressed a thick handmade quilt into Rayna's hands. He finally pulled Rayna through to their pew, then during announcements Pastor Tom himself beamingly pointed out the return of the honeymooners, which led to an energetic round of clapping.

Rayna, her cheeks slightly pink from all the attention, leaned over and whispered to him, "Bit of a celebrity here, eh?"

Ethan shook his head, "It's like this for everyone." Which was very much the truth. Whenever someone went through anything significant in life, good or bad, the community would surround them with comfort, encouragement or sympathy; whatever the situation called for. It was one aspect of small-town living that Ethan appreciated, but he knew it could be a little much for some.

He kept shooting looks at Rayna throughout the worship songs and during the sermon (which thankfully only had a few moments of exuberant fist banging, nothing too out there that might scare Rayna off). When they were dismissed from the service, Ethan's shoulders relaxed. It had gone fairly well; he thought. He turned to say something to Rayna but found she was already standing to go.

"I'll meet you in the truck, okay?" She awkwardly tucked the quilt under her arm and headed towards the door before he could say anything.

Ethan watched her shake off the many people trying to stop her for a chat as she made her way towards the front doors. He started to go after her when Daniel and Craig came up to him.

"Welcome home!" Craig said, clapping him on the shoulder. "A newlywed man! How was the honeymoon?" He wiggled his eyebrows suggestively.

Ethan shrugged Craig's arm off his shoulders. "It was good."

"That's all you have to say? It was good?"

Daniel grinned. "He doesn't want to brag to us unmarried folk."

Craig looked him over, his eyebrows shooting up towards his ginger hair. "Yes, he is looking very pleased with himself up there on his marital high horse."

"Well, I would be too," Daniel said. "Everyone's treating him like a bonafide hero for getting hitched."

"They're just relieved one of us made it out of bachelorhood," Craig said. "The population of Silver Heights was starting to not look so good."

Ethan snorted. "Are you guys done yet?"

"Where is the famed Mrs. Miller anyway?" Daniel asked, cranking his head, looking around.

Before Ethan could answer, Pastor Tom rushed in and vigorously shook his hand, congratulating him. A tide of people surged towards him, everyone wanting to visit. They all looked around, obviously wondering where the much-talked-about bride had disappeared to. Ethan ruefully waved goodbye to Craig and Dan and did his best to chat politely while slowly making his way towards the door. He finally pacified the last of the well-wishers and hurried out to the parking lot to his truck, where Rayna sat hunched in the passenger seat.

"Everything okay?" he asked, shutting the door.

"Yeah, sorry." Rayna rubbed her hand over her face. "I just... it was a little overwhelming."

"A lot of people wanted to meet you," Ethan said casually, trying to keep the annoyance out of his voice. He didn't enjoy being abandoned in there and having to make excuses for her when people asked where she went.

"I met a lot of people when we went in."

"They wanted to visit with you though."

"I know."

"You could have made a bit of an effort..."

"Okay, Ethan. I'm sorry." Her voice took on a hard edge. "I was uncomfortable, it was like everyone was staring at me the whole time. Can we just go, please?"

Ethan bit back his reply, deciding it wasn't worth the fight. He turned the key in the ignition, starting the truck. "Are you fine going to my mom's?"

Rayna sighed. "I'm kind of tired of visiting. Can we just eat somewhere in town?"

"The only place open is the Chinese restaurant," Ethan said.

Rayna wrinkled her nose. "No, not Chinese. Let's go by the grocery store and I'll get some stuff to make lunch."

"It's not open Sundays."

"Why?"

"Because it's Sunday."

"Is anything open?"

"Yeah, the Chinese restaurant."

"Great."

Ethan paused. "So...?"

"Fine! You win. Let's go to your mom's."

"We don't have to..."

"For fuck's sake, Ethan. Please, just go."

Ethan backed out of the parking lot and headed out of town. He tapped his fingers on the steering wheel; the sound filling the silence between them.

Finally, he couldn't stand the tension easing off her any longer. "You okay?" he asked.

"Stop asking me that," Rayna snapped.

Ethan stared at her, then flicked his eyes back on to the road. He was fairly certain the honeymoon stage was supposed to last a little longer than a few weeks. He looked over again at his stone-faced wife staring determinedly out the side window and felt a wave of unease. He didn't understand why she was suddenly acting moody. He had never known her to be like this before. As they turned off the pavement and hit the dirt road towards his parents' home, Ethan wondered briefly if maybe he didn't know his wife as well as he thought he did.

****

A few weeks later, Ethan had coaxed Rayna into helping with cows. He urged the quad to go a little faster, the wind whipping across his face with Rayna's arms wrapped firmly around his middle. The field rushed by in a blur of brown and green as around them gophers darted between their dug holes. More and more of the critters poked their heads up to investigate the loud roar splitting through the usually quiet air. A few confident ones scampered across the quads path, diving into their holes before the tire could catch them. A hawk flapped its wings threateningly from its perch on a fence post as it watched the activity on the ground and waited for its chance to pounce on its prey.

Ethan released the gas and rolled to a stop next to his dad, who was on his own quad. They faced the cowherd which mostly ignored them. Some cows were lying down chewing their cud, others were up and grazing as calves sprinted in between them.

"All right," Dad said, adjusting his baseball cap. "We're going to start with pulling twenty-five pairs. Just taking a couple at a time, got to make sure they're right."

"Sounds good," Ethan said. He leaned back into Rayna, "Ready for this?" Her chin grazed his back as she nodded.

"Let's get going," Dad said. "I'll try to pull some out and you two will chase them far enough from the herd that they won't wander back, alright?"

Ethan gave his dad a thumbs up. It was a perfect day for pulling pairs: the sun was up high in the cloudless sky and a slight warm wind trickled across his skin, keeping him just cool enough. It was going to be a long couple days of work ahead–moving the pairs to grass took a few weeks to accomplish. They had to make sure when they moved the groups they didn't separate a cow from her calf, as the herd would be divided into different grass pastures for the next few months. After they got them in from the field, they would sort the calves into one group and the cows into another. Then they would run the calves into the shoot and process them (make sure all the steers were castrated, give them all shots, tag the ones that needed it, etc.). Next they would load up the calves in the trailer, followed by the mothers, and haul them a few miles down the road to grass. Then they would come back and start the process over again.

Ethan was excited for today. He liked this work, especially quading around finding pairs. It was like a life-size game of memory. It also was the first time Rayna would be helping him with the cows. It was good for Ray to get out of the house. She had been a little aimless these past few weeks, and it had been affecting her mood. She was getting irritable a lot and Ethan felt like he was constantly saying things that made her even pricklier. Some fresh air and hard work would be exactly what she needed. He hoped, anyway.

He and his dad moved together in a familiar pattern, cutting through the herd, matching calves with the same tag number as their mother and separating them from the group. Rayna yelled in Ethan's ear and pointed excitedly whenever she spotted a pair. Her arms hung loosely around his waist and her soft breasts pressed against his back, making it hard for him to focus on the task at hand. When they reached twenty-five, they headed back towards the barn, pushing the chosen group down the alleyway and locking them in one of the pens at the end. Rayna leaned against the gate looking at the chosen pairs and Ethan enjoyed the sight of his wife in her cut-off jeans, showing off her summer tan. Her hair was up in a dark bun with a few curls escaping and swaying in the wind. She looked more ready for the mall than for work with her white sneakers and name brand t-shirt fitted tight against her. He would have to buy her a proper pair of work boots next time they went to the city.

"Done ogling your wife?" Dad said, coming up behind Ethan and making him jump. "Gonna be here all day at this rate."

"Sorry." Ethan cleared his throat and started forward, his dad's chuckle burning his ears. "Okay Ray, you will run this gate here." He led her a little ways down the alley and opened the gate for her. "Just stand here and we will separate them for you. Let the cows go by and open it for the calves."

"Okay," Rayna said, gripping the rusted blue gate. She eyed the cows as they trampled around the pen, bawling as they tried to locate their calves. "Are they safe? Like, do they chase you ever?"

"Sometimes," Ethan admitted. "But mostly they're safe. You don't need to worry."

Ethan left her there and waited for his dad to chase a few of the cows into the alleyway. With a cattle stick in hand, Ethan expertly separated them, keeping the calves back and letting the cows run past him. He glanced over his shoulder to see Rayna standing up against the gate, nervously watching the cows thunder past.

"Catch!" he called to her as a calf darted past him. Rayna stumbled as she scrambled to swing the gate open. Behind her a cow had seen the calves sprinting down the alleyway and she turned back around. Rayna sensed something behind her and looked over as the cow came pealing back. She panicked, swung the gate shut and jumped up onto it to get away from her. A couple calves took advantage of the opportunity and darted past Rayna to join the cow group.

Ethan huffed a sigh and shot a look at his dad who shrugged. He trotted down the alleyway to Rayna. "The cows aren't going to hurt you, Ray, you don't need to be afraid of them."

"Sorry." Rayna hopped down from the fence, her hands shaking. "They're a lot bigger up close."

"It's fine, let's chase these ones back."

Rayna followed timidly behind as they edged along the side of the alleyway to get behind the cows. They chased them back down and Rayna went back to her post. Ethan quickly sorted through them again, then his dad chased out a second group. Half an hour in and it was going fairly smooth. Rayna seemed to gain confidence. She had the gate open, letting a handful of calves run in when a cow bolted from the pen and tore up the alleyway towards her.

"Close!" Ethan hollered. Rayna swung the gate, but the cow got her head in and pushed past. The gate bounced off her hide and swung hard into Rayna, smacking her face. She clutched her hand over her mouth and doubled over. Ethan ran to her, "Rayna! You okay?"

She stood up, gingerly touching her lip dripping with blood. "*Fuck*, that hurt."

Ethan ignored the harsh word and examined her lip. "You have to keep your arms locked straight, so if they hit the gate it doesn't swing into you."

"Thanks for the tip," Rayna said sarcastically.

"She okay?" Dad called.

"Yeah, she's fine," Ethan answered. "Right? You're okay?"

"I'm fine," Rayna snapped. She opened the gate and slipped into the pen.

"What are you doing?" Ethan asked.

"I'm going to get the cow out."

"We can do that at the end, it's easier getting the cows out of the calf pen then the other way around."

"I'll do it now." Rayna strode determinedly forward. Ethan sighed and ran his hand through his hair, watching her cut across the pen. Just as she was halfway across, she caught the attention of one of the calves, who eyed her for a moment, then put his head down and charged.

"Look out!" Ethan yelled.

Rayna turned and saw the little terror running at her. She screamed and turned to run but the calf knocked into her, hooking his head under her behind and lifting her off the ground. Rayna yelped as she landed and staggered to her feet. She made it a few more desperate steps before the little guy got her again and lifted her a few inches up. Rayna landed and stumbled forward, grasped the metal fence and vaulted over, landing hard on the ground. Ethan and his dad stood stunned for a moment. Then his dad keeled over, roaring with laughter.

"Did you s-see that?" Dad gasped. "Lifted her clean in the air! Like a c-cartoon!"

Ethan fought his own wave of laughter. His insides twisted as he tried to keep a straight face. Rayna got up off the ground, her knee was gushing blood and torn up from landing on the gravelly dirt.

"Ray, you o-okay?" He couldn't hold it in. Laughter rippled from him.

Rayna limped towards him, blood trickling from her lip and oozing down her leg from the gash in her knee. "I'm going home," she said, lifting her chin with as much dignity as she could muster.

"No, don't go," Ethan said trying to put his arm around her.

Rayna shoved it off. "Don't. Touch. Me. I'm going home." She pushed past him and slowly hobbled to the barn.

"Ah, it's all right son," Dad chuckled. "She may need a bit of time to recover from that. Geez, that was funny."

The day wore on as Ethan and his dad worked together. Ethan pushed the calves into the shoot and systematically moved between them, sticking the needle deep down in their hindquarters and pressing the trigger, releasing the shot. He pushed the ones he got behind him and counted in his head how many he did while thinking about the day. It had not gone how he hoped it would. In his mind's eye he saw Rayna flawlessly handling the cows and enjoying being outside, working with him. She probably wouldn't want to come out again anytime soon. Ethan would reassure her that everyone struggles the first time they work with cows. It takes time to get used to them. She just needed to build her confidence. Everyone got chased now and then anyway. Not everyone got thrown in the air, howling like a rodeo clown, but still.

It was going to be fine.

He probably shouldn't have laughed.

He definitely shouldn't have laughed.

Still, she would be okay. Everything would come together soon. With that encouraging thought Ethan enthusiastically jammed the needle into the last calf and pulled himself out of the shoot. Things would be just fine. They always were in the end.

CHAPTER EIGHT: RAYNA

Rayna set the broom down and looked around with her hands on her hips. She had cleaned the bathrooms, tidied the entire house, thoroughly cleaned the fridge and swept and vacuumed everywhere. There was a chicken in the slow cooker for supper and the last load of laundry going in the dryer, and it was only two o'clock.

Now what?

Rayna made herself a cup of tea and sat on the porch swing, pulling her cardigan around her. It was a gloomy-looking day today. Dark, heavy clouds blotted out the sun and cast the world in a dim greyish hue. Rayna had found the weather here to be far less predictable than it was in Lethbridge. She could always count on Lethbridge to be dry, hot and excessively windy. Even in wintertime, there was more brown than white on the ground. Here, it was as if the weather took pleasure in being as obnoxious as possible. When Rayna had arrived in March, mountains of snow still littered the ground. Every time it seemed like spring had finally arrived and Rayna relaxed into its fresh embrace, she would wake up to more damn snow. It hadn't all disappeared until almost the beginning of May. Then the sun came out and nearly boiled everything in sight one minute, and the next thunder and lightning broke the sky and rain would gush to the ground. But just for a few minutes, then the birds would be back out chirping in the sunlight, as if nothing had happened at all.

Rayna sipped her tea, thinking. Every day was starting to feel the same and if she was honest, she was beginning to feel like her brain was leaking out of her head. At first, Rayna had loved the freedom of not being busy. She had nowhere to go and nothing she had to do. No assignments due or tests to study for. No job she had to rush off to and work late at. Rayna had spent the first month of her married life watching movies until late and sleeping in during the morning. But soon the novelty of doing nothing wore off, and in its place an intense boredom surfaced. In all her fantasizing about moving to Silver Heights, she had never expected to have absolutely nothing to do.

When Ethan suggested she come help with cows Rayna had been relieved, even excited. It was technically her ranch now too, and she wanted to learn how to help. But, well, it had been a disaster. Rayna had never felt so humiliated, like a bumbling idiot. Ethan had tentatively asked if she would come out again, but the thought of standing next to those monster animals who clearly hated her made Rayna feel sick.

She had entertained the idea of getting a job in town. Doing what she did not know. For the first time, Rayna thought maybe she should have finished her degree after all. At the time she couldn't have cared less. She wasn't passionate about it, and since she now had Ethan to support her, she didn't feel the weight of needing to earn money like she had before. When she had broken the news to her parents about her engagement, they had reacted so badly all Rayna wanted was to get out of the house. Now, with all the drama put aside, she felt a bit of regret. If she had her degree she would've at least had some credentials for a half decent job. What was she to do, bag groceries with the high school kids? It wasn't like there were a ton of options out here.

What she really should have been doing was taking advantage of all the free time to work on her writing. Her original plan was to help on the farm and finally start her first novel, but every time she sat down with her notebook, she couldn't think of a single sentence to put down. Absolutely nothing. It had never happened to her before. Usually she could always write *something*, a short story or a poem at least. It was like all her creativity had been leeched from her the second she moved out here.

Ethan was not overly sympathetic to her struggles. He was busy from dawn until dusk, it seemed, and he expected the same from her.

"There's lots to do," Ethan had said the other day. "My mom's always busy, why don't you go and see if you can help her?"

Rayna didn't bother to dignify this suggestion with an answer. She picked up the book she was reading and pointedly flipped it open.

Ethan tried again. "Why don't you go over there? She has lots going on, it would be good for you to get out and do something."

Rayna glared at him over top the page. "What do you want from me, Ethan? I clean your house. I cook your damn suppers. I'm doing all the wifey things. I don't want to hang out with your mother, all right?"

"Can you not swear, please?"

Rayna had thrown her book down on the coffee table, making Ethan wince. "You too now? Shit, Ethan! You knew who I was when you married me. Are you going to try to change me now too?"

"What are you talking about?" Ethan said bewildered.

"You and your mother! Criticizing everything I do! How I talk, how I dress..."

"How you dress?"

"Yes! Do you know what your mom said to me at church the other week? She said my dress wasn't 'praise worthy.' What the hell does that even mean?"

It seemed whenever Rayna saw her, Carol found some little comment to say about something she was doing wrong, and it was really starting to drive Rayna up the wall. So far, Rayna had kept from complaining to Ethan because she wanted to do what her *dear* husband asked and try to get along with his parents. Now here Ethan was complaining about her as well. It was getting to be too damn much.

"It just means it was too short," said Ethan.

"Did *you* think it was too short?"

"I honestly can't remember. She means well."

Rayna was on her feet now. "She doesn't *mean well*, and why are you always defending her? I am your wife! You're supposed to be on my side."

Ethan sighed and ran his hand through his hair. She noticed he did this quite a bit when they talked. "I'm sorry Rayna, okay? You're right. I'm sorry."

Rayna said nothing.

He stood uncertainly in the doorway, eyeing her like she was a rabid coyote. "I'm heading out now, okay? I'll see you tonight."

Rayna had stood frozen after he left, uncertain what to do next. She had been geared up for a fight and his quick apology left her feeling like a pot bubbling over. She didn't want him to be sorry. She wanted him to... what? Argue with her the way her parents did? Yell and scream and throw things? She didn't know what to do with his bloody apology.

That had been two days ago and things were still off between them, as they always seemed to be. She rarely saw him during the day since he was working and she barely spoke to him at night. It made her even angrier that he pretended not to notice when she was upset. He just talked cheerily about his day and carefully avoid asking how hers was.

Boring. That's how hers was.

Rayna rocked back and forth on the porch swing, setting her empty mug down. All their little fights weren't that big of a deal. They were about stupid stuff, ordinary, everyday, run-of-the-mill things. What was wrong with her that she couldn't let it go like he did? Why did she let this unfounded anger fester in her and spill over on to him?

A blue Dodge truck pulled up right then. Rayna got to her feet as a woman who looked to be in her mid-thirties got out with a bottle of wine in hand and came towards her. She looked familiar but Rayna couldn't quite place her.

"Hi!" The woman said, coming up onto the porch with her hand extended. "I'm Angie, we met at church a while ago."

"Oh, hi." Rayna dimly remembered her. "The pastor's wife, right?"

"Yes, that's me." Angie sighed dramatically. "I have my PhD in psychology and managed my own business for five years and around here I'm known as the 'the pastor's wife.' That's life though, isn't it?"

Rayna laughed. "And the pastor's wife brought me some wine?"

Angie looked down at the bottle. "Yes, I'm afraid I'm terrible at this job. When we got married he was an accountant, you know. So, I kind of got tricked into the role. Mind if we have a glass? It's five o'clock somewhere, as they say."

Rayna led her inside to the kitchen. They sat at the table and Angie poured them both a generous amount. Rayna couldn't remember much about Angie from church. Every week there were so many people coming up to her and wanting her attention she couldn't keep them all straight.

"How are you settling in?" Angie asked. "I wanted to come over sooner but I figured you needed some time."

Rayna shrugged. "I'm doing all right."

"It's quite the change though, isn't it? Not only being married, but moving here. I'm from Vancouver originally. It was basically a culture shock coming to Silver Heights."

"I couldn't wait to move out here," said Rayna. "It's a little different then I thought it would be, though."

"How did you think it would be?"

What did she think it would be like? In her dreams she saw herself standing in a long skirt like they wore in the early 1800s, feeding chickens, riding horses, herding cattle, staring at the unpolluted skies with Ethan's arms around her. In short, she envisioned a wild western romance movie. It obviously hadn't involved wearing pajamas till noon, lying on the couch waiting for Ethan to come home, almost being killed by a mini-cow and a mother-in-law who was convinced she was casting a spell over her son with her un-praise-worthy clothes.

"I guess I thought I would have a purpose. That my days would be meaningful," said Rayna.

Angie nodded, "I struggled with the same thing when I quit my job after having my third baby. Here is what I suggest, if I may be so bold after knowing you a whole five seconds. You need to take charge. Don't wait for things to happen, make them happen. Also, don't spend too much time alone. You'll drive yourself crazy overthinking life. You wouldn't be the first rancher's wife to be driven to depression out here."

"That's... comforting, I guess."

Angie laughed.

They visited for almost an hour before Angie had to get going. Rayna watched her pull out of the driveway and smiled to herself. She liked Angie. She reminded her a little of Chloe–both of them said whatever they wanted and seemed like happy people. She wanted to have that. That easygoing happiness they seemed so comfortable with.

Rayna looked around the empty house. Angie was right. She couldn't just sit around and wait for Ethan to come home. What was it that made her love it here? An image came to mind of the first time Rayna was alone with Ethan. It was a few days after they met at the wedding and he had taken her horseback riding. She remembered the feel of his hands on her waist as he hoisted her up in the saddle. How she had squealed and held on to the horn as she bounced gracelessly up and down while the strong, beautiful animal beneath her trotted onward. Ethan took her through the fields, telling her stories of his life there, explaining the difference between heifers, steers, cows and bulls. Rayna had fallen in love with the countryside as they galloped across the prairie, with the land stretching endlessly before them with no roads or houses or civilization anywhere on the horizon. It was a feeling of pure, undiluted freedom. After they returned and unsaddled Ethan had pushed her against the rough side of the barn and kissed her with such passion she felt dizzy. The spell of Silver Heights had been completely woven through her in that moment.

They had gone riding several more times after that, but not once since they were married. Ethan said he would take her sometime, but so far he had been too busy. Well, she didn't have to wait for him, she could take charge and go herself. Why not? He'd taught her how to saddle. She had even caught her own horse a few times. She could do it.

Her mind made up, she grabbed the cowboy boots Ethan had bought her as a wedding gift and got in her car. She drove the short distance over to the Big House, hoping Carol wouldn't be around to see her. She parked and hurried over to the barn. The horses were kept in a large pen beside the barn, thank goodness. She didn't know what she would have done if they had been let out to the fields as they sometimes were.

The Millers owned three horses. A buckskin gelding named Jack who was Chloe's horse, a feisty mare Ethan rode named Maybe (as in, maybe she would behave today, maybe not) and a shorter than average black gelding named Roman. Roman was who Rayna had ridden before. He was the closest to the ground, so she figured he would be the best choice for her, although when she got on him the ground still seemed a fair distance away.

Rayna found a halter in the barn then slipped through the gate into the pen. She crept forward towards Roman, one eye on Maybe, who kind of intimidated her. Maybe looked up, swished her tail indifferently and continued to tear the grass from its roots. Roman walked a little towards Rayna and sniffed her outstretched hand, his nose soft against her fingers.

"Hey boy," Rayna whispered, sliding the lead shank around his neck as Ethan had shown her. "Ready for a ride? Just you and me today."

It took a few tries to get the halter on right, Roman stood patiently until she finally got his nose through the right part and slid the top over his ears. Triumphant, Rayna took hold of the rope and led him out of the pen and tied him to the fence. She couldn't remember how the slip knot went, so she looped it around as best she could and pulled it tight.

"Here we go boy, we got this," Rayna murmured as she ran a horse brush down his gleaming hair. After she circled around and combed his other side, she went to the barn to get his saddle. It was a real western saddle, with a big horn that a cowboy would use for roping. Rayna staggered out, balancing the horse blanket on top. It was heavier than she thought it would be.

Carefully placing the blanket on his back, Rayna took hold of the saddle and attempted to lift it up, her arms trembling with the effort. Suddenly, the roar of a quad pierced the air, causing her to jump in alarm and bump into Roman, who swung away from her. The saddle fell in between them and Roman jerked back, making the wood creak as he yanked at his tether. Rayna stumbled backwards and fell, her heart hammering in her chest.

"Easy there!" Ethan killed the quad's engine and hopped off. "You okay?" He reached to help her up, but Rayna swatted his hand away.

"What the hell are you doing? Zooming up like that?" Rayna snapped. Roman's chest rapidly rose and fell as he eyed them nervously.

"Sorry, I didn't know you were out here. Here, I got it," he said reaching for the fallen blanket. With practiced ease he placed it on Roman's back, stroking him first in reassurance. He grabbed the saddle with one hand and swung it on.

"I can do it, you know," Rayna said brushing the mud off her jeans.

"I know," Ethan didn't look at her as he quickly did the cinch up.

A pang of guilt crept up her stomach. It really wasn't fair of her to be treating him like this. She didn't even know why she kept getting angry with him. It's like once she started she couldn't stop.

"Thanks," she said, trying to ease the fingers of resentment clinging stubbornly inside.

"Make sure you don't go galloping off into the sunset. He's pretty bulletproof, but he is still an animal and you haven't ridden for a while. I'd just take him for a walk."

His words squashed any effort Rayna was trying to make. "I know that. I'm not a complete idiot." The truth was, galloping off into the sunset was exactly what she pictured herself doing.

Ethan sighed and turned to look at her. *God, he's handsome.* The thought came unbidden to her mind as she looked up at his tall, powerful frame. Rayna wanted to go to him, kiss his lips and feel his muscular arms wrap around her and his hands slide down her body. It felt like it had been forever since they last touched. She held herself firm though, stubborn for what she knew was no good reason. What was wrong with her? It was like she was seeing how far she could push him until he snapped, until he got mad and yelled at her for being unreasonable. She knew what to do with that kind of reaction; she had a lifetime of practice.

He didn't say anything though. He just handed her the reins and stepped back, folding his arms across his chest. As gracefully as she could, Rayna put her foot in the stirrup, grimacing as her leg stretched to fit in it, then with a grunt she used the horn to pull herself up. Excited she had managed it on her own, she turned to grin at Ethan, but he had already turned away and was heading towards the house. Her insides clenched as she watched him go. She should call out to him, apologize maybe. Why did she have to make things so difficult?

"Let's go, boy." Rayna gave Roman a tentative kick in the sides. He let out a resigned sigh and started forward. "Oh, come on, I'm pretty good company." Rayna patted his neck. "Most days anyway."

She went the same route she and Ethan had taken when they'd gone riding almost a year ago. She got off once to open the gate to the cow pasture and left it open behind her. Most of the cattle in this field had been moved to grass, but there were still a few milling around with their noses to the ground as they munched on the now sparse grass beneath them. Their full udders with protruding nipples swung gently between their legs as gophers flittered back and forth and a jackrabbit sprinted across the field.

Tension leaked out of her shoulders as she breathed in the sharp, electric air that felt alive and bristling, like a storm was on the horizon. It had been a good idea to go riding. She needed this to remind herself why she loved it here. It was the land, the space, the sky and the fields stretching in all directions, melding together at the farthest point. The feeling of freedom surrounded her and filled her up, making her insides light and full of abandonment. She had longed to feel this way her entire life.

Rayna nudged Roman again, and they set off at a trot. She bounced hard in the saddle, trying to get the right rhythm like Ethan had showed her. The impact jarred her teeth together. Rayna urged Roman faster, and they hit a gallop. His strides became smoother and Rayna rose and fell with the pounding of his hooves. Laughter bubbled out of her as the ground flew by beneath them.

She and Roman were one, with the wind pressing against them, their hearts beating in sync and their blood flowing as one organism. She was Wyatt Earp, chasing the outlaws on his faithful steed. She was an Aboriginal, running wild over the untamed prairie. She was an eagle soaring through the air.

Rayna let out a loud whoop, releasing the wildness bursting in her chest as they came up to a hill. They flew up it and Rayna relaxed her grip on the horn, giving herself over to Roman's speed. She shouted at the top of her lungs, "I'm the queen of the wor-"

Her speech was cut off as they came down the other side and a cow was standing, like a deer in headlights, right in their path. Roman spooked, jolting to one side and the next thing Rayna knew was she was in mid-air with the ground rushing towards her. She hit with a bone-rattling slam, knocking the wind out of her lungs. Pain like she never felt before radiated from her shoulder.

Rayna wheezed and gasped, making an unearthly sound as she struggled to breathe. Tears streamed down her face as her lungs fought to bring air back into her body. Finally, she caught her breath and rolled over onto her back. She stared without seeing at the sky above.

"Shit," she hissed through clenched teeth, holding her shoulder. She groaned as she made herself sit up and look around. The cow stood a few feet away from her, snorting and pawing at the ground. Fear swept through her. The beast could sense the weakling in its midst, she was sure of it. That stupid little calf had seen it and had tried to do her in. Now this grown-up version would finish what it had started. She was sure the cow could do a more effective job mauling her than the calf had.

Oh, God, I'm going to die by cow. A cow is going to kill me. I'll be one of the stories the radio host talks about in the weird story of the day segment. Rayna panicked. If she had to die early, she preferred it was in an indisputably sad way, not in a shake-your-head-can-you-believe-it sort of way. Not a talk-about-around-the-dinner-table-with-a-laugh kind of death.

Rayna turned from the threat and caught sight of Roman a few feet ahead of her with his head down, munching grass contently.

"Come here, boy," she called desperately. She bit back a groan as she struggled to her feet and stumbled forward. She inched towards Roman, keeping one eye on the cow behind her. Just as she got close, the bloody useless thing jerked his head up and danced away from her.

"Stand still, you bastard." She tried again to approach him, but he snorted and started walking away.

Cursing, Rayna started after him, each step causing flashes of pain. As if he wanted to make her feel like the biggest idiot alive, Roman kept a few feet ahead of her, going in the general direction of home. He stopped a few times but as soon as Rayna got close he started walking again.

"Damn you to hell!" Rayna screamed at him. He ignored her and kept going forward as she trailed pathetically behind. The cows at least seemed uninterested in the human limping through their field trailing after a riderless horse. They glanced up as she passed but seemed to decide it would be too much effort to do something sinister.

They finally neared the barnyard and of course, there Carol was in the yard weeding the garden. She looked up as Roman lumbered by.

"What on earth happened to you? You poor thing," she said, getting up and going to Roman, who stood perfectly still for her like the angel he was not.

"1 fell," said Rayna through gritted teeth, still clutching her shoulder.

Carol looked coolly over at her, "Yes, I can see that. I was speaking to Roman."

"Course you were."

Carol smirked as she grabbed the reins. "Go sit in the house, looks like your shoulder is dislocated. I'll unsaddle then take you to the hospital."

"I'll get Ethan to," Rayna said stiffly.

"Ethan is busy working. In case you haven't noticed, no one has time to sit around and do leisure activities." *Like you do*, her words implied.

Rayna's stomach clenched in anger, but she said nothing. She waited on the porch for Carol to come get her, then stifled a groan as she slid into the truck. Carol whistled to herself as she drove. She seemed rather pleased with the situation, Rayna noted bitterly.

They didn't have to wait long in the emergency room before seeing a doctor. He checked to make sure she didn't have a concussion, then popped her shoulder back in (Rayna nearly biting her lip off to keep from screaming as he did so) and sent her on her way with some painkillers and her arm in a sling. With the pain in her shoulder dulling some, she could now fully appreciate how sore the rest of her body was.

"What were you thinking, going riding by yourself?" Carol said as they pulled out of the hospital parking lot.

"I was thinking I wanted to go riding and everyone was too busy working for leisure activities."

She shot Rayna a look. "It's not like the movies, you know. You can't just get on a horse and expect to know what you're doing."

"Why are you so determined to be miserable to me?" Rayna demanded. "I have news for you, I'm not going anywhere, so you may as well get used to it."

"At this rate, I won't have to worry about you leaving. You'll kill yourself doing something stupid first."

Rayna turned and stared out the window, too angry to say anything. Carol drove her straight home and put the truck in park in the driveway. Rayna went to open the door but Carol grabbed her arm, stopping her.

"I worry about my son," she said. Rayna opened her mouth to say something but Carol cut her off, "Let me finish. I worry about him, I want him to be happy and I just want what's best for him. Surely, you can understand that?"

Rayna stared at her for a minute, then nodded. Carol let go of her arm and Rayna gingerly eased herself out of the truck and walked stiffly to the house. She felt Carol's eyes on her until she shut the door behind her.

She stood and surveyed her home. The chicken cooking in the crockpot infused the air with a juicy aroma. Outside, she could hear the truck pull away and then nothing but some birds chirping back and forth and beyond that, the low mooing of a cow somewhere.

The phone rang, Rayna stared at it debating letting it go to voicemail, then limped over and picked it up.

"Hello?"

"Rayna, it's Angie. Are you okay?"

"What? Why?"

"I heard you got in an accident and broke your arm."

"It's not broken, I dislocated my shoulder. I fell off a horse... wait, how did you hear about it?"

"It came through on the prayer line."

"The what?"

"Prayer line, through the church. You know, if someone needs prayer it gets passed down the prayer line. Someone calls you and tells you and then you call the next person."

This town has a certified gossip chain. *Terrific.*

"Why is it on the prayer line?" Rayna asked.

"I think Evelyn Pratt, an elderly lady from church? You met her, I'm sure. Anyway, she saw you in the hospital, I think."

"Oh, for fuck's sake."

"Anyway, are you okay? Some of the ladies are going to drop off casseroles. I told them you are probably fine, but you know, any excuse to make a casserole..."

"I'm fine," Rayna said through clenched teeth. Now the whole town would talk about her even more than they already were. "If people ask, please tell them not to bake me anything."

"I'll try. Call me if you need anything."

"I will." Rayna hung up and shook her head.

She limped towards the bathroom and ran a tub full of scalding hot water and poured in a generous amount of jasmine bubble bath. Slowly, she removed the sling, hissing with pain as she did so. With a glass of wine in hand she eased herself in, sighing as she sank down to her chin, letting her hair fan out around her. She examined her freshly scabbed knee and gently twisted so there was no weight on her throbbing shoulder. She was an absolute mess.

Rayna sat in the tub, staring straight ahead until the bubbles started to disappear and the water cooled. Until the anger gave way to fear, and the fear got pushed down; buried where it couldn't do any harm.

CHAPTER NINE: CAROL

"There's nothing you can do, Carol." The exaggerated patience in Jim's voice grated against Carol's ears. She resisted the urge to throw her knife across the table at him.

"*I know*," Carol said. "Can't I just complain to my husband? I know there is nothing I can do, doesn't mean I can't talk about it."

Jim popped another piece of steak in his mouth, chewed, swallowed, took a sip of water then said. "I'm just not sure that complaining is worth the time it takes to speak the words. It won't change anything. Besides, I like her."

"Of course you like her," Carol said.

Men. So predictable. They liked anything with breasts and a cute smile.

Jim gave her one of those looks that said 'stop being ridiculous.' He had perfected it when they were kids. He always thought Carol tended to make a big deal out of nothing. Well, as far as Carol knew it wasn't a crime to *care* about things. She was allowed to have emotions that varied from his steady, laid-back attitude. An eternal optimist, that's what Jim was, and he had passed it down to their son. Carol knew better. She knew things didn't always work out, that this world could be cruel and hard and break your heart. She had been born knowing it, had seen it in her mother's dull eyes and in the lines of her father's face.

"Look honey, you're getting yourself all worked up for no reason," Jim said. "What's done is done, Ethan obviously loves her."

"Ethan doesn't love her, he was just lonely. He loved Mila," Carol insisted. Mila had been the perfect fit for Ethan *and* for their family. She couldn't imagine what went so wrong with them. One minute Ethan was talking about marrying her, the next Mila was moving out of town and he refused to talk about it. Carol always thought they would get back together in the end. They were *Ethan and Mila*, for heaven's sake. When they were growing up no one said one name without the other.

"Let it go, Carol," Jim said pushing back from the table. "Thanks for supper by the way, it was delicious." He gave her a peck on the cheek and cleared their dishes away.

Carol watched him load the dishwasher, her heart squeezing familiarly in her chest as she watched his dirt-stained farmer's hands carefully setting the plates in. Ever since they were newlyweds he had insisted on cleaning the kitchen if she cooked. He was always doing little things like that. Jim was the kind of man to carry her shopping bags without being asked and lift the heavy bags of cow's mineral out of the truck for her. The kind that always thought of her before he thought of himself.

It was one of the things Carol loved about him, his gentle, selfless ways. She had known Jim her entire life, she barely had a memory that didn't include him in it. They were born only a month apart, played together in the church nursery as babies and started kindergarten holding hands. Carol was an only child and Jim had an older brother who he didn't get along with very well. They grew up being each other's only real allies. He was the only good friend Carol had, even to this day. She was fine with that; she didn't need a lot of friends. She had her family.

"Chloe called me today," Jim said casually.

"Oh?"

"She's not coming home this month. Maybe next."

"Oh." Their daughter rarely called Carol anymore–it was always Jim whom she bestowed that privilege upon. Carol didn't know where she'd gone wrong with that girl. Was every mother-daughter relationship like theirs? Like walking on shards of glass? Carol could never say the right thing. Chloe took offense to nearly everything that came out of her mouth. She was constantly defensive and expecting Carol to think the worst of her. When did it get like that? Carol remembered the days when Chloe would crawl on her lap, her little hair in braids with fuzzies sticking out everywhere, and Carol would read to her, inhaling that baby scent which lingered into the toddler years. She missed those days, when her children had such an easy love for her and she for them.

People always warned her that being a parent of teenagers was the challenging years, but it was nothing compared to the murky waters of parenting adult children. They didn't need her anymore like they used to. They didn't have to listen to her advice, or ask her permission for anything anymore. Yet, she was still their mom. Was she supposed to just shut off her mom instincts? Leave them be to their own lives? How was she supposed to do that? It was the most unfair thing imaginable. She spent twenty some odd years being the rock that held her kids' lives together, and then suddenly she was supposed to sit idly by and do nothing?

"Carol?" Jim said, clicking the dishwasher shut. He looked at her with concern, he knew Chloe was a touchy subject.

"I'm fine. Just thinking," Carol said, waving her hand. "You're going to be late for the rec board meeting."

Jim glanced at the clock. "Ah, I forgot. What are you going to do tonight?"

Carol shrugged. "It's nice out, I'll do something outside."

Jim gave her a quick kiss goodbye and hurried out the door. She sat at the table for a minute longer, then went to the gun safe and grabbed her .22 rifle, an anniversary gift from Jim when they had hit the ten-year mark. Slinging it over her shoulder, she took a box of shells, stopped by the fridge to grab a Diet Pepsi, and headed outside. She climbed into the red Jeep with the doors and roof removed that they used as a farm vehicle and started it up. She drove out to the field where Rayna had been bucked off earlier that day. Carol smiled slightly at the memory of her daughter-in-law limping into the yard behind Roman, and killed the engine.

She loaded the rifle with as many bullets as it could fit, cracked open her Pepsi and leaned the gun on the side mirror. She looked through the scope. Aimed. Fired. The gopher she hit jumped in the air at impact and laid motionless on the ground. She took a sip of the pop and aimed again.

Dusk was prime time for gopher hunting. There were so many critters running around she barely had to move the Jeep forward. It was a relaxing pastime. With each thunk of a bullet hitting its target, she would pump the bolt-action expelling the shell, hearing it hit the floorboards with a satisfying clang. One time, many years ago, they took the kids to the Calgary zoo, and they all had been amused to see an area roped off for gophers as part of the exhibit. As far as ranchers were concerned, gophers weren't animals; they were pests who destroyed crops and created booby-traps for the cows. More than once Carol had seen a cow break its ankle in the holes the gophers had dug. If any city-slickers ever felt sorry for the little guys, well then, they definitely have never seen them eating each other's dead remains. They truly were a very unlikable rodent.

Carol slowly relaxed as she fired again and again. The summer air played pleasantly across her face as the sun made its way to the horizon. She used to come out here with Chloe after school. Chloe would reload the gun for her and count the hits she made. It had been years since she and Chloe had done anything like this together. The city had called her daughter away, seducing her with its bright lights and promises of a different life. All Carol had left was Ethan, and now a stranger was going to take him away from her as well. She fired her last bullet and heard the responding squeal. *We'll just see about that.*

CHAPTER TEN: RAYNA

April 1996

Two lines. Two pink lines.

Rayna sat on the edge of the tub and stared at the little stick. She blinked, then flipped over the box and double checked the instructions. Two lines meant positive. That's what it said. She carefully set the test down, stood up and looked at herself in the mirror. Her hand drifted lightly over her belly. *I'm going to be a mom.*

She didn't look like a mom. She looked... young. Moms didn't look this young, did they? They looked more...momish.

Her gaze dropped to her flat and innocent looking stomach. It seemed impossible there was a little life inside, swimming around in her uterus. Shouldn't she feel sick? Isn't that one of the first signs? In the movies the women always went running to the toilet and then with a shock they realized they missed their period and that's how they knew. Rayna didn't feel any different than usual. And yet... maybe there was something. Maybe there was a heaviness in her belly that hadn't been there before.

A baby. She was going to have a baby. What on earth was she to do with it? How did you even keep one alive? Oh God, she would never sleep again. And Rayna liked sleeping. No, that's not right, she *loved* it. She got excited whenever she got into bed and buried herself down into the covers like a mole. Some days, she would look at the clock and think, *only four more hours until I can curl up in bed.* How would she survive without sleep?

Rayna left the bathroom and paced back and forth in the kitchen. What should she do now? It felt like she should do something. Should she call a doctor and get it confirmed? Would they have to do an internal exam? Is that what they did? It seemed like a humiliating and uncomfortable experience to go through. Though, she supposed she would have to get used to people looking down there whenever they pleased.

She should tell Ethan. He would be thrilled. He had been hinting at kids for a little while now, but Rayna hadn't even been open to discussing it. For one thing, they were so young. They had plenty of time for starting a family. It wasn't the right time yet; they had only been married for a year. It seemed the choice wasn't up to them after all. Apparently, they really meant it when they said the pill was only ninety-eight per cent effective.

She wouldn't be the youngest person in the world to have a baby, and her situation was better than a lot of people when they became parents. So where was this anxiety coming from? Rayna poured herself a glass of water and took it to the living room. She sat on the couch and rubbed her hand over her face. This would be good. Babies were cute. She would be fine. Oh God, what was she going to do? *No, stop it! Get it together.*

She grabbed the phone and dialed her home number. It rang twice before she hung up. What was she calling her mom for? How would that help? Rayna supposed her mother could tell her what not to do. Most likely she would say something insulting like, 'you should have used birth control' then she would change the topic to herself.

Rayna tried to call her parents at least once a month. If she forgot, her mom would give her the silent treatment and refuse to speak to her when she called next. It wasn't the worst punishment ever, but it made Rayna feel like shit. It was something Ethan couldn't understand. He didn't get why she would call just to listen to her mother ramble on about herself, and exchange maybe two or three words with her dad. She was always in a bad mood after she hung up with them and Ethan would ask her why she called when she knew how it would go. Rayna would get angry and tell him she couldn't just cut them out of her life. They were her parents, and they still needed her.

She got angry a lot these days. That was another reason Rayna hadn't wanted kids yet. She needed to get herself figured out first and to stop sabotaging her marriage. Now she only had nine months to get her shit together. How the hell was she going to do that?

Rayna looked up, catching sight of the clock on the wall and she jumped. "Dammit!" She got up and started running around the house, trying to find her keys and her purse. She had forgotten her coffee date with Angie. They tried to meet up a couple times a month at the café downtown for a little chat. They had grown close over the past year. Angie was really the only friend Rayna had made so far, and she looked forward to their get-togethers. She hadn't realized how lonely she was before them.

Living half an hour outside of town hadn't seem like that big of a deal at the beginning. People commuted that far and longer to get across the city every day. But the distance here had an unexpected isolating effect. The only time Rayna really saw people besides the Millers was at church on Sundays. In the winter during the curling bonspiels, Rayna would go watch Ethan's team just to be around other people. She hadn't even enjoyed curling or understood how it worked, but everyone in town went to watch the tournament. Curling in this town seemed to be the equivalent of hockey to the rest of Canada. Rayna typically liked being by herself, but even she started to go a little crazy when it was too cold to go outside for a walk and the only sound was her own voice against the wind.

Quickly applying some make-up and changing her shirt, Rayna hurried to her car and went as fast as she dared down the gravel road. The mud and slush pulled at her car making her swerve dangerously. She parked at the café almost twenty minutes late. The bell above the door announced her arrival. Angie waved to her from their usual spot by the window with a pot of tea in front of her.

The little coffee shop was by far the best place in Silver Heights. It was an old-style house turned into a café with the scent of fresh baking swirling through the air, welcoming customers as they arrived. They served tea in individual teapots with matching cups for the tea drinkers, and specialty coffee for the others. Each table always had a little white vase with flowers and a big window flooded the room with natural light. It was a very quaint little shop, so out of place in the otherwise ordinary town of Silver Heights.

Rayna weaved through the tables and plunked down opposite of Angie. "Sorry! I know I'm late."

"I thought you stood me up for a minute there," Angie said. "I ordered a pot of the jasmine green tea we had last time, that all right? I'm kind of addicted to it."

"That's perfect," Rayna said, taking the offered cup. *Can pregnant people have green tea?* She stared doubtfully down. She had no idea what the rules were. She debated asking Angie, but then obviously she would know and Rayna wasn't ready to talk about it yet. Besides, Ethan should be first to hear the news. She just had to put it out of her mind for now.

Angie took a sip from her cup. "So, how was your week? Mine's been horrible."

"Why is that?"

"Helen got the flu on Monday. Typically, the other two followed. Puke everywhere! It was honestly like a horror movie," Angie shuddered. "I feel sick even talking about it. Of course Tom was no help, gagging whenever one of the kids ran to the bathroom. At one point all three of them were puking their guts out, I'm in the middle of it trying to keep everyone's hair up, and Tom walks out of the house! I was so mad. Finally, today they were well enough to go to school. Thank God for school."

"That sounds awful."

"Yes, it really was," Angie said seriously. "Anyway, what's with you?"

"What do you mean?"

"You look weird. Like on edge. What's going on?"

"Nothing."

"What is it? Come on, just say. Are you pregnant or something?"

Rayna looked at her.

"You are!" Angie gasped.

So much for keeping it secret. "I just found out. How did you know?"

"I guessed." Angie laughed. "I can't believe it. You said you didn't want kids for a few years. What did Ethan say?"

"I haven't told him yet. I literally just found out before coming."

"He doesn't know? You need to tell him!"

"I know," Rayna fiddled with her cup. "I will. I just haven't had time to process it yet. Please don't tell anyone." Then, to her astonishment, she burst into tears.

"Oh honey, it's okay. It's a good thing!" Angie pulled her chair around to sit next to Rayna and put her arm around her. "It will be fine, I promise. Motherhood is great. Well, it sucks sometimes, but it's also great. You'll see what I mean."

"I know," Rayna sniffed. "I'm sorry. I don't know why I'm crying."

"Hormones love, it's just the beginning."

"I don't know what to do. What if I'm a terrible mom? What if it hates me?"

"Rayna, listen to me. You will be an amazing mother. You'll love that little one so much."

Rayna wiped her face. "I know, I will. It's just, this wasn't planned, you know? I didn't have time to prepare."

"It's totally natural to be scared. It doesn't mean you're going to be a bad mom. And you know what? Hardly anyone feels totally ready when they get pregnant. Even if it was planned."

"I don't think Carol will be happy," Rayna said. "She all but threatened me not to have kids before our impending divorce."

"Oh, stop it. She did not."

"Yes, she did. When I moved out here."

"Well, that was a year ago. She will be so excited to be a grandma."

"I guess." Rayna suddenly had this horrible vision of Carol coming over and grabbing the baby out of her hands. She could just picture her mother-in-law trying to take over and order her around. Well, Rayna wouldn't let her–this was *her* baby. Carol couldn't take it away from her.

"Trust me sweetie, this is such a good thing." Angie clasped Rayna's hand.

"I know," Rayna rubbed her eyes. "Let's talk about something else. Is my mascara everywhere?"

"A little. Here I got it." Angie took a napkin and dabbed Rayna's face. "There, you look less like your eyes are melting now."

"Thanks."

The bell above the door dinged as a woman entered. Rayna watched her walk to the counter to place an order and mildly admired her long legs and blond hair swept back by sunglasses. Rayna wondered briefly what it would be like to look like that. She probably had an entirely put together life to go with her exceedingly beautiful looks. No unplanned pregnancies for her. She looked like the type that floated through life, collecting flowers along the way. There was something about her that seemed vaguely familiar to Rayna. She turned to say this to Angie when the woman looked in their direction and broke into a dazzling smile.

"Angie! Oh my gosh, it's been forever." She came sweeping over and bent to hug Angie who was caught in an awkward half standing position as she greeted her.

"Hey! What are you doing here? Visiting?" Angie asked, sitting back down.

"Actually, I'm back for a while. I took a teaching job covering Marie's maternity leave."

"Really?" Angie said. "Good for you!"

The woman smiled at Rayna. "Sorry, I'm being rude. I'm Mila Shaw. I don't think we've met."

Rayna shook her hand. "Rayna Miller."

"Miller?" Mila's eyes flickered over to Angie.

"Yes, this is Ethan's wife," Angie said.

"Oh. Right, I heard he got married." There was a slight pause, then Mila smiled again. "Well, I'm just grabbing a coffee. I'm unpacking right now. I'll see you guys around." She gave them one more glowing look than walked over to the counter to get her order.

Rayna watched her go and raised her eyebrows at Angie. "Mila? As in...?"

Angie nodded. "As in Ethan's ex."

So, that's why she looked familiar. Rayna had seen her picture in Ethan's photo album. Rayna glanced at Mila again. "Shit. She looks like a movie star. Her boobs are amazing."

"Aren't they? They're the most perfect round creations. I couldn't get boobs like that if I used all the padded bras in the world."

Rayna glanced down at her own generous chest. What she wouldn't give for a perky c-cup size that was cute and bouncy instead of floppy and saggy.

"This is just perfect," Rayna said. They both waved as Mila exited the café. "Absolutely perfect."

"Not like you have anything to worry about. You're carrying the man's baby," said Angie.

"Yup. He's really stuck with me now."

"Oh, don't be like that."

"I've been a bitch to him these past few days," Rayna said miserably. "I don't know what's wrong with me."

"What do you mean? And don't call yourself that."

"Sorry. I don't know. Everything is going good, then I get angry over something stupid and it goes on for days."

"Don't worry about it. Men know we can be a little irrational. It's part of the ups and downs of marriage."

"Yeah, maybe."

Or maybe Rayna just kept pushing him away because she didn't know how to be in a normal relationship. Maybe she was dysfunctional to the core and was going to bring a child into this life and ruin it forever.

Angie saw her distressed look and took her hand again, "You know what? This baby will be good for you guys. It will give you some stability."

"I hope so," Rayna said. She took a sip of her tea. "Can I drink tea, do you know? Is it okay?"

"I think so? You need that book, *What to Expect When Your Expecting*. It has all the answers."

Rayna set her cup down, her hand drifting over her stomach. *It's going to be fine*, she told the little being growing inside her. It would be. Maybe Angie was right, and this was exactly what they needed. Part of the problem was Rayna had been floundering this past year. She hadn't quite found where she fit and she was listless with her days. It was hard to stay positive when she was wasting away the hours before she could go to bed again.

But this could be it, this baby could give her the purpose she needed and maybe fix what was feeling so broken. Rayna put her hand more firmly over her belly, as if cupping the life inside. *We will be just fine, little one. I promise.*

CHAPTER ELEVEN: ETHAN

Ethan slowly guided the quad through the herd, keeping one hand casually on the tagging box behind him. He'd tagged two calves already this morning. In about ten days they would start dropping like flies and he and his dad would have to work around the clock to keep up. He liked this part of ranching; he enjoyed working with the cows, being outside and busy. They would start seeding soon and then there would be many hours spent in the tractor going back and forth across the fields. That was dull, long work so Ethan tried to enjoy being out in the open air while he still could.

Just over the hill, he spotted a cow standing some ways off from the bulk of the herd. He turned towards her and sure enough, as he got closer, he saw the steaming hide of a freshly birthed calf. Afterbirth still hung from its mother and swayed between her hind legs as she turned to face him. She bawled angrily when he drove between her and her calf. Ignoring her, he hopped off with the tagging box and set to work. It was nice when he caught the calves early, before they could run and he had to chase and wrestle them to the ground.

He quickly wrote the mother's tag number on a new one from the box and clicked it in the tagging gun. Positioning it between the two veins in the calf's ear, he pressed firmly down and yanked the gun away. The tag pierced the ear, and the calf let out a low moan in protest. He looked between the hind legs and grabbed one of the thick, green rubber rings and thumbed it onto the end of the castrator. Pulling it wide, he positioned it on the young steer's testicles and slid it off with a quick motion. Ethan released him. The calf got drunkenly to his feet and swayed unsteadily towards his mom, who was pawing and nosing the ground watching.

Ethan sat for a minute, his legs turning cold as the mud seeped into his jeans. He watched the mom lick her calf and sighed deeply, not wanting to get going just yet. It was a beautiful, crisp morning; the sun was already high in the cloudless sky and the air tasted thick on his tongue. It would be a warm one today. Hopefully, some mud would finally start to dry up. He checked the time on his watch and reluctantly got to his feet.

There was a lot to do today, as always. The seeder needed work to get it ready to go, he had fences to fix and the feed truck had broken down again. He had also promised Rayna he would look at the chicken coop in the yard– it desperately needed fixing and she was determined to buy hens this year. She seemed excited about it and Ethan was happy to see her enthusiastic for something.

He knew she'd had a tough time this past year. She spent too much time alone. It wasn't good for anyone to have so much idle time on their hands. He had tried his best to get her involved on the farm, but it had not gone well. She was timid around the cows since the incident last summer and was now too scared to be much help with sorting and chasing them. Then the one time he tried to teach her how to drive the tractor she busted down a fence, then was mad at him for 'expecting her to know what the hell she was doing'.

It really wasn't that hard. It wasn't his fault she didn't listen to him. She talked a bit about getting a job in town, but that didn't amount to anything. During the fall she had been busy cooking meals for the harvest crew. She hadn't seemed to mind it and had even seemed to enjoy trucking out the meals to the fields and eating with them amongst the cut crop stalks. She even rode with him in the combine a few times, but after harvest finished there was less for her to do again, and her melancholy came back in full force.

Ethan tried to encourage her to write, remembering that was something they had talked about before, but whenever he mentioned it she got royally pissed off and accused him of pushing her and how she would do it when she wanted to. So, he let it go, but he only saw her pull out her writing notebook twice, and even then she'd spent most of her time staring off into space.

Everyone said the first year of marriage was the hardest, so he figured it would get better soon. Sometimes, he feared she regretted coming out here with him. She would get quiet and moody for days and he was sure he would come home to find her things packed and her gone. Then one night she would turn to him and they would make love with a desperate hunger, both of them clinging to each other after, as if trying to convince themselves that they were fine. And things would seem fine for a while after that. Was this normal for a marriage? These crazy up and downs? Ethan didn't know, but he was sure getting sick of walking on eggshells in his own home.

They were in another low period right now. They had barely spoken for days, and he couldn't even remember how this one began.

The wind felt nice on his face as he drove the quad across the field. He pulled up to the shop and got off to get the fencing supplies. He would do that for a couple hours, then work on the seeder after lunch. He was just rummaging around for the pliers, grumbling under his breath at his dad for always putting them in a different spot, when he heard a vehicle pull up behind him. He turned to the unfamiliar SUV as a woman with long blond hair got out. A flash of attraction went through him. She was one of those obviously gorgeous women. Then, with a sickening jolt, he realized who she was.

She caught sight of him and froze, then with that familiar smile that used to pierce him to his core, she walked cautiously towards him. "Hey there, cowboy. It's been a while."

"Mila." Her name sounded foreign on his lips. "What are you doing here?"

Mila folded her arms across her chest and cocked her head at him. "That's not the greeting I was expecting," she said playfully.

"What *exactly* were you expecting?"

She winced at his harsh tone. "I guess I don't really know."

"The last time I saw you, you told me I was going nowhere and would accomplish nothing."

"I didn't say that."

"You implied it."

She stared at him for a beat then said, "You look good. Marriage suits you."

"What are you doing here, Mila?" Ethan asked again.

"I just came to say hi. We may run into each other now that I'm back."

"You're back?"

"Teaching at the school. I start Monday."

Ethan snorted. "Really. The girl who was too good for this town, crawling back to a lowly teaching position? What happened? Toronto wasn't all it was cracked up to be?"

"Life doesn't always go how you think it will," Mila replied coolly. "I met your wife by the way. She's pretty."

Ethan didn't answer. He turned and picked up the bucket with the fencing staples and hammer. Grabbing a roll of barbed wire, he moved past her and loaded them onto the quad.

"I hope we can be friendly at least. It's a small town," said Mila.

Ethan turned. "You want to be friends, Mila?"

"I've missed you, Ethan."

"I've barely thought of you."

"You're just trying to be hurtful. That's not like you."

"People change. We haven't talked in what? Six years almost?"

"You don't change, Ethan. I know exactly who you are. I've known you my whole life."

He looked evenly at her. "I used to think I could say the same of you."

They stared at each other. Mila broke the silence. "I have to say, I was a little hurt I wasn't invited to your wedding. That happened fast, uh?"

"I'm not discussing Rayna with you."

"Did you at least give her a different ring? Or is it mine that's on her finger?"

"I'm not doing this." Ethan turned and swung his leg over the quad and twisted the key. The engine's low rumble filled the air.

Mila raised her voice to be heard, "I wonder why you're still so angry with me, if you're just over it all."

"Don't flatter yourself." He pressed the gas and shot forward, feeling her eyes burning into the back of him.

He reached a place where the wire was down and swiftly jumped from the quad with a staple and hammer in hand. He grabbed the barbed wire and brought it up to the post, ignoring the scratches he was getting on his arms, and positioned the staple in place. He swung the hammer down hard, hitting it on a bad angle so it bent. He brought it down again, hitting it over and over, letting the sudden flare of anger he'd felt seeing Mila again ease out of him with every stroke of the hammer. The old wooden post began to splinter and crack beneath his strength. With one last smash he threw the hammer into the bucket and gripped the post in his hands, steadying himself. Immediately, he felt a rush of shame, then anger again that she should still have power to affect him.

The last time they were together was still burnt in his memory. His carefully laid plan, taking her to the bales where they had first kissed, the proposal, her rejection and the sting of her words. She hadn't wanted to be 'trapped' in a small town. Which really meant she didn't want to be trapped with him. She left the next day for Toronto and he hadn't talked to her since.

Everyone knew about it, how she'd rejected his proposal and fled town. It had taken a while to move on from that, but it was true he hadn't thought of her in years. It wasn't like he was clinging to some memory of her and Rayna was a substitute. The thought Mila was thinking that, even in the slightest, made Ethan clench his fists. It was just like her to think she was the star in everyone else's story. It made him disgusted to think he gave her any cause to think he still cared for her. Leave it to Mila to twist their simple conversation into whatever she wanted it to mean.

Well, she could hang on to that delusion if she wanted, but Ethan loved Rayna. She differed from Mila in almost every way–even their looks were opposite; Rayna was short and dark whereas Mila was tall and blond. Maybe that was part of the attraction when he first met Rayna. He knew she needed him. It was never like that with Mila. She was his childhood love, his high school sweetheart and his college romance, and then she had dropped him the second she could. Who did that? Who was that heartless?

Ethan let his breath hiss through his clenched teeth, then slowly forced his hands to relax. He would not let Mila affect him so much. He was caught off guard. He hadn't expected to see her ever again, let alone in Silver Heights. What had really thrown him was that quick spark of desire he had when he saw her. It was like instinct, like something ingrained in him. They had been together for so long, he'd never thought he would be with anyone but her.

Ethan closed his eyes, his mind unwillingly taking him back to the first time they held hands, the first time they kissed a real passionate kiss, not just the innocent kiss of childhood friends. The times her body was pressed against his, lying in the back of his truck till morning, whispered promises of forever, the way she used to nibble his ear and slide her hand under his t-shirt.

Ethan snapped his eyes open and shook the images away. A pang of guilt crept up his throat, making him feel sick. What was he doing, thinking of Mila when he was married to Rayna now? He loved Rayna in a more intense and real way than he'd ever loved Mila. He was sure of it. He suddenly needed to see her, to touch and kiss her. Almost to prove to himself that he was right. Ethan got on the quad and steered it towards home. He got there just as Rayna was pulling up.

"Ethan! What are you doing here?" Rayna said, getting out of her car. It was unusual for him to show up in the middle of the day like this–he usually had a quick lunch at his parents' place and kept working till supper. Rayna's dark curls were pulled up on the top of her head in that casual messy way Ethan liked. He felt a stirring deep inside him as he started towards her. Rayna's dark eyes looked at him curiously as he wrapped his arms firmly around her. He bent his head and kissed her hard, almost lifting her off the ground.

She kissed him back then pulled away. "What are you doing?"

"I wanted to see you," he said. His arm slid down her back and cupped her bottom.

"What's gotten into you?" She laughed then stopped at the look on his face. "Ethan, what's going on?"

"I love you, Rayna Miller. You know that?"

"Yes. I love you too. I know I've been difficult lately, but..."

"Stop. I don't want to get into it. I don't want to talk." He leaned down and closed the distance between them once more and she responded. Her tongue raked his, spurring the fire building in him. He hoisted her up so her legs wrapped around his waist and carried her easily into the house, the door banging shut behind them.

He took her to the bedroom and set her on the bed. Wasting no time, he pulled his shirt off and undid his belt, yanking impatiently at it. Rayna lifted her own shirt over her head and shimmed out of her jeans and underthings so she was bare. He kneeled over her and kissed her lips, then her neck and over the swell of her breasts, enjoying how she squirmed beneath his touch.

He moved down, kissing and sucking her stomach then, feeling bold, he moved even lower. He heard Rayna gasp as he kissed her there. His heart hammered in his chest–they hadn't done this before. He kept going until she cried out and grasped his hair, writhing against him. He grinned and slid back up her body, kissing her gently on the mouth before moving so he could go inside her. He moved slowly, letting it build before he lost control.

A few moments later he laid on top of her, his breath coming out in ragged bursts. They stayed like that for a while, tangled in each other's arms. Ethan moved off her and pulled her to him, so her mouth pressed against his throat.

"That was... nice." Rayna murmured against him, sounding shy. "I've never done that before."

A familiar spasm of irritation twitched through him that he felt whenever she mentioned, even subtly, that she had done things with other men. He didn't think it would bother him when they were first married, but he found more and more that it did. He pushed down those feelings and kissed her forehead.

He should get up and get going. The list of things needing to get done was pressing against his skull once more, but he found he couldn't will his body to move. He wanted to stay in this moment, just him and Rayna with nothing between them. Not Mila, not the mood swings of their marriage, not either of their pasts. And when Rayna whispered the news against his skin that they would be a family soon, and instant joy threatened to burst from his chest, he knew regardless of the roads they took to get there, everything was exactly as it should be.

CHAPTER TWELVE: CHLOE

Chloe eased back in her seat trying to stretch out the kink in her shoulders. Almost there.

The drive was a little shorter now that she had moved to Calgary, but it was still at least four hours until the shadowy image of the Silver Height's water tower came into view. A few more miles down the gravel road and she would be back home. Back to the place she could never truly escape from.

Ever since Chloe was young, she used to dream about the day she could leave. She would go for walks around the ranch to get out of the house, sit perched on the cold metal bar of a gate with her legs dangling and imagine that the scenery in front of her wasn't cows, but buildings. Buildings teeming with culture and restaurants, with musicians and actors and people bursting with passion. Chloe wanted to be there in the thick of it all, experiencing things no one in this town could dream of. She wasn't like Ethan, who fit in here as naturally as a bull moose did in the valley trees. Her brother never wanted a different life, never longed to explore somewhere other than where he was now. That wasn't the case for Chloe, not that there was anything wrong with staying in Silver Heights. Some people were suited for the country and small-town living; it's just she wasn't. She didn't want to stay in the same corner of the world that she had been born in. She wanted to live in different places, where the whole town didn't shut down after five p.m. and on Sundays. Where a cow crossing sign wasn't normal and she couldn't trace her blood relations to half the town.

It was always eerie coming back after being away for a while; nothing ever changed besides a couple people had slightly greyer hair and a few more lines on their faces. Every time as Chloe walked through town, people greeted her with hugs, remarked on how long she had been away and asked when was she moving home. Never was the answer. People had trouble accepting that. It was like she was doing something wrong when she said she wasn't planning on coming back. Like she was letting everyone down.

Chloe didn't even enjoy visiting all that much, it was like as soon as she entered the county she reverted to her old self, like she was a sixteen-year-old kid again. Her mom didn't treat her like an adult, constantly telling her to tidy her room and giving a list of chores to be done. Chloe didn't even live there anymore, so why was she expected to clean the bathroom when she came home? She even acted like she did as a teen, arguing with her mother, storming out of the house and taking long walks around the ranch. She'd sit on the bales, watching the sun dip down until she had to go back. Chloe wasn't like that in her real life in the city. She was capable and sure of herself. She had even landed a job at the top news station in Calgary almost as soon as her practicum had ended. Yet, no one here would ever see her as anything but little Chloe Miller, Ethan's runt sister and Carol's difficult daughter.

Chloe pulled into the driveway and shut the car off. She grabbed her duffel bag from the back and pounded up the steps to the house.

"Mom? I'm home," she called, throwing her bag down and kicking off her flip-flops. Her mom came to greet her, her fingertips black with soil from working in her garden.

"How was the drive?" her mom asked, giving her a hug.

"Fine. Long."

"Can you put your bag in your room, please? Don't leave it lying in the hall."

Chloe fought a surge of annoyance, as she had to whenever her mom told her to do something. She bent and picked up her bag and went down the hall to her bedroom. She threw it on the bed then wandered back out to the kitchen where her mom was pouring a glass of lemonade.

"Do you want some?" her mom asked.

"No thanks, I'm going to Rayna's soon."

"You just got here though. You're not gonna have supper with us?"

"No, Ethan and Ray are having a fire tonight." Chloe said.

"Your father would like to see you."

"Mom, I'm here for a week. You guys will see me lots."

"Only a week?"

"*Yes*. I told you, I start my new job next Monday."

"Right, I suppose you'll never come out after that," Mom said.

"It wouldn't kill you guys to come visit me now and then," Chloe pointed out.

"It's harder for us Chloe, we can't leave the cows with no one to watch them."

"Ethan could watch them."

"You could have taken a job a little closer to home. The *Daily*..."

Chloe's hands clenched into fists. *Here we go again.* "Mom, I'm not a newspaper reporter, I took broadcast journalism. I'm not going to work at the paper in town and cover the high school sports tournaments and the church potlucks."

"What would be wrong with that?"

"Mom, please. Can we not go through this every time I come home?"

"I just think you would..."

"*Mom.*" Chloe almost had to fight the urge to stomp her foot like a little girl. Why did this always happen? Why couldn't they just talk about easy things?

"Okay. Sorry for caring," Mom said. "Please don't roll your eyes."

"I didn't."

"Yes, you did."

Chloe sighed. It was the same every time. It was like they were in a conversation rut, it always turned into a bickering fight. She couldn't handle it, not today. "I'm going to go to Rayna's."

"Fine, I'll see you tonight."

"I'll probably be late." Chloe turned and headed back to the front door, leaving the stifling tension behind.

When she pulled up to Ethan and Rayna's place, a few trucks were already in the driveway. Chloe got out and walked around to the backyard where an impressive fire was shooting flames towards the sky. Pastor Tom and his wife Angie were tossing a football back and forth and waved merrily at her and yelled welcome home. Rayna and Ethan were sitting on a large rock next to the fire, and beside them Daniel was chopping more wood. He let the axe fall to the ground as she approached.

"Hey, Chlo." Daniel grabbed her in a bear hug, crushing her against his chest. "I had almost forgotten what you looked like!"

"Funny." Chloe grinned and turned to hug Rayna next. "Oh my gosh, I've missed you."

"I've missed you too!" Rayna laughed.

"How's it going?" Ethan gave Chloe a smile as he one-arm hugged her.

"Good. The drive was long," Chloe said, sitting down in a lawn chair beside them.

"Ah, if it isn't my long-lost love." The familiar voice floated up behind her and Chloe turned to see Craig walking up with a beer can in hand.

"Hello, Craig." Chloe grinned up at his freckled face, as familiar to her as her own. "Still rocking the Oilers hat I see."

He adjusted his baseball cap firmly over his forehead. "Never trade in a classic. Besides, a very good-looking girl gave it to me." He winked at her and she rolled her eyes.

"You'd think after I dumped you, you would have burned it." Chloe teased.

Craig looked horrified. "Burn it? And waste a perfectly good hat? Who knows the next time I can get a girl to buy me stuff."

"I'd buy you a hat," Daniel chipped in. "If only to cover that monstrous coloured hair of yours."

"You're just jealous of the ginger shine," Craig said.

Chloe laughed.

"I still can't get over how friendly you guys are for being exes." Rayna said.

"It was just a high school thing," Chloe shrugged.

Craig elbowed her, "Best days of your life."

"You wish," Chloe answered.

"She's too good for us now though," Ethan said. "With her fancy new TV job."

"Hey, you of all people need to be nice to me," Chloe said to her brother. "If it wasn't for me, you would still be single."

Daniel clapped Ethan's shoulder. "Are you kidding me? This stud? Ray's lucky she snatched him up when she did."

"Chloe's just jealous, she's worried no one will love her like I did," Craig said.

"You're all hilarious," Chloe said. "Ray, you want to go for a quick walk? Catch up without all these boys around?"

"We're men, thank you very much," Daniel said.

"Yes, definitely." Rayna gave Ethan a quick kiss and got to her feet. Chloe tried not to make a face. It was still weird seeing Rayna with Ethan.

"Off to catch her up on the juicy details, eh?" Craig called after them. "If you need any reminders, let me know!"

Chloe shook her head as Rayna laughed. They walked along the gravel road, crickets chirped in a nearby pond and the honking of geese filled the gaps between their words as a flock flew in v-formation across the dusky pink sky.

"It's beautiful here, isn't it?" Rayna said, watching the geese in their graceful flight.

Chloe looked around. All she saw was emptiness. "It's... slow."

Rayna nodded. "It is. You think that's a bad thing?"

"It's just not my thing," Chloe said. "But you're happy here?"

"Yeah, I am..."

Something in her tone made Chloe look harder at her. "What? Problems?"

"No, actually I'm..."

"What?"

"I'm doing good." Rayna said. "Better, I think. It's been a big change."

Chloe snorted. "I bet. You couldn't pay me to move back here."

"It's not that bad."

Chloe sighed. Converted. Silver Heights has claimed another one. It wasn't supposed to be this way. Chloe and Rayna had made plans. After graduation they were going to move to Calgary together and be roommates. Rayna would have got a job doing something (Chloe wasn't sure what job a business degree could get you, something with a bank maybe?) and Chloe would get hired at one of the TV news stations. They would continue enjoying life as they had in college; dating various boys, going out to the dance club Friday nights and lazing around till noon on Saturdays. That was the plan, and Chloe, at least, had stuck to it.

She snuck a look at Rayna. She was wearing cut-off jean shorts and a too-big plaid shirt hanging loosely off her with her hair pulled up in its usual curly bun. She looked... relaxed, was that it? Rayna had always given off a slightly strung out vibe–her shoulders always seemed tense, and she had a little frown etched on her face, as if she expected the world to crack open and swallow her whole. It was the first thing Chloe had noticed about Rayna when they met waitressing all those years ago, how she gave off an undeniable feeling of weight. Like gravity affected her more than rest of them. There was something about Rayna that had stuck with Chloe after she finished her first shift. Chloe decided right then that they would be friends; she was always drawn to people like that, people who needed a bit of sunshine. Now, looking at her friend, Chloe felt something almost like jealously. Silver Heights had done something to Rayna that Chloe never could for her. She didn't know what it was, but Rayna was different. Somehow, this city girl was becoming more a part of Chloe's home than Chloe had ever been, and for some reason it bothered her.

They turned around to head back towards the house, Chloe talking a mile a minute about things that didn't really matter; her new job, the apartment she was renting, movies she had seen. She tried to shake the feeling growing inside, the one she couldn't quite name.

That week Chloe was more restless than usual. By the time she had packed up her car again ready to leave, she was almost shaking with her need to get away. She pressed her foot down hard on the pedal and gravel spat out beneath her tires. She drove by Ethan and Rayna's house without slowing down, without stopping to say goodbye. She just kept going until Silver Heights was nothing but dust in her rearview mirror.

CHAPTER THIRTEEN: RAYNA

Rayna sat at the wooden picnic table in her backyard and read over the last paragraph she had written. She twirled her pen absently in her hand, enjoying the feeling of the sun warming her face and shoulders. Behind her, she could hear the soft clucking of her hens as they roamed around their pen with their funny little walk, their heads constantly bobbing as they ruffled their flightless feathers. She had bought seven mature chickens off one of their neighbours and she took great pleasure in gathering the eggs each morning.

When she went to the coop, she felt as she used to when she was a child running around the yard on Easter morning, finding the colourfully wrapped chocolate eggs scattered around the lawn. It was her grandma who would set up the elaborate hunt. The same giddiness would sweep over her now as it did back then when she set the warm chicken eggs in her bucket. It sort of amazed her that every morning there were fresh eggs waiting to be collected; that this hard-surfaced, edible food was being created every day in the bellies of her birds. It was one of those little wonders of life people never thought much about.

Rayna had been feeling productive these last couple months. She had Ethan till a vegetable garden out back and a bigger flower garden in front of the house. He was worried at first that it would be too much work for her because she was pregnant, but she waved his worries aside, assuring him women used to do far more work back in the day, and somehow, they had managed.

Her days were pleasantly busy, and they flew by now that she had a bit of a schedule down. After she collected her eggs and made breakfast, she spent most of the morning weeding the gardens before the heat of the day set in. She worked slowly, enjoying being outside with the feel of the soft earth between her fingers. There was something special about helping things grow and seeing the efforts of her labour sprout before her eyes. After a few hours of weeding she made lunch for her and Ethan, who had started to come home when he could. Then she dedicated a few hours to writing.

For almost a year Rayna hadn't picked up her pen, and she didn't know why. It was like the sudden changes in her life upset everything so much she wasn't herself for a while. Last month, while Ethan had been gone from dawn to dusk spraying and seeding and dealing with cows, Rayna had decided it was finally time to start again.

She thought of the baby she was carrying and imagined one day when her kids asked her what she had wanted to do with her life, and Rayna telling them her dream was to be a writer, and never having achieved it. The thought of her children knowing she never did the one thing she always wanted to do made her feel enough like a failure that it kick-started her to begin. She wanted to teach her children to chase their dreams and to be fearless. She couldn't tell them to do that and not do it herself.

After a year of writer's block, she was suddenly bursting with words just waiting to flow onto the page. It was as if a dam had broken inside her. She found once she started that it was easy to be inspired by everything around her. Being surrounded by nature and open space instead of traffic and people allowed her to explore her writing in ways she never had before. She started out slowly, writing a few descriptive paragraphs of the things around her; the way the winter reluctantly gave away to spring, how the newborn calves would chase each other around the field like pups as they sprinted up and down the hills with surprising speed. She wrote about the many birds she saw daily, flying in so great a number that at times they blotted out the sun. How the clouds hung fat and swollen over the fields that were slowly starting to sprout under the June heat, growing the food that fed the world.

She felt accomplished looking back and seeing the pages she had written, pages filled with her words that painted what she saw. That was what she was trying to be; a painter with words, an artist of the written language. It was challenging and hard, but it felt good to pour herself into something creative, like she was getting closer to the person she always wanted to be.

After her writing time, Rayna took an hour or so to relax, maybe read for a bit or go into town and visit Angie or call Chloe for a chat. Then she would start preparing supper, which she found she really enjoyed doing.

Rayna hadn't been much of a cook before she got married. Now she tried new recipes every week and made elaborate dinners and desserts. It impressed Ethan, and it made her feel like she was really contributing something to the life they were building–after all they had to eat just as much as they needed to make a living.

Rayna checked the time and sighed. She needed to get going if she was going to be on time. Tonight, they were going over to Carol's for supper. Rayna was supposed to meet Ethan there and they would finally break the news to his parents that they'd be grandparents this coming December. Ethan had wanted to tell them right away, but Rayna was firm about waiting. It was nice having a secret between just them (well, them and Angie, but Ethan didn't know that). Rayna wasn't ready for Carol to know yet, to have to endure the snide remarks and unwanted advice she was sure would come. She didn't have an excuse now though–she was just about thirteen weeks along and she was starting to show. Baggy shirts covered it for now, but soon it would be obvious.

After the initial shock wore off, Rayna found she was getting excited about this baby. She had even slowly started to turn the bedroom across from the master into a nursery and tentatively talk to the little fetus growing inside her. It was like things had fallen into place since she found out. Life seemed more enjoyable, and she felt she had purpose. She was going to be a mother, a *good* one. Her baby would always feel loved and wanted and important. Rayna would do this parenting thing right.

Reluctantly, Rayna flipped her notebook shut and went inside, thinking absently that maybe she should turn a few of her descriptions into a short story. She got ready quickly, fixing her hair into a bun and pulling on a flowery sundress. It was tight under her breasts then eased out a bit. Perfect for hiding her little bump and showed enough skin to irritate Carol, something Rayna made an effort to do whenever she saw her. Over the past year, Rayna had conceded that she would never live up to Carol's ridiculous expectations, so she went the other way and completely stopped trying. Their relationship had formed into the definition of passive-aggressive; a silent little war both their husbands wisely stayed out of.

Rayna silently cursed Ethan as she pulled up to the Big House. His truck wasn't there, which meant, despite her earlier threats, that he was late. She huffed a sigh and forced herself out of the vehicle. She knocked on the front door politely before letting herself in, something Carol had yet to master.

"Hello?" she called, slipping off her sandals and padding barefoot into the kitchen.

"In here," Jim answered. She followed his voice to the living room where he sat with Carol, sipping on iced lemonade.

"How are you guys doing?" Rayna asked, sitting down on the edge of the couch, her knee involuntarily began to bounce up and down.

"Doing good, yourself?" Jim said.

"Pretty good."

"Ethan is running a little late," Jim informed her. "He had to run to town to get some salt blocks for the cows."

"No problem." Rayna turned to Carol, "Is there anything I can do to help with supper?"

"I have it under control," she answered. "Would you like some lemonade?"

"Yes, thank you." Rayna could see Jim listening to the exchange warily and saw him relax when she took the glass from Carol and no blood was spilt.

"Nice day, isn't it?" He said cheerily. "What have you been up to lately, Rayna?"

Before she could reply, Ethan banged into the house. "Hi, sorry I'm late." He shot a nervous glance at Rayna, obviously worried she would be angry with him.

"I just got here," said Rayna, letting him off the hook.

"Yes, she didn't have to endure being alone with us for too long." Carol smiled, guessing correctly at their silent exchange.

"Now, let's not start," said Jim. "Supper is ready eh, love? Shall we go to the deck?"

"Actually, we're waiting for one more."

Ethan took the glass of lemonade from Rayna. "Who? I thought it was going to be just us?"

"Oh, just a friend I haven't had the chance to catch up with in a while."

"Well, before they come, we wanted to tell you..."

"Just wait Ethan, I need to check the roast." Carol got up and hurried to the kitchen.

Ethan shrugged at Rayna and took a sip just as the front door opened once more and a female voice called, "Hello?" This was followed by the appearance of long blond hair, tanned legs and exceptional cleavage.

Ethan choked on his lemonade, spurting it everywhere. "Mila! What are you doing here?"

"Carol invited me. She said you knew?"

"It must have slipped her mind," said Rayna dryly.

"I'm very busy, it's hard to keep track of who knows what all the time." Carol smiled, coming back in. "Everyone to the deck please, supper is ready."

The party shuffled awkwardly out of the living room, Ethan trying to catch Rayna's eye while she stared determinedly away from everyone and Jim looked like he wished he was somewhere else entirely.

"I'll say grace," Carol announced. Everyone bowed their heads obediently. "Lord, thank you for all you have blessed us with. Thank you for this beautiful day and for the chance to catch up with dear, old friends who have been gone far too long. Amen."

Rayna managed with difficulty not to roll her eyes. What exactly was Carol trying to do here? Make Ethan compare the two of them side by side and he'd realize he made the wrong choice? Make Rayna as uncomfortable as possible? This seemed like a whole new level of low in their little battle, and Rayna would be damned if she let her win this round. She turned determinedly to Mila as the dishes got passed around. "So, Mila, how is teaching going?"

"It's great! I'm loving it so much. A lot of the teachers who taught us are still there. Did you know Mr. Bolton is still teaching biology, Ethan? Remember how he would never let us sit together?"

Ethan grunted and attacked his peas with a little too much concentration.

"And why was that?" Carol encouraged.

Mila giggled. "He said we distracted each other too much."

She actually giggled, like a stupid little love-struck teenager. In that moment, Rayna was quite sure she might hate her.

"Well, fair enough. You two could barely leave each other alone back then," said Carol.

"Carol..." Jim warned in a low voice.

"Amazing how things change," Ethan said, grabbing Rayna's hand.

"Yes, it really is," said Mila.

"So, who's watching the hockey game tonight?" Jim tried bravely to change the subject. "Think the Panthers will step up, Ethan? Did you see the last game?"

"Ah, I missed it," said Ethan. "They're down two in the series, right?"

Jim nodded. "Colorado creamed them eight to one last game. Pity no Canadian teams made it this year. I still can't believe the Flames didn't even make it out of the quarterfinals. Do you watch hockey, Rayna?"

"Not too often," Rayna said. She shifted slightly as a light pain darted across her abdomen. She had been getting them a lot lately, and from what she read in the various books she had bought it was supposedly the ligaments stretching as she grew, but it was getting a little distracting.

"Let's give the hockey talk a rest," said Carol. "So, Mila, how long are you working at the school for?"

"I just talked to Marie the other day, and she isn't planning on coming back after her maternity leave. I might take the position permanently."

Perfect. Rayna stabbed at her roast. *Just absolutely perfect.*

"That's great news!" Carol grinned. "It will be like old times, won't it?"

"I'm pretty excited. I'm looking at buying a house in town. There's one for sale, Mr. Johnson's old place on the corner? It needs a bit of fixing up, but it's a good deal."

"I'm sure Ethan wouldn't mind lending a hand, would you, Ethan?"

He shot a look at his mom then said stiffly, "No, of course not."

"We're out of bread!" Jim said loudly, waving the empty bowl.

"I'll get more in a moment. What else are you up to Mila?" Carol asked.

"Actually, I'm writing a novel. I've got the second draft done and I have some author friends from Toronto who will give me feedback and help me with the next step."

"That's wonderful!" Carol said.

"Yes, wonderful." Rayna forced a grin. "Will you excuse me for a moment?" Before anyone answered, Rayna got up and hurried inside. She locked herself in the bathroom and stared without seeing at her reflection in the mirror. Her hands were shaking.

This was too much. Little Miss Perfect-In-Every-Freaking-Way was not only best friends with Rayna's mother-in-law, she was permanently moving back and writing a fucking book. It would probably win a Pulitzer and get turned into a movie. Then she would probably become rich and famous and use all her new-found wealth to build an orphanage somewhere. Meanwhile, Rayna would be penniless and unable to finish a single chapter in her own hypothetical novel. It honestly couldn't get any worse. Well, it probably could. She could walk out there and see Ethan making out with Mila while Carol cheered. That would be worse.

Rayna blinked back the sudden wetness in her eyes. Great, now she was crying for heaven's sake. Like a bullied schoolgirl, crying in the bathroom. This was ridiculous. She shook her head, fighting to get control.

"Hormones, it's just hormones," she reassured herself.

Rayna gripped her stomach as another twinge of pain came. She needed to calm down; this probably wasn't great for the baby. She ran some water and wiped her face, trying her best to get rid of the puffy redness around her eyes, then walked through to the kitchen where Carol was cutting up more bread.

"All right, dear?" Carol smiled.

Rayna stared at her.

"Go on out. I'm just getting more bread." She gestured to the cutting board.

"What the hell are you trying to accomplish?"

"What do you mean? And please don't swear."

"Why would you invite her here?"

"I don't need a reason to want to catch up with an old friend," she replied.

Rayna snorted. "An *old friend*? Why don't you cut the shit for once? You did this to get under my skin."

"Believe it or not Rayna, not everything that goes on around here is about you," Carol said. "And please, don't swear."

Rayna turned and went out to the deck with Carol following behind. An awkward silence had descended on the table during their absence. Ethan tried to catch her eye as she sat, but Rayna ignored him.

"We have some great news to share as well!" Rayna said, her voice louder than normal.

"Maybe we should wait..." Ethan whispered to her.

"What for? We are all such good *old friends* here." Rayna looked straight at Mila. "Ethan and I are expecting."

There was a shocked silence.

Jim cleared his throat, "Well, congratulations! That is great news."

"Thanks," Ethan said.

Mila looked thunderstruck. "Wow, that's... exciting guys. Congrats."

"Thank you, Mila." Rayna smiled widely. "We are so excited." She leaned over and kissed Ethan's cheek for good measure.

"You know, I just remembered I have a ton of papers to grade tonight." Mila stood up. "Would you excuse me, Carol? Thank you so much for supper. We will have to get together again."

"Of course," Carol said as Mila edged her way by the table.

"Mila, wait." Ethan stood up.

Rayna grabbed his arm. "Where are you going?"

He shook her off. "I'll be right back."

Rayna watched him leave after Mila, her cheeks flushed as she gripped her fork.

Another silence fell thickly. Jim cleared his throat again, "Thanks for supper dear, it was great. I have some... stuff I need to go do. Congrats again, Rayna." He smiled at her then got up and went down the porch steps and headed towards the barn.

Carol looked at Rayna. "When are you due?"

"December." Rayna tried to keep from turning and staring at the doorway. What was Ethan doing? Why wasn't he back yet?

"Rayna, I'm... I'm thrilled for you guys. I really am."

Rayna looked at Carol, surprised.

"I really am," she repeated. "A baby... it changes everything. It's... it's wonderful news."

"Oh, um... thanks."

"Although you might have considered waiting until it was a more appropriate time to announce it."

"I think it was the perfect time."

Carol smiled a little. "Maybe it was. So, how are you feeling? Are you taking your vitamins?"

Here we go. "Yes, of course."

"Everything has been going well?"

"Yes, I think so. I have been having some spotting lately, but I'm not worried. I have a doctor's appointment this week." Rayna shifted in her seat. This was the most personal conversation they'd had yet.

Carol nodded. "Good. I have a few books you might want to look at. For instance, did you know you shouldn't take hot baths? And make sure you don't carry anything too heavy, that can be bad for the baby."

Rayna listened to Carol ramble on and an unexpected warmth filled her chest, maybe something almost like a distant cousin to fondness. She thought she would hate all the advice, but wasn't this what a normal mother was like? Interested and concerned? It was sort of refreshing to have someone care in this way. Maybe this baby would fix more than just her and Ethan. Maybe it would be a fresh start for all of them.

Ethan came back cutting off their conversation. "Rayna, let's go," he said, not looking at her.

Rayna stood. "I should help clean up."

"No, don't worry about it," said Carol.

Ethan turned and left Rayna to hurry after him. She followed his truck home in her car with waves of anger, then worry hitting her in turn. What was his problem?

He waited for her on the porch of their house, his arms folded over his chest. Rayna cautiously got out of her car.

"Why did you do that?" Ethan glared at her.

"Do what?"

"Use our announcement like a weapon against Mila."

"I didn't! We planned on telling tonight."

"You meant to upset her."

Rayna swelled with fury. "Why does it matter? Why do you care?"

"You don't understand." Ethan's voice shook.

"Understand *what* exactly?"

"Mila and I, we have a history."

"*So?*"

"So, I would have liked to tell her my way."

"You're kidding me." Pain shot through Rayna's abdomen, but she ignored it. "You're worried about *her*? What about *me*? You go running after her like a whipped puppy. How do you think that made me feel? Your mother shouldn't have invited her in the first damn place!"

"Don't swear!"

"Dammit, fucking, hellfire!" Rayna screamed. "I'll swear if I fucking want to swear and people better stop telling me not to!"

"You are unbelievable. Every day you tell me what's wrong with me, but the second I say something to you, you turn into a victim."

Another pain rippled through Rayna's body, and she put her hand on her belly. "Well, finally! Finally, you're acting like a man and actually saying something! If I hear sorry from you one more bloody time, I swear I'm leaving."

"What do you want from me, Rayna?" Ethan came right in front and loomed over her. "You want me to yell at you? You want me to fight?"

"I want you to care! I want you to feel something!"

"I don't even know what you're talking about, and neither do you. I love you, Rayna. Why is that so difficult for you? Why can't you just make things easy?"

"So, I'm the problem?" Rayna's voice broke. "I'm the messed up one who is ruining your life."

"Stop it. That's not what I said."

Rayna pushed past Ethan and went in the house; the pain was now throbbing and not going away. She grabbed her suitcase and threw it on the bed.

Ethan came up behind her and sighed. "What do you think you're doing?"

"Leaving!"

"Don't be stupid."

Rayna whirled with her next words ready on her tongue, but the pain came stronger and she gasped. She knelt on the floor, her arms folded over her stomach.

"Rayna?" Ethan fell beside her. "Rayna, what's wrong? What's happening?"

Rayna shook her head and gasped again as another shot of pain hit her. Something was wrong. There was a wetness spreading between her legs. "Something is wrong." She rocked back and forth. "Ethan, something is wrong!"

Ethan went to get up, but Rayna grabbed him.

"Don't leave, don't leave, don't leave." Panic was seizing her now; the pain was coming in long sharp bursts leaving her breathless.

"I'm not leaving you Ray, we need to go to the hospital. It will be okay." He scrambled to his feet and bent down, scooping her in his arms. He tore from the room and burst outside. Gently as he could he placed her in his truck, then he stumbled as he ran around to the driver's side. They shot out of the driveway and turned onto the road, skidding on the loose gravel. "It will be okay, Ray." He said again. One hand clutched the steering wheel, and the other squeezed her leg. "It will be fine, just hold on."

****

Rayna learned a lot that day. She learned that pain could wrap around her entire body, that it could squeeze her so hard the simple act of breathing becomes impossible. Even when the physical reason for pain is gone, it doesn't fade away. It aches and grows roots, digging deeper and deeper until it penetrates the heart and stays there, vibrating and burning; taking over all her senses.

The doctor's words washed over Rayna in a meaningless jumble. They said there was nothing they could do. It just happened sometimes, no one knows why. Rayna didn't really care why; all she knew was that morning she was full of life, and now she was empty. Hollowed out like an egg with the yoke blown out ready to be painted for Easter. Except, she wouldn't be made into something beautiful, she would just be a shell; existing until the pressure cracked her, because there was nothing left to hold her together anymore.

CHAPTER FOURTEEN: ETHAN

It had been three weeks since they lost the baby.

For a precious few seconds that morning when Ethan stirred awake, he had forgotten. He forgot that their child, who had barely been at the beginning of life, was gone. That his wife was on the couch where she had been spending the nights and most days, the TV on but not being watched. He forgot the guilt that pressed down on him daily, but as he blinked at the morning light, it all came rushing back.

Ethan didn't move, he just let the sorrow eat away at him as he lay on the soft mattress, his hand resting on the empty space beside him where Rayna should have been sleeping. It was a strange thing, the sense of loss he felt. They didn't even know the gender, but he had already loved that baby so much. Or maybe it was the life they were expecting to have with the baby he had loved. The idea of a family, of Rayna and him tied together so permanently with a beautiful little baby their love had created. It was so clear this was what they had needed. The waters of their relationship had finally calmed and Rayna had been happy. Life had fallen into a peaceful routine and they were full of anticipation that it was just the beginning; then it was all gone. It felt like they'd lost more than the baby; they'd lost the thread of hope they had been pulling on that was supposed to unravel to something more.

Ethan couldn't fix it. Try as he might, he couldn't do anything to help them overcome this. He didn't blame Rayna for not talking to him and not wanting to lie beside him at night. What had he been thinking, yelling at her like that on the day it all happened? He should have been more careful with her, more loving. He was sick just thinking about it. What had they even been fighting about, anyway?

Mila.

She had been the start of it all.

It was ridiculous, and it made Ethan angry and ashamed to think of it, but when he saw Mila's face after she learned of the pregnancy he felt... what? Guilt? No. It was just concern, he didn't want her to feel hurt. After all was said and done, they used to mean something to each other. They used to be best friends. He barely had a childhood memory without her and Daniel in it. Ethan had gone after her just to make sure she was okay. It had been instinct. He thought of his conversation with Mila often, trying to figure out why it had made him so angry. Why it had made him lose control.

He had finally got Mila to stop in the driveway as she went to open her car door. "Mila, wait. Please wait a second," he had said.

Mila had turned and Ethan stopped, surprised to see a tear on her cheek.

"What, Ethan? What do you want?" She angrily brushed it away.

Ethan hadn't really known what he had been planning on saying. He shifted awkwardly. "I, well I guess I don't know."

"I shouldn't be surprised." Mila shook her head. "You married her, of course she will have your babies. I just...it's official now isn't it?"

"What is?"

"That you and I... we're really done." She laughed a little. "I mean I knew that obviously. This just cemented it, I guess."

"Mila," Ethan sighed. "We were done the day you left me."

"It wasn't though. We were just so young. I wanted... I had to do things before... well, it doesn't matter now."

They stared at each other.

"No, it doesn't matter now," he said quietly.

Mila had pulled herself up to her full height. "Well, I've moved on, anyway."

"Really."

"Yes, *really*. That's the other thing I wanted to tell you tonight."

"You don't have to keep me informed on your love life," said Ethan.

"I know that," Mila said. "But, well, it's Danny."

"What? Dan? Like Daniel Chase?"

"Like your best friend, Dan."

"Why?"

It was a stupid question, but it didn't make any sense. Dan and Mila? It didn't fit. Dan knew what Mila had done to him; he had sat with Ethan for hours that night after she left, loyally calling Mila every name under the sun.

"It just happened. He wanted to tell you, but I thought I should."

"Good for you guys." Bitterness flooded his mouth. "That's terrific, I hope you live happily ever after."

Mila had glared at him. "Like you have any right to be mad. At least I won't marry him after dating for a month."

"Yeah? Well, I'll tell him not to expect too much. In fact, I'll tell him when he gets sick of you to offer a ring and you'll start packing your bags."

"I don't need this." Mila yanked her car door open and got in. "Congrats on the baby."

She slammed it shut. Ethan watched her peel out of the driveway, the urge to hit something making his fists curl into tight balls.

Ethan didn't know what was wrong with him. Why it had made him so upset. It wasn't logical. He didn't love Mila anymore; he was married to Rayna. Yet, hearing that Daniel of all people had asked Mila out filled him with such anger. It had vibrated through him and spilled over in his argument with Rayna. It wasn't fair to her. He had no reason to go off on her like he had. Now, he couldn't help but feel his overreaction to his ex was partly to blame for his family being torn apart. So, no, he didn't blame Rayna at all for pushing him away.

Ethan forced himself to go through the motions. He got dressed in his old pair of work jeans, grabbed the first t-shirt he could find and pulled it over his head. He left the bedroom and went to the kitchen, poured himself a cup of coffee and gulped it down so fast it scalded his tongue. He ate a piece of toast with peanut butter and honey, made an extra piece and poured more coffee and brought it to the living room. He set it down on the coffee table in front of Rayna who laid on the couch, staring at the TV. He looked at her, wanting to run his hand down her cheek, but his arms dangled uselessly by his side.

"Need anything?" he asked.

"No."

He lingered a moment longer, trying to think of a string of words that might help, that might make her see how much he needed her, the old her. He didn't know what to do with this stone version of Rayna. He'd rather have the irrational, moody version than this empty shell before him. But he couldn't think of anything to say, so he let the silence stretch a little longer, then turned and walked out the door.

There wasn't too much he needed to be doing today. They were caught up with baling and spraying, so work was in a bit of a lull. Ethan couldn't stand not doing anything though–he had never been very good at being idle. He drove around and checked the fences, delivered some mineral and salt blocks to the herds, moved a fallen tree off of the fence line and spent an hour picking up baler twine in the field. He was in the process of cleaning and organizing the shop when the crunch of an approaching vehicle sounded behind him. Ethan turned and watched as Daniel got out and started towards him with his hands buried in his pockets.

"Hey man," Daniel stood uncertainly outside the doorway. "I've been trying to call you."

Ethan stared at him.

Daniel shifted his weight. "You doing okay? Everyone's been thinking about you guys. Mila said…"

Ethan barely registered what was happening as he dropped the wrench he was holding and his hand curled into a fist. In a quick motion he moved towards Daniel, drew back his arm and hit him hard in the jaw. Daniel dropped, clutching his face. Ethan stared down, stunned, then the next thing he knew he was sprawled on the ground with Daniel on top of him, swinging wildly. They wrestled on the ground, grunting as fists hit flesh. After a particular painful hit to his nose, Ethan shoved Daniel roughly aside and they lay beside each other, panting. He touched his nose gingerly and wiped away a trickle of blood.

"We haven't done that in a long time," Daniel said, wincing.

Ethan pushed himself up on his elbows, "You haven't been a dick in a long time."

"What are you so mad about? Mila?"

"No."

"Come on, man. I know it's a little weird."

Ethan just grunted. He didn't really want to talk about it.

Daniel pressed onwards, "Look, I don't want it to be awkward. I should have talked to you about it."

"It's fine."

"Besides, we are kind of even now."

"What are you talking about?"

"Rayna, when she first came out. You kind of stole her from me."

"What?"

"At the wedding."

Ethan shook his head. He had a vague memory of there being a bit of competition between them, but he would hardly say he stole her. "You're kidding right? There was nothing going on between you two."

"Obviously I was interested."

"Obviously she was fair game for both of us, and obviously I won."

"Yeah, well, obviously you and Mila are done now. So, what's the problem?"

Ethan laid back down. "Nothing is the problem."

Daniel was quiet then he said, "I always liked her, you know. Watching you with her all those years was torture, but you were *Ethan and Mila*. Everyone knew you guys would be together." He looked at him, "I never would have pursued her if I thought there was something left between you, I'm not that big of a dick. But you're married now so..."

"Yeah, I know," Ethan said gruffly. It wasn't a big surprise that Daniel had liked Mila. Every guy in town did back in the day.

They were quiet for a minute. Daniel sighed. "Hey, I'm sorry about the miscarriage. Is Rayna okay?"

"No."

"I was going to say, before you went all Rambo, that Mila and some ladies from church want to know if you guys need more casseroles."

"No, we've got lots still."

Daniel stood up and brushed the dust off his pants. "Will we see you guys at church soon?"

"I don't know. Rayna hasn't been ready to go anywhere yet."

Daniel nodded. "Tell her we're thinking of her." He felt the bruise forming on his jaw. "Good thing you punch like a girl, or my face would really hurt."

Ethan got up and watched Daniel get in his truck and drive away. His knuckles and nose throbbed, but he felt a little better than before. It felt good to hit something. He finished tidying the tools and gave the floor a quick sweep, then headed towards the Big House to get his truck, thinking maybe he would run to town and buy more mineral. When he got there, he found his dad waiting for him on the tailgate.

"Hey," Ethan said. "I was gonna zip to town for mineral. Need anything?"

"Have a seat. I want to talk with you a minute," Dad said, patting the space beside him.

Ethan hopped up beside him and waited for his dad to speak.

"Your face looks a little beat up," Dad observed.

"It's fine, it was nothing."

"How are you and Rayna doing?"

"About how you would expect," Ethan said.

His dad looked at him, waiting.

Ethan sighed. "I don't know how to help her. I don't know what to say, or do. She won't talk to me."

"There's no right or wrong way to grieve, for either of you," his dad said, rubbing his beard. "It's hard what happened–you need to be there for her though. You need to help pull your marriage through this. She may not admit it, but she needs you there."

"I don't know what to do," Ethan said.

Dad was quiet, thinking. "You know your mother and I, we told everyone we were pregnant as soon as we knew. We didn't wait until it was 'safe.' We wanted to celebrate the baby's life as soon as possible. Then, if something happened, we and everyone around us really had time to love it. You know? It meant something, even as just a little ball of cells it was a life already. I don't know what you need to do, but I know you need to let Rayna feel what she needs to feel and celebrate the life that was."

Ethan nodded, unable to speak passed the lump in his throat. Dad clapped him on the back and hopped off the truck, "I'll go pick up the mineral. Why don't you slow down for a bit?"

Ethan sat there long after his Dad drove off. He was right–they needed to commemorate their baby, a way they could start to feel some sort of closure instead of expecting each other to just move on. Slowly, an idea started to form. Ethan got in his truck and drove up to the shop. He grabbed a few supplies then got back in and drove around until he found what he was looking for.

CHAPTER FIFTEEN: CAROL

Carol knelt on the soft surface of her garden, patiently and methodically pulling at the weeds sprouting up between her carefully planted flowers. Gardening was one of the things she loved most about summer. She enjoyed burying her hands in the dirt for a couple hours each day and she loved the exhaustion that clung to her after, knowing she'd spent her time being productive. Years of labour had resulted in one of the most beautiful yards in Silver Heights. She wasn't being prideful in thinking this; it was a fact. She had flowers of all types and colours flourishing in her garden, from pink rose bushes to wild flowers, to Blue Eyed Mary perennials. She had built a pond to go under the wood bridge leading to the play set in the backyard, and lilac bushes she and Jim had planted themselves lined the road leading to the house.

She loved the lilacs most of all. When Carol was young, they had a beautiful row of lilacs right outside their back door. She and her mother would wander around them, cutting off enough to make a bouquet for every room. Their house smelled so strongly of that purple flower that her dad would often complain and cover his nose.

"Don't be such a grumpy old man," her mother would tease him. "It smells like happiness, doesn't it Carol? Refreshing, beautiful happiness."

Maybe that was why her mother had felt the need to put so many in their house. Maybe she thought she could chase away her demons with the smell of happiness. Unfortunately, lilacs had a terribly short season. They were barely in full bloom for three weeks before their colour was leeched out of them and their petals shriveled and crunched to pieces when touched. Just as her mom couldn't keep their sweet perfume, she couldn't keep the gloom at bay. Every year Carol would go out and collect lilacs for the vases, even when her mother stopped. Carol would carefully arrange some beside her mother's bed, and later, beside her grave when she had gone.

Carol still kept bouquets of lilacs in her house whenever they were in season. They were still her favourite flower. She stood up from her garden and stretched, pulling the tender muscles in her back. Jim came out of the house just then.

"How's the garden?" he asked.

"Growing." Carol smiled.

"Seen Ethan?"

"No, his truck is here though." Carol gestured to Ethan's Ford.

Jim nodded. "I'm gonna have a talk with him."

"What will you say?"

"Dunno. Something."

"Maybe I should be there."

Jim shook his head. "No, you know where you need to be."

Carol glared at him. "I need to be there for my son too, Jim."

"Be there for Rayna. That will be better than being there for Ethan. You know what it's like, being a woman going through all that. Besides, she doesn't have anyone here."

Carol brushed her hands down the sides of her pants, not looking at Jim. He was right; she knew what it was like, what Rayna was feeling. The shock and the loss. The utter helplessness. She knew all about it. All these years later and she still felt the regret, like a shard of glass in her heart.

"Hey," Jim said, coming up to her.

Carol tilted her head back and looked at the man she had loved her entire life.

"She needs you right now," he said, then bent and kissed her tenderly on the lips. "Go be the soft, loving woman I know is in there somewhere."

Carol swatted at him. He laughed and kissed her again then walked over and pulled Ethan's tailgate down and parked himself on it.

"All right, I'm going," Carol said. She turned to go to the house, then stopped and went towards the road where the row of lilac bushes waited. She would cut a few and bring a bouquet over to Rayna's. If anyone needed the scent of happiness, it was a woman who had just lost her baby.

****

Carol pulled up to Ethan's house and got out, cradling the vase of lilacs in her hands. She noticed the garden out front was a tangled mess of overgrown weeds and she shook her head. Really, even if the world's gone to pot, there was no reason to let the garden suffer like that. She trudged up to the door and pushed it open, stepped inside and paused letting her eyes adjust to the dim. The curtains were all drawn, blocking the sunlight and casting the house into a depressed darkness. It took her a moment to notice Rayna curled up on the couch. Rayna looked at her and blinked, like she wasn't sure if Carol was real or not.

"Still not knocking, I see," Rayna said.

"Hello, Rayna." Carol shut the door behind her. She moved into the house and placed the vase on the coffee table beside an uneaten piece of toast and a mug of cold coffee. "I'd ask how you are, but clearly the answer is not well." Carol's gaze swept over Rayna, taking in her frizzy curls, which had turned into a ball of puff from going unwashed. "How long are you planning on pining away like this?"

"Please, go away."

Carol turned and grabbed the toast and coffee. She brought them to the kitchen and threw out the old food and placed the dishes in the dishwasher. Then she went back to the living room and firmly yanked the curtains open, shut the TV off and whirled to face Rayna. The girl did look terrible. Carol shook her head.

"Rayna, I know you're hurting, but this isn't healthy. You need to get back on your feet now."

"Leave me alone." Rayna sat up now and was glaring at her.

Carol ignored her. "I'm very sorry you have to go through this, the pain of losing a child..." Carol shook her head. "I wish to God it didn't happen. But it did. We cannot change it. You can't let it wreck your life."

"Stop," Rayna said, her voice shaking. "Stop talking like you know anything."

"I had a miscarriage too, I'll have you know. Between Ethan and Chloe," Carol said evenly.

Rayna looked up, surprised.

"Unlike you, I didn't have the luxury to mope around for a month. I had Ethan to take care of." Carol stopped. She sounded a little harsh. Something about this girl brought out the worst in her. She tried again, this time with a softer tone. "Look, Rayna, it's not something many people can understand, losing a child so early. I know you can't just move on from it, or pretend like it never happened. And you shouldn't. You *should* grieve. But you need to know it wasn't your fault, Rayna. Just like it wasn't mine."

"What you went through, it wasn't the same." Rayna looked at the floor. "This was my fault." Then she began to cry.

Carol stood for a minute, not sure if she should try to comfort her or wait it out. After making a split decision Carol went to the kitchen again and brought back a glass of water. "Here," she said, sitting down beside Rayna and pressing the glass into her hand. "Have a drink."

Rayna took a small sip, her shoulders shaking, but she started to calm down. Carol passed her a Kleenex and waited for her to wipe her face, then said. "Now, why exactly do you think it's your fault?"

Rayna glanced at her then looked away. "When I found out I was pregnant, I wasn't sure if I wanted it. I didn't think I could do it. And maybe I wouldn't have been a good mom." Her next words came out in a small voice. "Maybe this was for the best."

Carol's heart squeezed painfully. *Oh, Rayna.* She looked at her and for the first time she thought she might be seeing the real Rayna. Not a confident, sexy temptress who'd ensnared her son and was trying to take him away from her. But a sad, broken girl. What had made her this way?

Carol sighed. "Rayna, that's ridiculous. You're allowed to be scared, that doesn't mean you didn't want your baby or that you wouldn't be a good mom. My children were all planned, and I was scared every time. I know it's hard to believe, but this is a very small part of your life. There will be more ups and more downs. You will get pregnant again and the odds are you will carry to term and have a baby. Then maybe a few more after that."

"So," Carol clapped her hands. "Here is what you will do. You will take this day to be as miserable as you need, do whatever you need to let it all out. Then you will wake up tomorrow, get dressed, shower and start fresh."

"Do I get a say in this?"

"Well, what's the alternative? Be miserable forever? That won't fix a single thing, you will only hurt yourself and Ethan. And maybe you're fine with hurting yourself, but I believe you love my son, and I would like to think you wouldn't want to do that to him."

Rayna paused then said, "Why do you care? Why are you doing this?"

Carol stood up. "It may come as a shock to you, but I'm not a complete monster." She headed for the door, pausing as her hand twisted the handle. "We are praying for you, by the way. You may want to try it. It's what helped me to get going again. And for the love of all that is holy, take care of that garden. It's not its fault you decided to become part of the couch." With that, Carol turned and left.

Rayna would be all right. Carol knew it because as much as she hated to admit it, she saw something of herself in the girl. They were both women who knew how to get tough when they got beat down. They had to be, to get through whatever it was life threw at them. Some women didn't know how to do that. They wallowed in the gloom and let it seep in and destroy. Not Carol–she made it her mission for that to never be her. Rayna was the same; she had that look in her eye. She had fallen now, but she would get back up again. And if she didn't, well then Carol would just have to drag her up. For Ethan's sake, of course.

CHAPTER SIXTEEN: RAYNA

Rayna sat still until the sound of Carol's vehicle faded away. Then she pulled the blanket tight over her again and flopped back down on the couch, her safe place of late. She wanted to stay there forever, unmoving, letting the world go on without her. Unfortunately, she was getting hungry. She regretted not eating that piece of toast Ethan gave her before Carol had cleared it away. It seemed like too much energy to get up and find something in the kitchen, so she just stared at the coffee table. She was exhausted. Angie had stopped by again yesterday and the effort it took to sit up to talk made her dizzy. Rayna appreciated it, but the truth was she didn't want anymore visits. She didn't want to talk about it; she didn't want to be reassured, or comforted. She just wanted to be left alone. Of course, Carol would come by without asking. Without considering if Rayna even wanted her there. She may have thought she understood, but how could she? Carol said it wasn't her fault, but Rayna knew the truth. She didn't deserve to be pitied or comforted or to feel better and move on.

No. She deserved this ocean of nothingness she was currently floating in. She deserved the dull aching pain thumping against her chest and the weight which settled on her body, making her shoulders sag. The past month had reduced her to three emotions; sadness, anger and numbness. The sadness had been first and the most consuming. Rayna had barely moved from a fetal position. The pain of grief was so great it tore through her body.

Anger was next, as great as the grief and as destructive. She had hated everyone; the doctors, the visitors, Ethan and mostly herself. She felt betrayed by her own body; it had failed at the one task she was genetically designed to do, keep a baby safe and growing. Finally, the sweet relief of numbness set in and she felt nothing. She let it shroud her and protect her. If she didn't move too quickly or think too much, it held firm and kept her safe. She had been content to stay that way until Carol came and suddenly her armor cracked and fell apart, leaving the tears a clear pathway to come again. Now she just felt drained.

She wanted to stay on the couch and never leave it, huddled in her protective nest. She would have too, except her body was not in sync with her mind and the urge to eat was growing harder to ignore. When was the last time she had eaten? Breakfast yesterday maybe? Rayna sighed. Keeping the blanket wrapped firmly around her, she slid her feet to the floor and pushed herself upright. Her head immediately felt heavy and her vision distorted. She swayed on her feet, waiting until the head rush subsided some, then moved with deliberate slowness to the kitchen, passing the hallway to the bedrooms.

Her eyes lingered on the closed door of the second bedroom. She hadn't gone in it since that day. It was a terrible physical reminder of what could have been. How long would it sit like that? Frozen, waiting for a little life that was no longer coming. Rayna shuffled forward, firmly putting it out of her mind before it could trigger another bout of tears. She half-heartedly ate part of a banana and a piece of plain bread, having no patience or energy to toast it.

After her pathetic meal she made her way back to the couch and sat hugging her knees to her chest, thinking. Angie and Carol had both said the same thing to her–she needed to accept it and start living again. Carol was right, Rayna didn't really want to hurt Ethan, and she didn't want to stay miserable forever. She just wasn't sure how to move forward. She thought of what Carol threw over her shoulder about praying as she left. Rayna had never tried it before, but maybe she should. There had to be a reason all those people kept going to church every Sunday, right? Rayna straightened. What the hell, she would give it a go.

She cleared her voice nervously, not sure how to begin. "Hello? God?"

Immediately she felt foolish. Maybe she should try something else, ease into this whole prayer thing. Rayna let the blanket drop from her shoulders. She went to the bedroom and found her writing notebook and a pen. Taking them with her, she went out to the yard and sat in her usual writing spot at the picnic table. She stared for a minute at her garden. Weeks of neglect showed a shocking change. Weeds had sprung up and crept over her hard work, making it almost impossible to tell the difference between what was supposed to be there and what wasn't. She imagined the vegetable garden out back was just as bad. How quickly things could change; one minute everything is carefully tended, planned and structured, the next it was an out-of-control mess that barely resembled what it once was.

Rayna flipped open to a blank page, her pen hovering above the paper. Then she let the words fall.

Dear God,

I hardly know where to begin. I can't help but feel it's all been a big mistake. Moving here, marrying Ethan. I thought it was the right decision; I thought it was the answer I needed, that I would finally belong somewhere. I had hoped this would be it, the place I was searching for, but it's not at all how I imagined. It seems like from day one nothing has gone right. The people here are nice but I can't shake the feeling they are one thing and I am another. I thought the baby would fix it–I know that is a lot of pressure to put on a baby, but then I couldn't even do that. I can't help but feel it was my fault. Maybe I needed it too much, or I wasn't careful enough. Why did it happen? Will I ever know? How do I move on from here?

In my head I see my ideal life, and it is so far from what I have. I feel like I'm constantly chasing something I will never catch. I feel like I'm playing pretend, trying to fit into this role that was clearly made for someone else. I want to believe this was the right thing; I want to believe my life with Ethan will be enough. What if it isn't? Where does that leave me? The thing is, this was my dream, to be out here and with him. Now, I don't know what I dream of. I don't know what I want. But it's too late, anyway. This is the path I chose. What if I shouldn't have? What if I should have finished my degree, got a job and lived a different life? Some days, I wish I had. Then I would only have myself to worry about. Selfish I know, but it is true. Marriage is so romantic, but you never consider how restricting it can be. I feel like I can barely make my own choices, and those that I make are wrong.

I don't know if I'm making sense; I don't know if you're listening or what you might do about it all. I don't even know what I would want you to do. I guess, maybe, if you could help me get control of my feelings, that would be a start. If I could stop this spinning and be able to think clearly for once. If you could help me be happy, I really want to be happy...

Rayna let the words pour from her pen. She let her doubts and fears and hurts spill out until she was pleasantly empty. It was like putting the words down in a physical way helped her to process exactly what was going on inside her and start letting it go.

When she felt she had no more to say, she closed her notebook and just sat, listening to the surrounding sounds. To the breeze whistling lightly through the branches of the trees and to the chirping of the birds who always seemed to be there. She could hear cows mooing in the distance and the low rumble of a vehicle rattling down the gravel road somewhere.

Sounds of life.

Carol was right (surprisingly). It was time to stop punishing herself, time to rejoin the living. Starting with a shower.

As she got up to go inside, Ethan pulled up in his truck. She watched him walk towards her, noticing with a bit of a jolt that this was the first time she had properly looked at him since it happened, and he wasn't looking great. He had let his stubble grow and there seemed to be a bit of a slouch in his shoulders. He looked defeated. And it was her fault; she had been punishing him as much as herself. The thought made shame trickle through her. Despite what she had written a few moments before, seeing him in front of her there, she knew she loved him. So why did she try so hard to push him away?

"What happened to your face?" Rayna asked as he came closer and she could see a bruise forming under his eye.

"Nothing. How are you doing?" he asked tentatively.

Treating her like glass. Well, that's what she had made him do. "Better." She offered a small smile.

"I want to show you something." He gestured to his truck, "Can you come for a ride?"

Rayna nodded and followed him to his truck. They drove for several minutes until he turned off onto a dirt road Rayna hadn't been on before. "Where are we going?"

"Almost there," said Ethan.

Rayna stared out the window as the flat prairie fields started to give away to rolling hills. Ethan turned into a field and parked on the edge of a coulee. He got out and led Rayna carefully down the side. Rayna grabbed onto tree branches to help her move down the steep slope until they came to the bottom. A trickling creek moved slowly through and the sounds of crickets chirping filled the air.

"It's beautiful," Rayna said, looking around. "I didn't know there were places like this in Silver Heights."

"I should have taken you here before. The valley stretches on for miles. We own this section." He took her hand and guided her further in. He stopped in front of a pile of stones with a handmade wooden cross.

Emotion burned in her throat. "Ethan... did you?"

"I thought we should do something. It didn't feel right not doing anything." He looked at her nervously. "It's a little strange, I know..."

"No, it's perfect." Rayna bent and ran her hand down the cross. "It's perfect." The tears came again and this time she didn't fight to hold them in. Ethan came up behind her and wrapped his arms around her. She leaned into his chest, the feel of him making her cry harder; it had been so long since they last touched.

"I'm sorry," he murmured into her hair.

She couldn't speak, so she just shook her head.

"I love you, Rayna."

"I love you too," she turned to face him. "I want us to try again for a baby, maybe not right away, but eventually. I want to have a family with you, Ethan."

He brushed a tear from her cheek, "I want that too." He kissed her lightly on her forehead. "We will be okay."

They stayed that way for a while, holding each other. Then Ethan drove her back and dropped her off at the house. Rayna watched him drive away, then she knelt by her garden and started to clear away the weeds to make room for the life trying to grow beneath the mess.

PART TWO

CHAPTER SEVENTEEN: RAYNA

December 2001

"Oh da... drat," Rayna quickly corrected herself and looked around for her eldest daughter. Emma had a habit of picking up on Rayna's bad language and storing it until Ethan was around. Although Rayna liked to think her daughter was a sweet innocent who didn't know better, she was certain Emma liked to get her in trouble. Emma was busy though, imparting her three-year-old wisdom upon Grace who frowned at her big sister as Emma importantly lectured her on why she couldn't have the soother.

"It's for babies," Emma informed her. "You're not a baby, so you can't have it." Grace frowned at the soother waving in Emma's hand. Emma didn't have a problem when she had to give up the bottle and soothers, but Grace was a little more stubborn. Especially since Ben was born. She would often steal his soother from his mouth, something Emma was quick to report on.

"Girls, why don't you draw me a picture?" Rayna called, sensing a battle on the horizon. She stopped to gather the broken pieces of the ornament she had dropped and place it back in the box. The afternoon had started out well enough. The girls had been excited to help with the Christmas decorations, but as time went on and Rayna's extensive collection of décor kept coming out of boxes, their enthusiasm turned to boredom. Now, they were merely watching and licking the broken candy-cane pieces that had fallen onto the floor as Rayna decorated the tree.

"I don't want to," Emma said quickly, her default answer for anything Rayna suggested.

"I don't want to," Grace repeated, still eyeing the soother.

Rayna sighed. "How about a Christmas one for Daddy? He would like that."

Emma considered this, then finally deemed the suggestion acceptable. "Okay, Grace come on!" She hauled her sister by her hand and led her to their bedroom. That would keep them busy for all of ten minutes. Rayna shook her head and turned back to the tree. She hummed along to Burl Ives' bass tone as he solemnly sang *Silent Night.*

She hung the last ornament in the box and stepped back to review her handiwork. The tree, which was real this year much to Ethan's disapproval ("It makes such a mess," he had grumbled as he dragged it through the front door, leaving behind a trail of pine needles.), exploded with handmade crafts from the kids and herself, with red and silver circular ornaments scattered throughout. It looked a little chaotic with the mix of paper snowflakes, lifesaver strings, candy canes and a string of colourful lights, but Rayna loved it. It very much summed up her family at the moment.

The phone rang and Rayna hurried to answer it before it woke Ben, who was slumbering in a laundry basket on the table.

"I got it!" Grace yelled, stumbling from her bedroom with a piece of paper and crayon in hand.

"No, I got it." Rayna snatched the receiver before Grace could reach it. "Hello?" Grace shot her a pouty look then retreated to her bedroom.

"Hey! It's Angie."

Rayna stilled. "You finished it?"

"I did."

"And?" She held her breath.

"I loved it. It was so good."

"Really? It wasn't boring? Did you care about the characters?"

"I did, I couldn't put it down. I don't think I've ever read a book so fast before."

"You're not just saying that?"

"I'm not. I was fully prepared to give you a very brutal and honest review. Have you showed anybody else yet?"

"No, you're the first. Ethan hasn't even read it. Although, he doesn't like reading so he probably never will."

"We've got to get this into the right hands." Angie paused. "You know who you should give it to..."

"Don't say it."

"She has two books published and a third coming out. Obviously, she knows what she's doing."

Rayna gripped the phone hard against her ear. Over her dead body would she give her manuscript to Mila. She could just picture her sitting there all smug with her books around her. Mila just *knew* the right people, that's why she got published. It had nothing to do with her writing. Even as she thought it, Rayna knew it wasn't completely true. She had read both books Mila had written (she had borrowed them from Angie, no way would she have bought them and given Mila her money) and to her disappointment she had actually liked them.

Angie sighed on the other end. "You need to get over it, you are both my friends and..."

"I'll think about it." Rayna interrupted. She didn't want to go over this tired conversation again. "Thanks so much for reading it."

"Anytime! What are you up to?"

"Decorating."

"Seriously? Just now? We had everything decorated before December even hit."

"We are late this year, usually I get Ethan to..." The sound of the door opening and a voice calling hello cut Rayna off. "Hey, I think Chloe is here. I got to go. I'll see you tonight."

"Don't be late!" Angie warned.

Rayna hung up and turned around as Chloe entered the living room.

"Rayna!" Chloe dropped her suitcases and swept Rayna up in a tight hug. She smelled as expensive as she looked, with her long black button up coat, silver hoop earrings and brand name jeans. Rayna ran her hand down the wrinkled shirt of Ethan's she had thrown over her sweat pants that morning and wished she had dressed properly. Or had at least showered. Her hair was a frizzy mess, and she was uncomfortably aware she didn't even know where her deodorant stick was.

"You look amazing," Rayna said.

"It looks like Christmas threw up in here." Chloe observed spinning around.

"Aunty Chloe!" Emma came tearing out of her room, followed closely by Grace.

Chloe laughed as she bent and hugged them. "My favourite nieces! Guess what? Aunty brought you some Christmas presents." They squealed as Chloe pulled out two colourfully wrapped gifts.

"Put them under the tree," Rayna instructed the girls as they grabbed them from Chloe.

"Can we open them now mom? Please?" Emma begged.

"Pleeeease?" Grace echoed.

"Maybe tonight after the Christmas concert," said Rayna.

They jumped up and down and ungracefully hurled the presents under the tree. "Go finish your pictures okay?" Rayna said. They darted back to their room laughing and yelling. Rayna looked at the presents, "I hope those weren't breakable."

"They aren't. It's only Barbie dolls. So, this is Benjamin!" Chloe peeked over at Ben, who was blinking resentfully at them having been woken by all the noise. "Oh my God, what a cutie! How old is he now? I can't believe this is the first time I'm seeing him." She lifted him up carefully and cradled him in her arms.

"He's almost four months."

"He looks exactly like Ethan. Don't you think? Same nose. Emma looks like Ethan too."

Rayna nodded her agreement. Emma bore a striking resemblance to her father. The same coloured hair and blue eyes, she was a Miller through and through. Little Grace on the other hand was a mini Rayna, dark curly hair that was wild and untamable most days and dark brown eyes. Both girls however were identical in their tendency to be stubborn and irrationally crazy. Rayna suspected this came more from her than Ethan. She prayed Ben would get his father's easygoing nature along with his nose. Just one calm child would be nice.

"Sorry I haven't been out more, things have been crazy busy," said Chloe.

"Do you want tea?" Rayna led her to the kitchen and started the kettle. "How is work going? We saw you on the news the other night."

Chloe beamed. "The holiday shopping story? That was just a puff piece. I will cover more serious stuff in the New Year. My boss really likes me, it's been incredible. Things are moving so fast now. I mean it's about time, I've paid my dues." She kissed Ben on the cheek. "That's right Benny! Aunty is going to be a famous TV reporter. Yes, she is!"

Rayna smiled a little as she filled their mugs with steaming water. "That's awesome, Chloe."

"Thanks!" Chloe said. "So, how are you? How's the mom life?"

"It's good," Rayna said. "Not as glamorous as a TV reporter, a little more puke and less sleep."

"Don't be so sure," Chloe said seriously. "I had to cover the opening of this gay club and right as we finished this guy puked all over me." She shuddered. "Still, I can't imagine being a mom right now. I can barely imagine being a girlfriend!"

"Ya it's..." Rayna searched for the right word. "Busy."

"But don't you get bored? Being home all day?"

"Um, well there's a lot to do."

"I guess cooking and cleaning and stuff, right? Man, I couldn't be a stay-at-home mom. I think I would feel so unfulfilled, you know what I mean? Like, I would go crazy."

"Ya..." Rayna's face flushed. "It's not for everyone I guess. I'm working on some writing too. I just finished a draft for a novel, actually."

"Oh, ya. That's a cool hobby, something to pass the time."

Rayna was spared having to answer by the arrival of Ethan. He came through the door shaking snow out of his hair. "Hey, Chloe! Nice news story last night."

"Daddy!" Two voices screamed at the top of their lungs as they launched out of the bedroom. Every time Ethan came home it was like he had been gone for days. He laughed as he bent and hugged them and gave exaggerated praise on the drawings they stuffed in his hand. Grace's looked like a bunch of squiggling green lines, but Emma's might have resembled a tree. The noise proved too much for Benjamin who opened his mouth and let out a loud wail. Rayna took him from Chloe and hugged him to her.

Chloe made a show of covering her ears. "Maybe I should stay at mom's" she grinned.

"Maybe you should," Rayna said, feeling irritated. "Girls! Bath time!"

"Nooooo!" Grace shouted, running as fast as her two-year-old legs could take her.

"Ethan can you get them started? I need to feed Ben," Rayna called over Ben's increasingly loud cries.

"I'll do it!" Chloe started after her nieces.

Rayna noticed they listened a lot better to Chloe than they did to her. Little traitors.

Rayna took Ben to her room and sat on the bed as she nursed. Ethan came in, still clutching the drawings.

"You know we have to leave in an hour."

"I'm aware."

He eyed her frizzy hair and sweat pants. "O-kay..."

"I'm aware Ethan. The girl's dresses are laid out, it won't take us long."

"Isn't Emma supposed to be a sheep or something?" Ethan stripped off his shirt and bent to look in the dresser mirror. "Do I need to shower?"

"She's a shepherd, they keep the costumes at the church. You could probably get away with wetting your hair down."

Ethan peered critically at his image. "I'm going bald," he announced as he moved his head side to side.

Rayna raised her eyebrows at his mass of wavy brown hair. "You're the hairiest man I've ever seen." Her eyes drifted pointedly down his chest.

"I think it's starting to recede. My dad's bald."

"Isn't it the mom's dad that determines baldness? Was your Grandpa bald?"

"I don't know. He died when I was a kid, I'll have to ask."

"Well, I think you're safe, anyway."

"For now," Ethan frowned, patting it down. "Will you still love me if I go bald?"

"You're not going to."

"But if I do?"

"We will shave your chest and put it on your head."

"Ha, ha." Ethan turned away from the mirror. "Is he done? I can take him, you should probably shower."

"Probably," Rayna said sarcastically. She handed Ben to Ethan who patted him on the back to burp him. Rayna paused in the doorway to their bathroom. "Chloe thinks my life sucks."

"What do you mean?"

"She thinks I'm wasting my life being a stay-at-home mom."

"She said that?"

"Pretty much."

Ethan grinned. "Want me to beat her up for you?"

"Maybe, let me think on it."

"Oh, before I forget, four more chickens are dead."

"What?" Rayna said. "Seriously?"

"Blood and feathers everywhere, I think it was a weasel this time."

"Damn it!" The chickens had not been panning out. This was the third bunch Rayna had bought and each time they barely made it through the winter. "I'm done, I can't deal with them anymore."

"Maybe you should switch to a less fragile animal, like turtles."

"Funny," Rayna said, shutting the bathroom door.

One hour, a traumatic hair-combing episode and a frantic hunt for shoes later they were finally ready and out the door. They got to the church as the first carol was being sung. Angie swept over to take Emma to the other kids, shooting Rayna an exasperated look. Angie got stuck organizing the program this year and wasn't dealing well with the pressure.

"The Three Wise Men have all lost their gifts," she hissed to Rayna. "And I can't find the bloody baby Jesus doll. It's a disaster."

"Do you need help?" Rayna asked, pulling Grace's coat off.

"No, no. Go sit and enjoy this train wreck." Angie grabbed Emma's arm and hauled her away.

Ethan grinned and winked at Rayna as he setup the video camera at the back. Rayna took Grace's hand and led her into their usual pew. Ben was happily sucking on his soother so she left him in his car seat beside her. Chloe had gone to sit with Carol across the aisle who waved to Grace.

"I sit with Grandma," said Grace as she tried to move past Rayna.

"No, Grace. Not now." Rayna grabbed her and swung her on her hip, grunting at the weight. When did she get so big? Soon she would join Emma with the preschoolers. It always amazed Rayna how one day she would look at her children and they would differ completely from the previous week. Life was moving far too fast now. She wanted to slow it down and capture the moments instead of letting them fade into the forgotten place unremembered memories go.

Rayna sang along to the carols while looking around the church. It was decorated nice for the holidays. Red bows were strung along the end of the pews and the stage boasted a tall, impeccably decorated Christmas tree. It's white Christmas lights winked and twinkled in the dim lighting.

'Joy To The World' was followed by one of Rayna's favourites; 'O Come O Come Emmanuel'. She especially liked when the men and women split, each singing a verse then joining again for the chorus. When the men sang alone, their deep voices rang out powerfully against the old church walls and vibrated through the wooden pews. It sent chills down her spine. She didn't think there was a sound more beautiful than voices raised together as one, singing so loudly they overpowered the instruments. Even though she had been attending church for years now, she still felt a little out of place. Like a guest on Sunday mornings more observing then taking part. Their ways were still a mystery to her, as was their faith. But at times like this, she was almost sure she glimpsed the God they all spoke of, the one she tried to talk to now and then.

The music faded away, and the spell was broken. There was a rustling and coughing as people sat and Angie nervously made her way to the front. Rayna put Grace beside her brother and tried to smile encouragingly at Angie. She had confessed to Rayna that she dreaded public speaking. Rayna found this a little ironic considering how Angie was usually so outgoing. She felt bad for her now though, watching as Angie's hands trembled as she gripped her piece of paper.

"Good evening," Angie started. She paused and cleared her throat, then began to read. "In those days, Caesar Augustus issued a degree that a census should be taken of the entire Roman world. And everyone went to their hometowns to register. So, Joseph went up from Nazareth to Bethlehem, the town of David. He took with him Mary, who was pledged to be married to him and expecting a child."

There was a twitter of laughter as a young boy came down the aisle shyly holding hands with a girl who had a pillow stuffed under her shirt. They made their way onto the stage and as the story unfolded other little kids in homemade costumes joined them. Rayna smiled when she spotted Emma amongst the shepherds. They had towels secured by headbands around their heads and bathrobes as part of their costume. They smiled tentatively at all the adult eyes as they dutifully used sticks to tap the children who were baaing and crawling on their hands and knees like sheep. By the end all the children were on stage kneeling and listening to Angie finish reading. (Baby Jesus was a rolled-up towel and the Three Wise Men were clutching a coffee mug, a Bible and a toy from the nursery).

Angie finished reading and folded up her paper. "We will now take up a special offering that the children decided would go to towards our missionary friends in Kenya. If the ushers would come forward?"

Two teenage boys shuffled to the front and Angie handed them the offering plates. She prayed quickly then nodded to her daughter, Helen, at the piano who started to plunk away at the keys. The children started singing 'Away In A Manger' in their small tuneless voices. Ben began to cry. The reason Rayna discovered quickly was because Grace had taken the soother from him and was happily sucking on it.

"Grace, give that back to Ben," Rayna hissed. Grace shook her head no. Ben began to cry louder and a few heads turned their way. "Now, Grace!" Rayna tried to grab it from her but Grace darted to the other side of Ben. Rayna huffed a sigh and started to unbuckle Ben from his seat. Just as she pulled him up he let out a stream of vomit that landed largely down the front of Rayna's dress. Rayna groaned and bit back a very undignified word.

"Grace-give-me-the-soother-now." Rayna tried to speak quietly, but Ben was having a complete meltdown. She reached over and grabbed the soother out of Grace's mouth, who immediately began to wail. The offering plate had made its way down her aisle and her neighbour, old Evelyn Pratt, held it tentatively, eyeing the vomit with her nose wrinkled. Rayna reached for the plate just as Grace launched herself over the car seat and tried to grab the soother from Ben again.

"No, Grace!" Rayna firmly pushed her back down. Where was Ethan when she needed him? She reached again for the plate but Evelyn had it still, apparently too distracted by the drama to see Rayna trying to grab it from her.

"Grace, stop it!" Rayna said trying to shush her. Ben opened his mouth letting the soother drop and another wave of half-digested breastmilk came forth with such force it splattered against Rayna's neck and down the back of the pew.

"Oh, for fuck's sake! Give me the damn plate!" Rayna yanked the plate from Evelyn's startled hands and thrusted it at the usher who stood with his mouth open. Helen stumbled in her piano playing. The children stopped singing and stared wide-eyed. There was a second of silence before Helen hastily began playing again. Ethan hurried over, picked up Grace and took her out to the entryway.

"Excuse me," Rayna murmured to Evelyn as she stood and held Ben with one hand and the car seat with the other. She made her way out, heat radiating off her cheeks.

As she passed them she heard Chloe say to Carol with a little laugh, "Some things never change."

Ethan was kneeling in the entryway talking quietly to Grace who still had tears streaming down her face. He looked up as she passed with his eyebrows raised, but she quickened her step before he could say anything. She cleaned herself up as best as she could in the bathroom, then hid in the nursery until the program ended. Then with as much dignity as she could muster, she hurried and got her coat on and went to wait in the van for Ethan. He came a few moments later holding both the girl's hands.

Ethan glanced over at her as he pulled out of the parking lot. "Well, that was..."

"Don't."

"Mommy said a bad word," Emma announced.

"Yes, she did." Ethan agreed.

"She said fuck," Emma continued.

Ethan whipped around. "Don't say that Emma!"

"What's fuck?" Grace asked.

"A bad word! Don't say it!" He glared at Rayna.

She turned around in her seat. "Girls, I'm sorry for what I said, that's a grown-up word okay? Little girls aren't allowed to say it."

They drove in silence for a bit then Emma said, "Damn is a bad word too."

Rayna could feel the tension throbbing off Ethan by the time they got home. He was so rigid as he helped the girls get ready for bed she was surprised he didn't snap in two. She waited on their bed nursing Ben, preparing herself for the inevitable scolding she was going to get. He came in just as she finished and was placing Ben in the bassinet at the foot of the bed.

"Chloe texted, she's visiting some friends and will be in late."

"Okay." Rayna eyed him, waiting.

He got ready for bed without a word and slipped under the covers beside her.

Rayna sighed. "I'm sorry, Ethan. I don't know what's wrong with me."

Ethan didn't respond. Tears sprung to her eyes, and she shook her head. "I don't know why I do these stupid things. I wish I could be better."

"It's just..." Ethan started, then stopped. Then he snorted and began to shake as he fought to keep the sudden tide of laughter in.

"Stop it! It's not funny." Rayna swatted him, which caused him to erupt in great bellowing laughs. Despite herself, she began to laugh too.

"I think I got it on camera," Ethan gasped. "All those stunned kids... I can just imagine what they're asking their parents tonight." He clutched his sides as another round of laughter hit.

"It's... not... funny," Rayna wheezed between her own laughs. Ethan turned and pulled Rayna to him. "I wish I was differ-"

"Stop that," Ethan frowned. "I wouldn't have you any other way. Although I would prefer if the girls didn't have such a large vocabulary..."

"I'm trying."

"You know, the girls were exhausted when I put them to bed."

"Oh?"

"I doubt they would wake up even if a train came through here."

"Really... Ben's a heavy sleeper too," Rayna said, smiling with anticipation.

"It would be a shame to not take advantage of it, wouldn't it?" Ethan said, shifting so he lay on top of her.

"It would," Rayna agreed. She ran her hands down his back as he kissed her. They moved quietly, kissing and caressing until Rayna quieted the tornado of thoughts and feelings that were constantly swirling inside her and let herself be consumed by her husband's touch.

CHAPTER EIGHTEEN: RAYNA

Rayna tilted her head back and smiled. The night sky was so covered in stars it almost looked staged, like she was staring at an exaggerated painting of the night instead of the dazzling real thing. There were so many stars dancing around the full silvery moon that it was impossible to focus on only one spot. Her eyes constantly moved between the bright lights as she tried to take it all in. The sheer vastness of it made her chest ache. No matter how many times she had stared up into the stars, it never ceased to amaze her. It was a beautiful reminder of how small she was in this big, deep universe, how truly insignificant her life was in the grand scheme of things; and how much she didn't yet know. She thought it was a little unfair of God to make his most incredible creation so far out of reach, and for it to only be visible when most people were dead asleep. There were so many things humans missed out on because they weren't looking.

The wagon hit a large bump and Rayna grabbed the straw bale she was sitting on to keep from falling. Angie swayed beside her as Jim pulled the trailer through the fields with his tractor. The hayride was a very popular part of the annual party held at the Miller ranch on New Year's Eve. Every year friends and neighbours would gather to celebrate the beginning of the New Year. There was always a roaring bonfire to help keep everyone passably warm, an outdoor rink Jim spend weeks perfecting for the ongoing hockey games, and enough food and hot drinks to feed the entire town. Kids would whip around the backyard playing capture the flag, apparently immune to the cold, and the evening usually ended with a pathetic yet appreciated display of fireworks.

Rayna loved New Year's Eve. She liked the symbolism of the end of something turning into the beginning of something else. She always felt like she could really start fresh. Shake off her old self and begin again. The year ahead seemed to stretch in front of her with mysterious possibilities. Her optimism admittedly would fade after a couple of days when the disappointing realization sunk in that, although the number at the end of the date had changed, nothing else really had. Still, there was something about tonight. Something that made Rayna sure this year just might be different than the rest.

Angie's voice cut through Rayna's silent reflections as she yelled at her son Liam to sit back down. Rayna turned with a start, looking with a slight panic for her own kids. She remembered a second later that they were at home in bed, with Carol watching over them. Rayna didn't leave them often, and this was the first time she had left Ben since he was born, but it was good to get a break. It was a nice change to not have to worry about two little toddlers and a demanding baby for a few hours, although she felt as though she was missing a limb or something. She leaned back and sipped her mug of hot chocolate and tried to relax. It was only for a couple of hours; they were all sleeping anyway. Surely Carol would be fine...

"So," Angie turned to her after making sure Liam had listened. "Let's get going then, shall we?" She reached into her pocket and brought out a notebook, fumbling trying to open it.

Rayna groaned. "You still have that? I was hoping you lost it."

"Of course I didn't. I keep this in a very secure, special place."

"Why do you make us do this every year? It's just depressing."

"It's important to have goals."

"We never stick with them."

"Well, that can be our first one then. *Stick to New Year's resolutions.*" Angie scribbled it down with her pencil, her frozen hands made her writing childish. "Okay, last year you said you wanted to write more, and you did! So, there you go." She frowned, reading further. "You also said you were going to swear less. You can keep working on that... I said I would lose some weight, that didn't happen. And I was going to cut down on coffee, which I did! Pretty good year for us. Progress!"

"We also said we would watch less TV, and you wanted to learn piano and I was going to stop keeping a drawer full of chocolate to snack on," Rayna read off the list.

"We may have been a little too ambitious last year. Anyway, moving on."

Rayna laughed. "Fine, fine. This year I want to... well, I want to have a better relationship with my parents."

"How is that all going?"

"It's been okay. I try calling once a month still and I send them pictures of the kids. I invited them to come out here, and they said they would next month."

"That sounds positive."

Rayna shrugged. "We'll see if they even come. It would be a first."

Angie nodded and wrote it down. "I actually, seriously, will lose weight this year. And I want to have a monthly date night with Tom."

"That's a good one." Rayna thought for a minute. "I want to be more accountable with writing. I get into it for a few weeks then taper off again. Which is probably why my novel took so long to finish."

"How are you going to do that?"

"I don't know. I wish there was a writing group or something in town."

"You should start one," Angie said. "There's bound to be a few people who enjoy writing. I can think of one in particular."

"No."

"Yes! This is perfect. My other resolution is to get you to be nicer to Mila. Two birds with one stone."

"Stop it. I'm not mean to her."

"You're not nice."

"She's the one who flirts with my husband."

"She does not. This is a good idea, Ray."

"No, it really isn't." Rayna couldn't think of anything worse than sitting across from Miss published-two-books-and-has-a-third-coming-out, while she held her pathetic unedited manuscript and asked for tips.

"You really need to stop this. Put away your pride and see what happens. You've been going on lately about how you're worried you won't accomplish anything and you're just a stay-at-home mom..."

"That's because Chloe turned up at Christmas like a fu... frickin' poster-child for the modern-day woman and made me feel like I'm an anti-feminist loser."

"You're exaggerating."

"You didn't hear her. She pretty much said I'm wasting my life."

"She didn't. And you aren't. Geez, Ray, you can't let other people's life choices affect you so much. Everyone is on their own journey, there's no right or wrong way to do life. Unless you're a serial killer or something."

"So, your advice is 'don't kill anyone' and I'll be fine."

"Exactly. I have full confidence you will manage it."

The hayride completed its loop and pulled up in front of the farmyard to unload.

Jim came around the back to help people down. "Had fun ladies?" he asked them with a grin.

"We did. Thanks Jim." Rayna smiled. "Do you want me to get you some hot chocolate before you go again?"

"That was the last one, only twenty minutes till firework time," Jim said brightly. "Tell Ethan if you see him I'm going to start setting up."

Rayna and Angie headed towards the bonfire to warm up. Pastor Tom was standing at the end warming his hands and smiled as they approached. The blazing heat radiating off the large pyramid of crackling wood instantly thawed Rayna's frozen face and made her backside feel even colder. She rotated in a slow circle, trying to distribute the heat.

"How was the hayride?" Pastor Tom asked.

"Good," Angie said. "Liam ran off somewhere, where are the other two?"

"Helen is inside, she said she's too cold. Jake is somewhere," Pastor Tom said, looking around.

Strong arms wrapped around Rayna and the distinct smell of old sweat made her wrinkle her nose.

"There you are," Ethan said in her ear and kissed her cheek.

Rayna wiggled away from him. "You smell."

"Sorry, it's my hockey gloves." Ethan smelled his hands and grimaced. "Where have you been?"

"On the hayride. Your dad's gone to set up the fireworks."

"It's that time already?" Ethan checked his watch. "2002 is almost here! I better go. Hey Dan! Are you coming? Fireworks?" Ethan hollered overtop Rayna's head.

Rayna turned to see Daniel and Mila walk up.

"Yes! I brought some too to add. Where are we setting up?"

"Backyard, where's yours? In your truck?" They turned together and headed off towards the driveway.

"I'll help too," Pastor Tom said. He kissed Angie briefly. "Happy New Year, babe." Then he hurried after Daniel and Ethan.

"Boys and their toys," Angie grinned. "Mila, we were just talking about you. We have an idea to run by you."

Don't you dare. Rayna shot Angie a look, but she ignored her.

"Oh? What's that?" Mila said. She looked chic with her knee-high leather boots and her button-up black coat pressed delicately over the swell of her pregnant belly. Her cheeks were rosy from the cold and her hair fell elegantly passed her shoulders from under her beanie style toque. Rayna reflected that if she didn't look like a photo-shopped supermodel all the time it would be easier to like her.

"Rayna wants to start a writing group," said Angie.

"*We* want to start one," Rayna said quickly. If Angie was hell-bent on forcing this, then she could damn well come.

"That would be awesome. I used to go to one in Toronto, it really helped me get my first book done."

'My first book done.' Please keep reminding us, Rayna thought while managing to put a horrible fake smile on her face.

"Rayna actually has a book done too," Angie said.

Rayna almost went against Angie's advice and committed murder right there.

"Oh really? What's it about?"

"It's just a rough manuscript," Rayna said.

"It's really good," Angie went on ignoring her. "It's a murder mystery set in London during the Blitz. You should read it."

"That sounds interesting, I love anything to do with history." Mila smiled tentatively at Rayna.

Liam came up just then and tugged on Angie's arm. "Mom, Jake fell and got a bloody lip." He gestured to his younger brother, who was behind him holding a bloody mitt to his face.

"Oh, for heaven's sake," Angie sighed. "Come here, Jake." She grabbed his hand and pulled him towards the house.

Rayna watched Angie walk away and shifted uncomfortably. She glanced at Mila who gave her a little smile.

"So, writing group. That would be good," Mila said.

"Yeah."

There was an awkward silence, then Mila tried again. "If you want, I could read your book and give you feedback? I really like doing that type of thing."

"Um, well it's only a rough draft, it's not very good yet," Rayna said. She wished one of her kids would come to her bleeding so she had an excuse to leave.

"I'm sure it's better than you think. I always think my books are terrible until I read over them again and realize they aren't too bad. It's helpful to get feedback too, then you kind of know where to go with it."

"Okay, sure. I'll bring it to church this week." Rayna said. *Now please, shut up about it.* Mila's niceness was really starting to irritate her. Rayna would take the olive branch and give her the stupid thing. It would keep Angie happy. Plus, as much as she hated to admit it, she really could use feedback from someone who knew writing.

Much to Rayna's relief, Daniel came running over and cupped his hands to his mouth. "Everyone! Fireworks are over there!" He pointed behind him to the backyard. "Countdown starts in five minutes!"

The crowd shuffled obediently forward, shivering as they left the heat of the fire behind. They hunched together, stomping their feet and tucking their hands in their armpits for warmth, waiting for the big moment. Someone with a watch gave the one-minute warning then led the group in the ten-second countdown. Shouts of "Happy New Year!" filled Rayna's ears and the first firework went off, whistling through the air and exploding in a bright, fiery show of red sparks. There was a slight delay before the next one went off; the operation never ran quite as smoothly as the movies, but everyone oohed and awed with exaggerated enthusiasm in a show of support. One firework went off a little closer to the ground than expected and they could see the outline of the four men running for cover to gales of laughter.

Rayna grinned looking at all the neighbours and friends pressed together–her feeling about a good year coming felt stronger than ever.

****

"This is a terrible idea."

"No, it's not," said Angie firmly. "It's a great idea."

Rayna scowled at her, bouncing her knee up and down. She looked at the clock. "She's late."

"She's not. There's three minutes till seven."

Rayna threw down her pen on top of her notebook. "Why are we even doing this?"

"Because. Stop complaining."

"You could have got a few more people to come at least."

"You could have too," Angie shot back. "I'm not the president of this thing, I'm not even a writer."

Rayna snorted and glanced at the door again. The library wasn't very busy this evening, only one or two others were slowly meandering around the shelves. She had hoped Angie and Mila would have forgotten about the writer's club, but a few weeks after New Year's Angie had informed Rayna their first meeting would be the first of February. Rayna hadn't talked with Mila since she had handed over her manuscript the following Sunday after the party. She'd tried not to think about it, but she had been in a state of anxiety ever since. Why hadn't Mila gotten back to her yet? Was it so terrible she didn't know what to say? Was she laughing at her? Telling her Toronto friends what an untalented loser her ex had married? The more Rayna thought about it, the more convinced she was that Mila was doing this to her on purpose; torturing her just for sport. She probably hadn't even read it yet. Rayna was about to tell Angie her suspicions when Mila came in and hurried towards them.

"Hi! Sorry I'm late." She shrugged out of her coat and delicately sat down with her hand resting on her bump.

"You're right on time," Angie said. "How goes the pregnancy? You look amazing by the way."

"Thanks," Mila beamed. "It's going really well. It's so cool feeling the baby kicking and moving. Danny's been the absolute best. He won't let me do a single thing around the house."

Angie snorted. "Enjoy it while you can, by the second and third they stop the royal treatment."

Mila laughed.

"So, should we get started then?" Rayna asked, fiddling with her notebook.

"Actually, I invited someone else to join," Mila said. "I hope you don't mind."

"Who?"

The door opened again before Mila could respond and in walked Craig, his red hair glistening with snowflakes and a big grin on his face. "Ladies! Sorry I'm late, I brought beverages." He held out a tray of hot drinks then looked around quickly. "We can have drinks in here, right? I've never actually been in here before."

"For sure. Thanks, Craig," Angie said.

Craig sat down and handed them out. "I got two teas and two coffees. I haven't missed anything have I?"

"No, we haven't started yet. I didn't know you liked writing, Craig." Rayna took one of the cups and her spirits lifted considerably. She had grown to like Craig over the years and was glad it was him who'd come. He would help make this evening a little less awkward.

"I do a little, nothing serious. Mila mentioned the group in passing and I thought, well why not?"

Angie turned to Mila. "Since you've been in a writing group before, we thought maybe you could give us a rundown of how it worked?"

Mila shrugged. "Well, it was pretty simple. We met every two weeks and whoever wanted to would share what they had written and then we would offer some critique. Sometimes we would do writing exercises or organize a workshop weekend. Maybe since there are so few of us, we could each take a turn heading up a meeting? We could all read what we brought, then the person in charge could lead some kind of writing exercise or something?"

Angie nodded. "That sounds great, only can we just meet once a month? I think that's all I will be able to handle." Everyone nodded their agreement.

"Great," Mila said. "Everyone brought something to read tonight? Angie, want to start us off?"

"Sure. Writing is a new thing for me, so I just wrote a little poem to share tonight." She cleared her throat then read:

I don't really do much writing,
But I'm here so my friends quit their fighting.
For they both have kissed the same man,
So, their rivalry began
But they need to get over it because this town is small
And the awkwardness is driving me up the wall

She leaned back and smiled sincerely. Rayna glared at her, feeling her cheeks heating. Mila bit her lip, looking like she might laugh.

"I liked it," said Craig, breaking the silence. "Very honest piece, and it rhymed which was very poem-ish."

"Thank you, Craig," Angie said sweetly. "It was from the heart."

"Uh huh. Thanks for that Angie," Rayna said dryly, careful to avoid looking at Mila. "I'll go next? I just have a little story thing. Flash fiction, I guess it's called. I titled it *Legacy*." Rayna shifted in her seat as she flipped open her notebook to the right page, her hands shaking slightly. She was nervous to be sharing her writing, it was like she was putting herself on display, exposing her most vulnerable side. She had debated sharing a short story she was currently working on, but she didn't feel she could handle critique on it yet. She'd settled on an old piece she'd written a few years back; it was short, so she didn't have to talk long. Taking a breath, she began to read.

Hanging from a rusty nail in the rickety horse barn was an old, worn-out lasso rope. The cowboy who wielded it had long since passed on, leaving the ranch to his descendants. Back in its glory years, expert hands had used the rope nearly every day. It cut through the air, landing perfectly around a calf's neck. Pulling tight, it would keep the animal secure while the men rushed forward to brand their mark in its hide. The lasso would then get coiled back up, where it would wait, like a cobra ready to strike, for its next chance to prove its worth. The shifting nerves of the snorting horse and the strong hands of the cowboy would vibrate through its fiber. Years of progress had rendered this method of work less efficient. Now the lasso sat like an old forgotten friend, a silent witness to the comings and goings in the barn. Its once taut strands were limp, and gifts from the pigeons roosting in the roof decorated the exterior. Dust had settled deep into its threads, turning the colour to a depressed grey. It had become such a part of the barn no one would ever think of moving it. It belonged there much like the windows, the wooden planks and peeling paint. If only that old lasso could speak and educate the people hurrying by about their very own history. It would tell captivating stories of long nights on cattle drives, camping on the trail, fighting through the best of what Mother Nature could conjure... But it just hangs there, a memento of days past.

Rayna finished and looked up nervously.

"That was awesome. Good descriptions," Craig said.

Angie nodded. "Nice Rayna, I liked it a lot."

Mila smiled at her, "It was great. I love flash fiction pieces, they're like little glimpses into a bigger picture."

"Thanks," Rayna said, feeling herself relax.

Of course, they would be positive about anything she read. She didn't know why she was so nervous. Thinking maybe next time she would bring her new story, she turned her attention to Craig, who went next. He shared a spirited piece about a hunter who had gotten lost and had to spend the night in the woods. The story took an unexpected twist when the character saw a ghost and ended up discovering a murdered body. The writing was surprisingly good and Rayna gave him some honest praise afterwards. Mila gave a bit of advice on a few things which Craig happily jotted down, then she shared a bit of the new novel she was working on. It was centered on a journalist who gets romantically involved with an aspiring actor. After they finished, Mila led them in a writing exercise where they had to write a scene from a first-person perspective and then again from a third-person view.

An hour later, Rayna was walking to her van feeling rather excited. It had been fun to sit and talk about writing with others who liked it too. She even found that she had maybe ever so slightly enjoyed Mila's company.

Maybe.

Rayna had reached her van when she heard Mila call out behind her, "Hey, Rayna!" Rayna turned and waited for Mila to make her way carefully over the iced pavement, one hand protectively over her large belly.

"I have been bursting to tell you, but I didn't want to say in front of the others because, well I don't know. I wanted to tell you in private," she said breathlessly. "First off, I'm sorry it's taken me so long to get back to you about your manuscript. But I had a really good reason. I read it in about three days. I really loved it. I immediately sent it to my agent, Maggie. She just got back to me today and Rayna, she loved it too! She wants to represent you and get it published!"

"What?" Rayna stared at her dumbfounded. "What did you say?"

"Your book is going to be published! Maggie thinks she knows a publisher who will be interested. I didn't want to tell you until I knew it was going to happen."

"You're... you're kidding right? This is a joke?"

"I'm not, Maggie will call you this week, 1 think. So, keep your phone near you."

"1 can't believe... wow Mila. Thank you!" Rayna laughed. "1 can't believe you did this for me."

Mila shrugged. "Consider it an apology for... well, you know."

"For being the worst ex-girlfriend my husband could have had?"

"Something like that." Mila smiled.

"Well, thank you. Honestly, you have no idea what this means to me." Rayna said. Published. She was going to be a published author! All those years of dreaming and now it was right in front of her.

When Rayna got home, she went to her bookshelf and ran her finger down the spine of her grandma's old novels, as she used to do when she was a little girl. To think soon she would have her own sitting right there beside it. Fierce joy coursed through her, making her hand tremble. She knew this would be her year. Finally, everything was going as she always imagined it would.

CHAPTER NINETEEN: ETHAN

Ethan checked the monitor that showed the weight in the back of the silage truck then raised the radio to his lips. "We're full."

"Roger that, I'm gonna run a few bales to the heifers," his dad answered.

Ethan watched the tractor back away from the silage truck in his review mirror, then he jolted forward towards the field. He bounced excessively in the driver's seat–the truck's shocks were starting to go, along with the heat and the radio. It wasn't worth buying a new one yet though, as much as Ethan would have liked to. It still got the job done even if it offered very few comforts to the operator.

Ethan hopped out quickly to swing the gate open, then continued on. Even though it was fairly warm outside for a February day, his breath still rose in a white cloud before him, and his fingers were numb gripping the steering wheel. He came across the herd just over the second hill. They were spread out in all directions, but as soon as they heard the silage truck rumbling across the snow they started running towards him. They trailed behind, calling out as they waited impatiently for the food to drop. He pressed the brake and was immediately swarmed, the cows pressed on every side of him pushing to get to the front. Ethan flicked the switch, lowering the spout, and turned on the unload augurs so the silage spilled onto the ground. He inched forward slowly, leaving a trail of fermented fodder mixed with mineral and grain behind him. The cows lined up shoulder to shoulder on either side as they ate greedily, their backsides facing outward and their heads down, creating a solid wall of warm red and black hides.

Sometimes he amused himself by making little designs, zig-zagging back and forth or going in a great big circle, but he didn't have time to fool around today. Today was *the* day. The day his in-laws would make their grand appearance. Not once in his almost six years of marriage had they shown any interest in his family. They barely ever called Rayna, but her mom would be furious if Ray went too long without calling them. They had gone to see them a couple times, but never once had they offered to come out and visit.

When Rayna suggested she once again invite them out, he had said sure. They weren't likely to say yes, anyway. But lo-and-behold they did, and Rayna had been on edge the past week trying to get ready. On edge was being kind. She had turned into a complete maniac and Ethan thought it would have been better if they'd rejected her again instead of agreeing to come. He tried to be supportive; this was important to Rayna so by default it was important to him. Yet, he wished she could just let them go. He hated the way she reverted to this uncertain, timid girl around them.

Maybe he was being too pessimistic. After all, they were coming. Maybe it was a sign things would get better. And maybe this year pigs really would learn to fly. Who knew?

It probably didn't help much that Ethan knew they didn't overly like him. To be fair, he didn't think Alice and Greg liked much in this world. The first (official) time Ethan met them was also when he asked for their daughter's hand in marriage. He knew it would have been hard for anyone, meeting their only daughter's boyfriend at the same time he was asking to take her away. But he never could forget the way Alice had sneered at him and laughed like it was the most absurd thing she had ever heard. Greg hadn't said much, which Ethan learned quickly was his usual response to situations.

The unofficial first time he had met them was through the doorway of their house the night he had surprised Rayna. He couldn't think of that night without wanting to break something. It was best to keep that memory blocked away if he had any hope of doing what Rayna wanted and try to make an effort with them.

He thought he might be able to handle Greg for a week, but Alice had a way of sneaking in these underhanded insults that Ethan didn't quite realize were rude until he thought about it later. The whole thing was too much drama for him, but he would be supportive. He would power through the awkward visit and hope the week went by quickly.

He finished the load then brought the silage truck back to the shop and parked it. They'd managed to get all the chores done in a little over two hours today. Not too bad. He got in his truck and drove the short distance back to his house. He sat in the driveway for a minute, enjoying the peace and quiet while he still could. Sighing deeply, he forced himself to go up the steps and inside and was immediately assaulted.

"There you are! What took you so long?" Rayna snapped, rushing past, her hands covered in yellow rubber cleaning gloves and grasping the mop.

"Sorry, I tried to…"

"Ben! No!" Rayna sprinted across the room, nearly tripping over the bucket of soapy water to grab Ben, who had vomited and was rolling around in the mess. "I just finished mopping. You've got to be kidding me."

"I got him." Ethan gently lifted Ben from her arms and took him to his bedroom for a quick wipe down and a change of clothes. When he came out again, he found Rayna standing on a chair, dusting the top of the bookshelf. "They won't look up there you know."

"If you're not going to be helpful, then you can leave."

Ethan quirked his eyebrow at Ben, who gave him a big gummy smile. "Where are the girls?" he asked, gently setting him down again.

"In their room." Rayna hopped down and walked quickly to the kitchen.

Ethan went to the girls' room and cracked the door open. Emma and Grace looked up from their game of Barbies.

"Hi, Daddy." Emma said. "Do you want to hide in here too?"

Ethan bit his lip to keep from laughing. "No, I'm gonna help your mom. Thanks for the offer though." She shrugged as if to say 'suit yourself' and turned back to their game.

Ethan left them to it and cautiously approached Rayna. "What can I do?"

"Empty the trash, and can you give Ben his bottle?"

Ethan went to the cupboard to take out the formula they had recently switched to. He frowned. "Ray, what's this?"

"What?" Rayna looked up, distracted from scrubbing the countertop.

"Why did you buy all these bottles of wine?"

"That's the kind my mom drinks."

"So? Why would you encourage that?"

Rayna's face flushed. "I'm not *encouraging* it. You don't understand, she can't go without. It will be worse if she does."

"I don't think we should supply—"

"Don't give your opinion about something you know nothing about."

"Fine." Ethan grabbed the formula and shut the cupboard door. "What time is the blessed event occurring?"

Rayna glared at him. "They'll be here in an hour."

Ethan resisted the temptation to take up Emma's offer after all and retreat to her bedroom. He watched Rayna fly around the house, cleaning and re-cleaning everything in reach. Finally, just when he was trying to stop her from taking the broom out again, there was a knock at the door. Rayna whirled around, carefully tried to flatten her hair, then opened the door.

"Mom, Dad, you guys made it!"

"Barely," Alice said, giving her daughter a stiff hug. She looked the same as she always did, light brown hair streaked with grey twisted up into a bun, her face lightly lined with wrinkles. "It was damn hard to find. You really live out in the middle of nowhere, don't you?"

"Greg, how are you?" Ethan shook his hand then turned to Alice. "Always nice to see you, Alice."

"Ethan, you look the same as ever." Her eyes flickered over him.

"I'll take that as a compliment."

"Take it however you want." Alice turned back to Rayna. "You've almost lost all the baby fat."

Rayna looked down at herself. "I'm getting there..."

"You really have been popping them out, haven't you? Ben is your last, right?"

"Um..." Rayna glanced at Ethan.

Ethan clenched his fists. Two seconds in the door and already he had to fight the urge to leave the room. He might have to drink some of that wine in order to get through this. Before Alice could say anything else, Emma and Grace came cautiously into the room, their little faces arranged in a curious expression as they looked at their grandparents.

"Hi Grandma. Hi Grandpa." Emma gave them a little smile.

Greg bent and gave the girls a hug, "You both are so big. Where is my grandson?"

"Napping," Rayna said. "He should wake up soon."

"This is for you." Grace shyly handed Alice a piece of paper with some scribbles on it.

"Well, these are lovely, thank you." Alice smiled. She ran her hand over Grace's curls, "Oh dear, what a rat's nest your hair is. Why don't you get a brush and I can see what I can do."

Grace looked uncertainly at Rayna who said quickly, "It's fine. She needs to have a bath tonight. Girls why don't you go watch a show?" Emma and Grace darted away, taking advantage of the rare permission to watch TV in the middle of the day.

Rayna led her parents into the living room. "Do you guys want tea? Coffee?" She watched them look around, wringing her hands.

Ethan wished she would take a breath and relax. It was getting painful watching how tense she was.

"I'll take a coffee," said Greg.

Rayna hurried to the kitchen. Ethan sat down on the couch and tapped his knee watching his in-laws. "So, what have you been up to Greg?"

"Not much, working mostly."

"Would you guys like to go on a tour of the ranch after lunch?"

Greg nodded. "Sure."

"I think I'll pass," said Alice. "It's freezing out here, and I'm not a fan of cows. Do you people notice the smell of cow manure out here? Or I suppose you get used to it."

Ethan gave her a tight smile. Rayna came back and handed her dad a mug of coffee and shot Ethan a look.

"It's a nice place you have here," Greg said.

Rayna looked around, "Sorry the house is a bit of a mess."

"Well, you do have three children," Alice frowned. "Maybe you should try to get a housecleaner, it would help make this place a little more livable."

That was about all Ethan could take at the moment. He stood up. "Greg, why don't you take that coffee to go and we'll head out on the tour now." He didn't wait for a response but went to the kitchen to find a travel mug. One week was looking a lot longer than it had this morning.

****

Ethan leaned back on the bed, arms folded as he watched Rayna try on another sweater and stare at herself in the mirror, twisting this way and that. He felt a familiar warmth of pleasure as his eyes traced her form. Her body was different than when they first got married–her curves were slightly more pronounced since being pregnant, and her breasts hadn't fully lost their plumpness from breastfeeding Ben yet. The effect was one Ethan rather liked.

"Come here," he said.

Rayna frowned at the expression on his face, "We don't have time for that."

"I can be quick."

She snorted and pulled the sweater off and tossed it on the floor. Selecting another, she tried it on and turned to face him. "What do you think of this? Does it look okay?"

"It looks better off."

"Stop it." She turned back to the mirror and started piling her hair up into a bun.

He watched as she pinned the escaping pieces with bobby pins, wishing she would leave her curls down and wild. He liked it best when he could slide the curls between his fingers.

"We're just going to Mom's, you don't need to dress up," he said. His mom had invited them and over for a late supper that evening to spend time with Rayna's parents while they were out. Thank goodness they had; Ethan wasn't sure he could take another evening of sitting around waiting until he could politely go to bed.

"I'm not dressing up," Rayna said. "If you're done getting ready you should go visit with my parents."

"No thanks."

She shot him a glare. "It wouldn't kill you to try a little harder with them."

"I am trying."

"No, you're not. You've barely been here."

"I've been here as much as I can, Rayna. I still have to work."

"You've barely talked to them."

"Neither have you."

"What are you talking about?" She turned and faced him with her hands on her hips. "I stay up every night talking to Mom."

"You sit with her every night while she drinks and complains to you. The rest of the day you're running around like a paranoid clean-freak scrubbing the place down and telling the kids to be quiet."

As soon as the words were out, he wished them back. Her lips thinned as her eyes narrowed, colour rose in her cheeks and he braced himself.

"A *paranoid clean-freak*?"

"Sorry," he said, swinging his legs down and getting up. "You're right, I'll go visit."

"Don't do that."

"What?"

"Be a jerk and then try to get away with it."

"I'm sorry. I shouldn't have said anything."

"But that's what you really think."

Ethan sighed. They had reached the point where the conversation would start to spiral into something else, and he wouldn't even know what they were talking about anymore. He should have kept his mouth shut, but the past three days had turned his wife into an unrecognizable person and he couldn't stand around and watch it any longer.

"I don't want to fight Rayna, please," he said. "Let's go have a nice time tonight. You're telling everyone about your book, right?"

She stared at him for a moment, debating whether to let the argument go. Finally, she answered, "Yes," and turned back to the mirror to adjust a few more curls.

"That's exciting," Ethan said, trying to keep things friendly.

She rolled her eyes. "Let's just go, please."

Ethan followed her out of the bedroom. Greg and Alice were standing in the kitchen, the air between them thick as they glared in opposite directions. They had obviously been arguing about something. Ethan exchanged a look with Rayna then cleared his throat. "Ready to head out?"

"Let me check with Helen quick," Rayna said, going to the living room where Helen was watching TV. The kids were in bed already, so there shouldn't be much for her to do. Ethan went out and started the van to let it warm up. A few minutes later they all piled in and drove over to the Big House.

They pulled up to the house and his mom quickly ushered them in out of the cold. "Hi! Come on in." She shot Ethan a nervous smile when he passed her and he gave her an encouraging wink. His parents had spent little to no time with Rayna's mom and dad and he knew she would be anxious for it to go well.

The table was set with the tablecloth usually reserved for special occasions and the food was ready and waiting. His mom had gone all out with an oven-roasted chicken, potatoes, carrots, poppy seed strawberry salad with roasted almonds and homemade buns. The lights were dimmed and the room lit by candlesticks.

"Smells amazing Mom," Ethan said, leading the way to the table. He sat in the same spot he always had growing up, at the end opposite of his dad.

"Mind if we say grace?" Mom asked as everyone sat.

"Not at all," Greg answered.

She nodded and bowed her head. "Thank you, Lord for this day, for this food and that Alice and Greg could come and visit us. Amen." There was a murmur of amen around the table and a shuffle as the food was passed around.

"I don't think we've really seen you since the wedding," Dad said. "Still working as a petroleum engineer, Greg?"

"Yes, not much has changed. Alice has a new job though," said Greg with a bit of steel in his voice.

Ethan caught the look Alice shot her husband. Obviously, whatever had been the problem back at the house had followed them here. He started eating a little quicker. If things went south he didn't want to go home hungry.

"That so? Needed a change of pace?" Ethan's dad asked.

"Something like that," Alice answered. "I'm working at Shoppers Drug Mart now. The hours are better, and they were downsizing at my old job."

"Yes," Greg interjected. "They let go all the people who didn't bother to show up half the time."

Dad coughed to hide his discomfort. Alice glared at Greg then said, "I have an illness. It keeps me from work sometimes."

"Oh, I'm sorry to hear that," said Ethan's mom.

Ethan could feel Rayna's leg stiffen beside his. He tried to change the subject. "This tastes great, mom."

"Thank you, Ethan."

Silence descended on the table, broken only by the clatter of utensils against plates.

"I have some news," Rayna said, fiddling with her fork. "I got an agent for my manuscript. She called me last week, it looks like it's going to get published."

"That's awesome!" Dad said. "Good job, Ray."

Ethan smiled and took Rayna's hand. "It's been a long time coming. She's been working really hard on it."

"When will it come out?" Dad asked.

"Hopefully this summer," said Rayna. "My agent found a publisher already so things are coming together quickly."

Alice looked at Rayna. "I didn't know you were a writer."

"I want to be," Rayna said with a little smile.

Alice snorted, "Well, don't hang all your hopes on it." She turned to the rest of the table. "Rayna's grandmother fancied herself a writer. Didn't get her anywhere. She could barely afford to pay the bills after my dad died, but she wouldn't give it up and get a real job. I'm not that surprised Rayna would try to follow in her footsteps, actually. She was always obsessed with that woman. Like she was God or something."

Rayna looked as if someone had slapped her, "I... well I..."

"It was almost unhealthy," Alice continued. "She wasn't the greatest influence, you see. We actually had to keep Rayna away for a while."

"That isn't what happened," Rayna said. Her hand trembled under Ethan's.

"Oh? How would you know? You were just a little girl."

"Drop it, Alice," Greg warned.

"She has all these grand delusions, I think we should finally set the record straight," Alice turned to Rayna. "Your grandmother was one of the most selfish people I have ever known. She put herself before everyone else, always thought she was better than everyone around her. She even..."

"What I remember," Rayna said, her voice rising, "was she was more of a mother to me than you ever were."

Alice's eyebrows rose, and she laughed. "Really? You're proving my point. You had no idea who she really was."

Mom watched the exchange and interrupted, "I think the book is a wonderful thing, Rayna. It really is an accomplishment."

Alice nodded, "Oh yes, for a country housewife it really is something."

Mom's eyes narrowed. "What doesn't that mean? For a country housewife? What does that mean, exactly?"

Alice shrugged. "Nothing, just that you don't have much going on out here."

"Well," Mom huffed. "It may seem that way to you, but folks round here work harder than you city people ever will. And Rayna has done a fine job, raising her babies and writing a book and helping on the farm..."

"Ah, yes, the babies. Like a broodmare, isn't she? I was just telling her I hope Ben is the last. There comes a point when there is one too many, doesn't there?"

Rayna stood up. "I think we are done here. Thank you, Carol, for supper. We should head home and make sure the kids are okay."

"There's dessert..." Mom said, standing as well.

"No, we should go. Thank you, though." Rayna moved around the table and headed for the door. Ethan got up and went after her, leaving Greg and Alice to follow.

The ride home was unbearably awkward. Ethan could feel tension rising like steam from the three of them. Not a word was spoken. When they finally pulled up to the house, Ethan launched himself out of the vehicle, wanting to get some air, but the heaviness swirling around them followed them into the house.

Helen was still in the living room watching TV. She stood up as they entered. "That was quick," she said.

"Yeah, early evening. Thanks, Helen." Ethan fished out his wallet and handed her some bills without paying attention to how many.

"No problem, they slept the whole time," Helen cheerfully tucked the money into her back pocket. "See you later, Mr. Miller." she said over her shoulder as she left.

He waved and shut the door behind her.

"I need a drink," said Alice, going to the kitchen.

"Of course you do," spat Greg. "You can't even stay off it for one night, can you Alice?"

"Dad..." Rayna began.

"Like you have a leg to stand on," said Alice, coming back in with a water glass full of red liquid. "You think because you drink in private no one knows you're drunk all the time? Please." She took a sip and glared. "What were you thinking, acting like that over there? You went out of your way to embarrass me, bringing up my job. You know the only reason you haven't been fired yet is because your cousin is your boss and he is too much of a fuckin' pussy to fire your ass."

"Not even waiting till you're drunk to get nasty, are you Alice?" Greg retorted.

"Mom, Dad, please let's just go to bed," Rayna pleaded.

"Stay out of this." Alice rounded on Rayna. "You're no fuckin' better! You always—"

Ethan stepped forward, fury coursing through him, "Enough!" All three jumped, clearly startled he was still in the room. Alice's wine slopped onto the floor. "That is enough. You cannot talk to Rayna like that. Not under this roof. This is our home, and whatever this is," he gestured between Greg and Alice, "it will not happen here. You...you need to go. I think it's best you leave this house. Now."

"Excuse me? What did you just say?" Alice stared at him.

"There's a motel in town if you want to stay there tonight, but you're not staying here."

"Ethan!" Rayna said.

"No, Rayna. I'm not having this in my house. Around my kids. I won't have this around you anymore." Ethan looked directly at Greg. "Please, get your things."

Greg looked levelly back. There was a heartbeat of silence then he turned and went to the spare bedroom. He came out a moment later with their suitcases. Alice stood dumbfounded with her glass in hand. "Let's go, Alice." He gestured to the door.

Alice set her glass down, "Well... you really know how to pick them, Rayna." She turned and without a glance at Ethan walked out of the house.

Greg went to follow, then paused in the doorway. He looked back at Rayna. "It's a good life, what you got here." He turned to Ethan like he was going to say something, but he just gave him a nod and slipped out, shutting the door behind him.

Rayna sank down on the couch. Ethan sat beside her. "I'm sorry, Ray." He pulled her to his chest and rested his chin on her head. "I didn't mean to overstep. I couldn't..."

"I can't believe you kicked them out." She started to shake. He thought she was crying until he realized the choked gasps were actually laughter.

He pulled back uncertainly, "Are you okay?"

"I'm... fine... It's just... That couldn't have gone any worse, could it? Your mom's face..." She covered her face with her hand trying to stifle her laughter. "What a mess." Then the laughter gave way to a sob and suddenly there were tears soaking her cheeks. "What a mess, what a mess," she repeated, rocking back and forth.

Ethan pulled her towards him again, "It's okay Rayna, it's okay." He didn't know what else to say, so he kept repeating it, holding her tightly against him, wishing it was enough.

CHAPTER TWENTY: CAROL

Carol couldn't stop thinking about it.

She kept replaying the conversation with Rayna's parents over and over again in her head. The way Alice had treated Rayna in front of everyone. The way Greg sat there, sullen and angry, egging on whatever it was that had made Alice on edge. She wasn't sure why it bothered her so much, but it had just seemed wrong. There was nothing Carol wouldn't do for her children, nothing. Yet Rayna's mom had treated her own daughter worse than dirt. She had treated Rayna like she was nothing.

Her own mother wasn't perfect, but she had loved Carol. Not enough maybe, but she had. There had been many good times mixed in with the bad; spontaneous picnics on warm summer days, listening to her mother read stories while they nestled by the fireplace, creative birthday cakes and lavish Christmas dinners... Yes, Carol's mom had loved her. She clung to these memories when she thought of her childhood and tried to make them shine brighter than the dark times. The times when her mom couldn't get out of bed. When she would stare straight through Carol and her hair hung in strings around her face. But that was life, wasn't it? There was always the good and there was always the bad. She just had to choose to focus on the good. Despite all that had happened, Carol had managed to rebuild her family with Jim and her children. She also had her faith. So, it had all worked out in the end.

The supper had disturbed Jim as well–he'd always had a soft spot for Rayna. Last night when they were getting ready for bed, he'd been more worked up than Carol had seen him in a long time.

"We need to talk to those people," Jim had declared as he'd folded the blankets back and climbed onto his side of the bed. "Can't let them treat her like that."

"Oh Jim, you can't save everyone," Carol said.

"She deserves better," he grunted. "I don't like the way that woman talked to her. And that was in front of us. Imagine what she says behind closed doors?"

"I know Jim, but there's nothing much we can do. So don't even think about going over there and causing trouble. They'll be gone in a few days, anyway."

"I always knew there was something off about them. Remember, they were drunk at the wedding?"

"I remember."

Jim shook his head. "Must have been terrible growing up with them."

Carol didn't answer.

Jim sighed. "Well, she's got us now, that's something at least." With that he turned over and went to sleep, as only a man can do when there's something heavy on his mind.

Carol, of course, was up until the night had faded away to the early hours of the morning. She felt... possibly guilty. She could admit she had been less than welcoming to Rayna when she'd moved out here, and though the gap between them had lessened after the grandkids arrived, there was still an unnaturalness to their interactions. While Carol suspected Rayna's home life hadn't exactly been great, she'd never thought there was something more going on.

Something damaging.

Something Carol had missed because she was so concerned with Ethan and what marrying someone from such a different background would mean for him. Carol had flopped and turned, crushing her pillow beneath her as she tried to push the unwanted thoughts from her mind, but they kept flooding back.

She supposed now, it had probably been the Lord nudging her last night. Probably trying to tell her what an idiot she had been. Carol sighed. She hated being wrong. She paced around the living room now, replaying the scene at supper and thinking about her conversation with Jim. Finally, she stopped pacing, grabbed her coat and boots and headed out to her truck. There was no sense driving herself mad, she decided. She needed some answers, and Rayna was going to provide them. She drove the short distance over to Ethan's and marched up to the door and opened it.

"Hello?" Carol called, shaking the snow off her shoulders and stepping out of her boots.

"Hi, Grandma." Grace came tearing out of the kitchen, a piece of toast in hand. "Mom! It's Grandma."

"Grandma!" Emma rushed past her sister and threw her arms around Carol's legs and exclaimed, "I missed you!" Carol smiled down at her dramatic granddaughter and ruffled her hair.

Rayna came through to the living room with Ben on her hip. "Hi Carol. Please, come on in."

Carol bit back a grin at the hint of sarcasm in her daughter-in-law's voice. "I thought we could have a cup of tea. Ethan mentioned your parents had gone?"

"Yes, they're gone." Rayna didn't look at her as she said that. She led them all back into the kitchen. The girls chattered away, pulling on Carol's arms.

"All right munchkins, can you give your mom and I some alone time?" Carol asked, gently shaking them off. Immediately there was a gale of protest. Carol held up her hand. "If you can play quietly for twenty minutes, I'll give you a treat. Okay?" After a bit of debate this seemed to be a reasonable deal and the two little girls sullenly headed to the living room. Rayna placed Ben in the high chair and handed him pieces of cut up toast. Carol moved around the kitchen, fixing them both a cup of tea and sat down.

"I'm sorry for last night," Rayna began. "I know you went through a lot of trouble cooking."

Carol ignored her, determined to stick to her agenda. "I got the feeling last night that I don't know you very well," she said.

"What do you mean?"

"I don't know much about you. Where you come from."

Rayna shifted uncomfortably. "... And? You want to?"

"I do."

"Why?"

"Because we're family, aren't we?"

Rayna's eyebrows rose.

"Don't be difficult," Carol said. "You're married to my son, you're the mother of my grandkids. That makes us family."

"Does this mean you've finally accepted me?"

"Don't be dramatic."

"I'm just teasing." Rayna picked up her tea and took a sip. "What do you want to know then?"

"Your parents..."

Rayna's face hardened. "I don't want to talk about that."

"Why?" Carol studied her. "You don't need to be ashamed of your past."

"That's really something coming from you," Rayna said. "My past is exactly why you have never liked me."

"That's not true."

"Please." Rayna snorted. "The second you saw me, you decided I wasn't good enough for either of your kids. You think I didn't notice?"

"I'm not going to apologize for wanting the best for my children," Carol said. "Put yourself in my shoes, why don't you? Your only son marries a girl he hasn't even known for a year yet, a girl who obviously doesn't have the same beliefs..."

"You mean because I wasn't some perfect goody-two shoes? Because I did things differently and didn't meet your ridiculous standards?" Rayna fumed.

Carol sighed. "This is off topic. I'm trying to make an effort here, Rayna. I'm trying to understand you."

Rayna went silent, thinking. "Fine," she said. "My parents... have issues. They drink, as I'm sure you figured out. They weren't around for me much growing up."

"And your grandmother?"

"What about her?"

"You were close?"

"Yes, she tried to help and my mom wouldn't let her. So, I wasn't allowed to see her again and then she died." Rayna leaned back. "What else do you want to know?"

"Why did Ethan propose to you?" Carol asked.

"He wanted to marry me."

"I talked to him that day, and he said you hadn't even discussed it yet. Then he goes out there and comes back engaged. Why?" It had bugged her all these years, not knowing. She suspected now, but she wanted to finally hear the truth.

Rayna tapped her finger on her tea mug then said, "Do you remember when I moved out here, you said Ethan only married me because he saw someone in need of saving?"

Carol vaguely recalled that. She nodded.

Rayna took a breath. "That's why. I was in a bad situation at home, and he wanted to save me."

Carol leaned forward. "Can you tell me how it happened?"

Rayna tapped her glass again, thought for a minute, looked up and told her.

CHAPTER TWENTY-ONE: RAYNA

On the night Rayna got engaged she had been working at the restaurant. She got home around 8 p.m. from her shift, tired and sore and wanting to do nothing but sink in the bathtub for a while then go to bed. She had let herself into the house and shrugged out of her jacket. She could hear the TV on and followed the noise to the living room.

"Mom?" Rayna had called, rounding the corner. She froze. Her mom was in her usual spot on the couch, but sitting beside her was a man Rayna didn't recognize.

"What are you doing here?" Mom had said, her words heavy with drink.

"Who is this?" Rayna said.

"Don't be rude, this is a... friend from work."

"Nice to meet you." The man smiled at her, his hair slightly ruffed and the top button of his shirt undone.

Rayna looked him over, and her eyes flickered back to her mom. "Where's Dad?"

"I don't know. Out."

"He could be back any minute."

"So?"

Rayna stared at her, then she looked at the man. "You need to leave."

"Rayna!" Her mom tried to push herself up but only succeeded at nearly tipping off the couch.

The man steadied her. "Don't worry Alice, I need to get going anyway." He got up and moved past Rayna, giving her a wink as his hand ever so casually brushed her hip. "See you around."

Rayna clenched her fists and waited until the door slammed shut, signaling his exit. "What the hell are you doing Mom?"

"Don't talk to me like that," her mom snapped.

Rayna swallowed her reply; her words would fall on deaf ears, anyway. The house was a mess; used plates and cups littered the table and the floor, and books and clothes were strewn everywhere. Rayna bent and began gathering the dirty dishes then took them to the kitchen which was an even bigger disaster. She fought to swallow her anger, but it was beginning to spill out of her.

"Did you even go to work today?" Rayna asked, trying to keep her voice even.

No answer.

Rayna set about cleaning. She loaded the dishwasher, scrubbed the pots in the sink and put the empty bottles into the recycling. When she finished, she passed her mom without a word and went up the stairs to her bedroom and slammed the door.

"Dammit!" Rayna cursed, kicking over a pile of clothes. She shut her eyes and clenched her fists, trying to get her anger under control. How many times had she been in this situation? Countless. Her mom did it just to light a spark, just to get under her dad's skin and try to make him feel something. Maybe to make them both feel something, to see if they still could under all the numbness the drinking had created. Had they always been this way? Testing and pushing and fighting until someone broke? Rayna knew what would happen when her dad found out, like following lines in a play. Things would get bad and she would be right in the middle. Ready and waiting until the next break in the storm to gather the pieces and attempt to form them into some semblance of normal.

Rayna breathed in.

Then out.

She bent over and picked up the clothes she had kicked, then flopped on her bed and shut her eyes. She must have dozed off, because the next thing she knew the sound of something crashing downstairs made her eyes fly open. She was halfway down the stairs before she fully realized she was awake.

"You stupid bitch!" her dad's voice had roared, shaking the walls.

Rayna went around the corner and stopped when she saw her parents standing across from each other, their faces red and their feet spread apart in battle stance. Her dad twisted a man's coat in his hands, and behind him the wall had a red stain from where her mom's wine glass had shattered after it missed his head.

"You shut your mouth!" her mom screamed.

Rayna moved in between them. "Guys, stop. Let's go to bed."

"You shut up." Her mom turned to her, her eyes wild. "You told him, didn't you? You did this!"

"Don't you talk to her like that. She's not the one whoring around," Dad snarled, starting forward.

"Don't come near me!" Mom grabbed a lamp and threw it as hard as she could. Rayna and her dad ducked just in time and it smashed to pieces.

"Mom, calm down." Rayna rushed forward and grabbed her mom's wrists before she could find anything else to throw.

Mom started screaming as if Rayna's hands were made of fire. "Let go of me! Let go of me!"

"Christ, Alice shut up!" Dad said.

Rayna looked over her shoulder at him, "Go upstairs Dad, now!"

Her dad gave his wife a look of pure disgust, but he listened and left the room.

"Mom. Mom listen to me, you need to calm down." Alice's eyes were wild, but she stopped fighting as Dad disappeared. Rayna took a breath and released her wrists. "Let's get some water…"

But her words were cut off as Alice swung her fist, hitting Rayna hard on the side of the head. Rayna staggered into the bookshelf, knocking some to the floor.

"This is all your fault!" her mom screamed. She pulled Rayna's hair back so hard Rayna's eyes watered. The next blow came suddenly, whipping her head around. The taste of iron filled Rayna's mouth, and she fell to her knees, clawing at her mother's hand still gripping her hair.

"Mom, Mom, please," Rayna gasped.

"Fuck, Alice! Leave her alone." Dad had come back in and was trying to pull her off. Her mom let go and tried to strike Dad, but he grabbed her shoulders and slammed her into a wall. A picture fell and crashed to the floor.

"Stop! Please!" Rayna got to her feet and grabbed her dad's arm. There was a frantic knocking on the door. *No, not the police.* Rayna stumbled as she turned around. The neighbours must have called them. Her parents froze. Her dad stepped back.

Rayna wiped some blood away from her mouth. "I'll get it," she said shakily. "Dad, for God's sake, go upstairs!"

There was more knocking, Rayna turned her back on her parents and hurried over to the door. She swung it open and came face to face with a startled Ethan. Rayna blinked, sure the sight of him had to be some sort of hallucination. What was he doing standing at her door close to midnight?

"Rayna, is everything okay? I heard shouting and..." He paused, his eyes widened as he registered her split lip. His hand drifted up, touching the side of her face, and Rayna grimaced and pulled away. There must be a bruise forming where her mom had hit her.

"What are you doing here?" There was a loud ringing in her ears.

"Who is it?" her mom called.

"No one," Rayna said. She pushed Ethan backwards and followed him outside before pulling the door shut behind her. The winter air played across her bare arms and she shivered.

"What are you doing here?" she repeated.

"I... I came to surprise you."

"How did you know where I lived?" Rayna demanded. Her heart thudded in her throat. She had never taken him to her home, she had been careful not to.

"Chloe told me. Ray, what's going on? Was that your parents? What happened to your face?"

"I..." Rayna started, but she heard her parents' voices begin to rise again, the sound drumming against her spine. She sent a panicked look over her shoulder; she needed to get rid of Ethan and get back inside before things escalated again. "You need to go," she said.

"Not until you tell me what's going on," Ethan said. "Did your dad... did he do this to you?"

He reached again for her face, but she moved past him. "Come on." She took his hand and led him down her steps to her car parked on the side of the street. She got in the driver's side and he climbed into the passenger's. Rayna started the car and blasted the heat. At least she got him away from the house, but as she watched him look around she immediately regretted her decision.

"What's this?" he asked, pointing to the backseat at the blanket and pillow she kept stashed there. "Rayna, do you sleep in here? Are you sleeping in your car?"

"No," Rayna said. "Just... sometimes. When it's bad. You shouldn't have dropped by unannounced Ethan, you should have told me you were coming."

Ethan ignored her. "What's going on? Are you in trouble?"

Rayna shook her head. The lies she had told her whole life were ready and waiting to make excuses, but suddenly she felt exhausted. She couldn't fight it any longer, she didn't want to. She started crying.

"Hey, it's okay." Ethan took her hand and squeezed it. "Tell me what's going on, Ray."

Rayna wiped her eyes and sniffed. "My... my parents are alcoholics. God, it sounds so fucking simple just saying it. But it's not, it's messy and complicated and not something you go around talking about. I mean, the drinking is just the tip of the iceberg. My mom is so selfish, and my dad... It's complicated."

"Does he... does he beat you?"

"No, it's not like that. My mom just gets worked up when she's really drunk. It's like Dad triggers her. I'm the only one who can calm them down. My mom pushes until my dad snaps, I have to keep them separate or Dad loses control and... but he doesn't mean to. Mom just..."

Rayna stopped. She wasn't explaining it right. It wasn't something she could easily put into words. She never would describe her mom as abusive, she just lost control sometimes, and when her dad tried to defend himself he forgot how strong he was. It didn't happen too often, and over the years Rayna had learned how to diffuse the situation before it went too far. The key was to separate them, give them both time to cool down. But sometimes not even she could smother the fire burning her mother's veins. Rayna gingerly touched her lip. Sometimes even she wasn't enough.

"Would they ever consider divorcing?"

Rayna shook her head. "I don't know. I wish they would. It's like... I guess they just have gotten used to it? It's their normal. I don't know. I guess they support each other's bad habits. I don't know if they would be better off or not if they did, actually. It's just twisted."

Ethan stared at her, then he asked, "Why don't you leave?"

"You think it's that easy, do you? You think I haven't thought of that? I've tried, okay. It's not that simple. I'm going to leave, I have a plan."

They were quiet for a minute, and Rayna started to feel ashamed of her outburst. "I have left before," she said quietly. "Once when I was ten, the bus dropped me off, and I just kept walking past the house, past the end of the cul-de-sac. I kept going until I found a park and I sat down on a bench. I don't know why I did that. I didn't want to go home, I guess. I stayed there until a policeman found me and brought me back. The last time was when I turned twenty. I promised myself I was done with them, but I came back after a few weeks. I didn't have enough money for rent and school and... they need me. It's hard to explain, but they do."

Who else would keep them from tearing each other apart? Who would keep her mom in check? Make sure the house was livable, and the fridge had food on the bad days? The hard thing to admit was that she knew on some level she needed them too. They were one big, dependant mess. Rayna stared down at her hand intertwined with his. She didn't expect him to get it. She barely did herself.

"I'm sorry, Ray," Ethan finally said.

Rayna had given him a little smile. "It's fine, honestly I'm fine. It's just a bad night. It's not always like this. Anyway, as soon as I graduate and get enough money I'm gonna leave for good. I'm done for real this time."

"You need to get out of there now." Ethan gripped her hand harder. "I can help..."

"No, you can't." Rayna pulled her hand from his. "It's not your problem, Ethan. It's mine. You can't fix this."

He wanted to; she knew that. She could see it on his face that he wanted to *do* something. Something that would make everything be okay. But there was nothing to do, no action to be taken. It just was the way it was.

They had both been quiet, staring at the street. Rayna looked at the doorway to her house. So similar to all the others. It almost looked like a normal house with a normal family living there. Though who was to say what was normal? Maybe behind one of those other perfectly normal looking doors, a girl was crouched behind a couch listening to the screaming fights of her parents. Maybe there was a father filling the garbage with empty vodka bottles. Maybe that's what normal was. Maybe this was all life had for her.

"Rayna," Ethan said, breaking both their train of thoughts. "Make it my problem."

"What?"

"Marry me."

"Don't be stupid," Rayna said automatically.

"I'm serious, Ray." Ethan stared into her eyes. "I love you, I want to marry you. Why wait? You can't go on living like this, and I don't want to go on living without you. I want you with me every day, not six hours away."

His words lit something in her, something dangerously close to hope. He could protect her, she knew he could. And Lord help her, she wanted to be protected. She wanted to fold herself in his strong arms and stop worrying for once in her life. Could it really be possible? Doubt washed over her as quickly as the hope had come. It couldn't be this easy, nothing ever was for her.

"We can't Ethan," Rayna had said. "We can't just get married. We've barely been together."

"So? It doesn't matter what others think, all that matters is me and you. We can wait till you're done school if you want, or you can finish later. Just marry me, Rayna."

Rayna looked back at the house, then turned to study him, her heart slamming against her ribcage. "You're serious, aren't you?"

Ethan put his hand around her neck and pulled her to him, kissing her firmly. "Completely," he said.

Rayna rested her forehead against his. "Ethan... are you sure?"

"I'm sure that I love you, Rayna Parker. I'm sure you don't need to live like this. Marry me. Come live with me and leave all this. We will figure the rest out as it comes."

So, that's what she did.

****

Rayna told all of it to her mother-in-law, who listened patiently until the end. They were quiet after, listening to the girls' laughter as they played with their toys in the living room. Ben looked from one to the other, thoughtfully chewing his piece of toast.

Carol finally looked up. "Thank you for telling me."

Rayna nodded.

Carol took a long drink from her mug, draining the rest of her tea, then stood up. "I think I know you a bit better now," she announced.

"Is that all you wanted?" Rayna stood as well, picking up Ben and holding him on her hip.

Carol nodded then looked at her. "You have us now. Jim and I. It's something at least."

Rayna watched her leave the kitchen, thinking that might be the closest she ever got to an apology from her mother-in-law.

It just might be enough.

After Carol left, Rayna went to the living room, sat on the ground, and watched the girls run around playing. Ben stared wistfully at them as they raced in and out of the room, their games changing every two minutes.

"Don't worry, Benny," Rayna said, running her hand down his chubby cheek. "You'll be walking soon enough, then you can play too." Ben gave her a smile then flipped over onto his stomach. Rayna felt a sense of pride as she watched him roll on the carpet and listened to the sound of her daughters' easy laughter. They were all having a good childhood. A happy, healthy, from-the-books childhood. Her parenting methods were probably far from perfect, but she tried to shelter her children from seeing her at her worst. She made a point not to fight with Ethan in front of them, and if she was having a bad day, she tried to put her best foot forward.

That's what parents should do. They should protect their children. So why hadn't hers? When Rayna had held each of her babies for the first time, she'd felt such a gut-wrenching attachment to each of them. More than that, she had an overwhelming urge to protect and spill as much love onto them as she could. Did her mother never feel that way?

Sometimes Rayna looked at her children and wondered how polar-opposite her life would have been had she been raised differently. What if her parents had been normal, happy people who'd showered her with kisses, come to her events and made her feel like anything was possible? Who would she have turned out to be? Someone better or someone worse? In all honesty, she probably wouldn't have ended up here, marrying so young and not even finishing school. She probably would have had a successful career like Chloe or something.

Rayna's thoughts kept tumbling; the possibilities of what life could have been spread out before her. What if she had never been separated from her grandma? Or if her grandma hadn't died so soon from that heart attack? What would a little bit more love done in Rayna's life? Her grandma would have loved Silver Heights. Rayna was sure of it. It was exactly her kind of place; it had room for a person to discover themselves and enough inspiration to feed the creative side. A wave of longing swept over her. She wanted to see her grandmother so badly. She would have loved Ethan and the kids. She and Rayna could have sat together on the porch and shared what writing they were working on. They could have encouraged each other and told story after story.

Rayna shook her head and pushed herself to her feet. She went to the kitchen to start cleaning up after breakfast. There was no point in dwelling on the "what if's" and "could have been's." No point at all. Besides, she wouldn't change anything if it meant she wouldn't have ended up here with Emma, Grace and little Ben. She told herself this as an unexpected tear threatened to fall. Then she did what she always ended up doing. She straightened her back, wiped her eyes and pushed all thoughts of her parents, the past and the hypothetical futures firmly out of her mind. There was no point thinking about it all, absolutely no point.

CHAPTER TWENTY-TWO: JIM

Today was going to be a good day.

Jim could feel it in his bones. It was a beautiful, clear March morning. The snow had left early this year, and the geese had already returned, which was the true sign that winter was over. It was a bit of a worry that the winter moisture was already disappearing. It could mean a bit of a dry spring, but Jim tended not to worry too much before he had to. He never saw the sense in wasting time worrying about things that may never come to pass. Besides, all his years as a farmer taught him he really had no control over the weather, and whatever would be would be. It was as simple as that.

Jim drove the tractor this morning, as he usually did. He pulled up to the pen by the barn just as Ethan got back from his last load and hopped out of the feed truck. Ethan opened the gate for him so he could go in and drop two bales into the feeder for the bulls, who were lounging on the straw bed in the corner of the pen. They rocked to their feet when they saw the bales and lumbered over to the hay, their powerful legs moving slowly through the mud pulling at their hooves.

Ethan had bought four bulls in the past two weeks to add to the three they already had. Jim was proud of his son's choices—he had developed a real eye for good livestock over the years and their herd reflected it. The bulls were strong and stocky, their thick bodies proportionate. Their muscles strained against their hide as they moved with their manhood hanging proudly between their legs. Ethan swung the gate shut after Jim backed the tractor out. He was waiting for him as he climbed down the ladder.

"They look good, don't they?" Jim said, hopping to the ground.

"They do," Ethan nodded.

"How's Rayna?" Jim asked, as he often did since her parents' visit last month.

Ethan shrugged. "She's fine."

"I've been worried about her."

"I know."

"Working on her book?" Jim prodded. He had been concerned the negative feedback she had got from her mother had discouraged her from pursuing it. There was nothing so sad as wasted talent.

"Yup. She's been working closely with an editor to get it ready for print."

"Good." Jim nodded. "Tell her I want to read it."

Ethan snorted. "I don't think I've ever seen you read a book before."

"Someone's got to encourage her," Jim said firmly. "Those parents of hers... Got a lot of good in them, I'm sure."

Ethan laughed and shook his head. Jim always said someone had 'a lot of good in them' whenever he didn't like them. It was his attempt to not talk bad about anyone, which was defeated by the obvious sarcasm. "So, who's left? Heifers?" Ethan asked.

Jim nodded. "They need a couple bales. Then I think we should fix that fence in the east field, get it ready to move the bulls. I don't want them standing in this muck for too long."

"Sounds good, that whole side needs to be redone, eh? The posts are pretty much rotten."

"It does. Why don't you head that way and start taking it down. I'll deal with the heifers then bring the post-pounder and meet you there."

Ethan nodded and headed for his truck. Jim climbed back up the ladder and twisted the key so the machine shuddered to life beneath him. Swinging the wheel, he directed it over to the stack of bales piled three high and lined up so the bucket was square. Opening the claw as wide as it would go, he drove forward slowly until he gently bumped against the bales. Then he squeezed the claw shut, its teeth sinking down into the soft hay, securing it. He tilted the bucket, heavy with its new burden, and backed up. The tractor jolted forward as he switched it into high gear, and the mud, thick with gravel, crunched beneath the massive wheels as he headed down the road towards the heifer pen. He could see Ethan's truck in the rearview mirror, going the opposite direction to the bull field a little ways down. After they got the fence in decent shape, they would move the bulls there, where they would stay until June. Then they would get turned out to their designated cowherd for breeding.

Allan Jackson's new song, *Drive,* came through static on the radio, and he turned it up a bit and mumbled along to the words he knew. The tractor rumbled over the Texas gate and the heifers surged forward, trying to grab bites of the bales as he released them and let them roll away. He got out and took the knife they kept in the toolbox with him. Working quickly, he sliced the baler twine and pulled it off. Then he got back in and used the bucket to push the bale so it unraveled for the heifers to eat. He left them to it and went back to the shop to hook up the post pounder and load the bucket with some new wood posts. He grabbed a fresh roll of barbed wire then got back in and made his way down the road to the bull field.

Ethan had made good headway on the fence. Most of the staples had already fallen out, so there weren't too many left to pull. They worked silently side by side, getting rid of the rest. Then they tied the ends of old barbed wire to the quad and pulled it away to be gathered up and thrown away. They started to work on the new fence, taking their usual positions. Ethan ran the tractor, inching it forward until the post-pounder lined up with the rotting posts. They were so old Jim just had to jiggle them a little and they pulled out of the damp earth. He placed new ones near where the old ones were and used the post-pounder to slam them a good few feet into the ground. They moved the length of the field until they met the corner, then strung three rows of barbwire across the new fence line and tightened it so it scraped against the wood. Then came the mundane task of walking from post to post, hammering the staples to secure the wire. They started at opposite ends and moved slowly towards each other. Jim's hand was beginning to cramp when they finished the last few posts.

"Looks good," Jim said, looking down the fresh fence line. "Should keep them in at least. The other sides are good for a bit yet. What time is it?"

Ethan checked his watch. "Almost noon."

"Let's break for lunch. Want to come over?"

"I better go home and see if Rayna needs help. She's having some kids over this afternoon for Emma's birthday party."

"Oh geez. I forgot. How old is she now?" Jim was never much for keeping dates of important things straight. He left all that for Carol to manage.

"She's four," Ethan said with a hint of pride in his voice. "Though she told me very firmly she wants to be five. We said she could be next year."

"Four." Jim shook his head. "I remember when you were that young."

Time was flying by at an increasingly intimidating speed. Jim never felt old and being called Grandpa had seemed absurd when the grandkids first came. He was only in his fifties; it wasn't like he was even considered elderly yet. But he supposed compared to his son, old was what he was, if not what he was on the verge of. It was an odd time of life, watching his friends with their greying hair and lined faces. The conversation, which years ago used to be about what sports they were playing and girls they were dating, was now what body parts hurt the most and what the grandkids were up to. It was like he'd blinked and suddenly his youth was gone.

Jim shook his head again. "Life is funny, isn't it? We're probably coming for supper tonight then, I suppose?"

"I think so."

"I think your mother got her a blanket with an airplane on it." Jim said, remembering the gift Carol wrapped yesterday.

"Emma will love that. We gave her a toy airplane this morning, it's her latest obsession."

Jim laughed. "Well, isn't that something. Takes after me, eh?"

"What do you mean?"

"I always wanted to be a pilot. Did you know that?"

"Really?" His son looked at him, surprised.

"Since I was a kid," Jim said with a grin. "I always thought it would be pretty cool."

He still did, actually. Besides a brief time in his teens when he had wanted to be a professional hockey player (like almost all young Canadian boys did, but a blown out knee ended that dream pretty quickly) he had always envisioned himself in a cockpit. Even now he often thought of flying, of what it would feel like to soar through the sky with the wind around him and the ground far below. Like right now, with barely a cloud in the sky–he couldn't help but think today would be a good day for flying. Maybe one day he would know what it felt like. Perhaps when he retired, he would finally do it, if he ever retired.

"I had no idea," Ethan said. "Why didn't you do it?"

"I knew your mom didn't want to leave Silver Heights, and I wanted your mom. Plus, your uncle wanted nothing to do with the farm and someone needed to take it over."

"Do you regret not doing it?"

Jim shrugged. "This is a good life too." He looked around and nodded, "Better than sitting in an office somewhere with florescent lights instead of the sun on your face."

It was a good life, one he hadn't minded for the most part. He could have done with making a little more money; it would be nice not to worry about making ends meet all the time. Funny how farming was such a vital part of the world, yet it was so difficult to make a living doing it. They had done all right over the years though, and there were things he did love about it. Like how each change of season brought both a feeling of newness and a refreshing predictability. With fall came harvest and selling the calves. Winter was filled with feeding cows, hauling grain and preg-checking. Spring brought calving, seeding and new life. In the short summer months, there was moving cows, fencing, baling and spraying. Jim enjoyed breathing in the new air every few months; warm, brisk, cold, then brisk again. On and on it went, the moments blurring into days, which melted into months then turned into years. It wasn't a bad way to spend one's life.

Ethan's cellphone rang, interrupting them. He pulled it out of his pocket and flipped it open.

"Hey, Dan." He listened for a minute then smiled. "Wow, congrats. Very exciting... Yeah, course. I can't wait to meet him... Okay, see you later." He hung up and stuffed it back in his pocket. "Dan and Mila had their baby. Justin Paul."

"No kidding? That's awesome. Funny how that ended up, eh? Mila and Dan together and having a baby."

"Yeah, funny. You know Mila and Rayna meet every month for a writer's group? Mila actually helped get her an agent."

"Huh. You know, I liked Mila when you two were together, but I'm glad you found Rayna. She's better suited for you."

Ethan gave him a wry grin. "Only took you six years to say."

"Well, your mother had some strong opinions. And I don't like to cross her." Jim laughed. "Those two are pretty similar, don't you think? Stubborn and headstrong... Don't tell them I said so though."

"I wouldn't dare," Ethan said. "I better get going, the kids will be over soon. See you in a bit." Ethan headed for his truck and took off out of the field towards his home.

Jim got back in the tractor and made his way slowly towards the Big House. There was a dark figure on the road ahead of him, as Jim got closer he saw there was more than one. He realized with a jolt it was the bulls, and that they were trotting down the road towards the heifer pen.

"No, no, no," Jim muttered, urging the tractor to go faster. It would be a disaster if they got in and bred them early. He pulled over and jumped out to the ground and ran towards the barn. He grabbed a cattle stick and hopped on the quad, noticing as he did so the gate to the pen was wide open. Ethan must have forgot to chain it shut. Jim took off down the road towards the bulls. He gained ground and flew past them. Skidding to a stop, he yanked the quad around and went up to the first bull.

"Get going! Let's go! Turn around!" He waved his arms, getting the bull's attention. The bull snorted and tossed his great big head, half-heartedly turning to go the other way.

Jim looked over and watched as two bulls went into the ditch beside the heifer's fence, put their heads down and started pushing against each other. Their nostrils flared as they snorted with their hooves pawing at the ground. Jim groaned. This wasn't good. Fighting bulls were likely to break down any fence in their vicinity when they got going.

Jim gunned the quad over to them. "Break it up!" He tried to nudge one with the quad, yelling and banishing the cattle stick, but they ignored him and continued to bear down against each other. Obviously, they believed their testosterone match was far more urgent than the human yelling at them. Jim jumped off the quad and used the stick to hit their faces, desperately trying to break them up by getting them to turn their heads away.

It happened in an instant. One of the bulls turned, his head down and he rammed into the side of Jim, slamming him into the fence post behind him. Jim slumped over and reached for the post to keep from falling. The bull turned to continue his fight with the other and his back end swung into Jim, hitting him again. There was a sickening crack, and he fell to the ground. The fighting bulls pushed each other above where he lay. His world became a whirlwind of hooves, pain and the sound of wild animals snorting above him, as his body was dragged between their feet. The bulls moved and hit the fence, the metal wire snapped beneath their weight, releasing them into the heifer field.

Jim laid on his back, pain radiating from every part of him. He couldn't breathe. It hurt, everything hurt. He could feel a trickle of blood run down his chin. The thought drifted across his mind as he stared into the clear, blue sky before darkness overtook him: *Today would be a good day for flying.* Then he closed his eyes.

CHAPTER TWENTY-THREE: RAYNA

Rayna sat stiffly next to Ethan in the front row of the church. Behind them, friends and family filled the pews wearing various shades of dark clothing, like a gathering storm cloud on a summer's night. Their voices filled her ears as they sang hymns in clear, sharp voices. They sang about grace, peace and joy. Things Rayna did not feel as she stared at the giant picture of Jim, sitting amongst the dozens of bouquets littering the stage.

It was a good photo of him; he was smiling, a genuine smile that reached his eyes and a black cowboy hat sat pushed up on his forehead. When was that taken? A year or two ago? Rayna tried to peer back in time to when the camera's button was clicked. Jim probably just said something he found funny and was laughing at his own joke. He wouldn't have known in that moment his funeral picture was being taken. It made her angry, that this innocent, beautiful memory full of life was turned into the symbol for his death. That he didn't even see it coming.

That's the way it went though, wasn't it? Her own funeral picture could very well be taken already. The one everyone would stare at while her body sat under several feet of freshly dug earth. The one that would freeze her in time and preserve the way she looked instead of letting her grow old. No one knew when their time was up.

What a strange thing death was. Everyone knows they won't live forever, in theory anyway. But when death happens, it feels like such a great shock. Like something terrible and unnatural occurred, when really, it's one of the most natural things in the world. At least in the sense that no one can escape it.

Still, it wasn't supposed to be Jim's funeral today. It should have been another regular day of working and hearing Jim's little teasing comments. They weren't supposed to be here, sitting shoulder to shoulder at the front of the church after walking down the aisle like a morbid bridal party. Just one short week ago, Jim was living and breathing, talking and laughing. The injustice of it made Rayna want to scream. She gently took Ethan's hand in hers and squeezed it, needing his strength to anchor her as it always did. But his hand sat stiffly in her own, holding none of his usual warmth. He was distant and contained and Rayna couldn't shake this foreboding feeling she had. Like waiting for thunder to rumble across the sky after lightening had flashed.

He had been like that ever since the hospital, when Rayna had finally gotten there and found him sitting in the waiting room. Ethan had left the party after Carol had called him asking if he knew when Jim would be home for lunch. Rayna had a terrible feeling watching him drive away. Then the next thing she knew, she was getting a frantic call from Carol saying Jim was on the way to the hospital. It had taken her a while to get away; she had to wait for Angie to come watch all the kids before she could race to town. She knew it was bad when she saw Ethan's face, the way he stared through her as he tried to register her questions about what had happened.

What happened, she had finally learned, was Jim had extensive damage from being hit by the bull then trampled. He had severe internal bleeding, several broken bones, and a collapsed lung. It was already too late by the time Ethan had found him lying broken in the ditch. Her heart squeezed thinking of the moment when Ethan saw his father lying there. The sheer terror that must have coursed through him as he'd realized what had happened. She wished she could take away his memory of that moment. It was obviously haunting him. It probably always would.

As the last hymn ended, there was a shuffle as the congregation sat down. As the final key of the piano died away the only sounds were the constant sniffing of noses and quiet, gasping sobs. Ethan and Carol shared identical looks of blankness as they stared straight ahead. Emma and Grace sat between them, being uncharacteristically still, as if they sensed the despair around them. Chloe sat on Rayna's other side, her body shaking as tears fell down her cheeks. Rayna grasped her hand as Pastor Tom got up and stood at the pulpit. He began to speak, his voice strained as he tried to force words of hope past the obvious lump in his throat.

Rayna couldn't concentrate on anything he was saying. She let his voice wash over her as she peeked around at the people gathered to say goodbye and honour Jim. She had never seen the church so full before. People were spilling out of the back and standing against the walls. All these people were here because Jim had affected them in some way with his easygoing, laid-back manner.

Rayna hadn't even realized how much she had liked Jim, how much she had depended on his presence. He had always made her feel comfortable and accepted. He had been more like a father to her than her own dad ever was. Now he was gone.

Jim was gone.

The thought struck her in a new way and suddenly the pain that had been building in her chest exploded. She shook and trembled as the tears came, gasping as she struggled to get enough air to breathe. Ethan leaned over and put his arm around her, still staring straight ahead. It was done automatically, a reflex to her tears, but she was grateful for the solid grip of his hand on her shoulder. It helped steady her some before she descended into hysterics. She shook her head, trying to collect herself and push her emotions down.

After the program ended, Rayna followed Ethan and the others into the common area where refreshments had been set up. She sat in the back corner, gingerly nibbling on an egg salad sandwich and watching as people came in. The room filled up quickly, sound rose as people chatted, some in dull solemn tones, others with loud, brash laughter.

Angie came over, holding Ben, and sat down beside her. "How are you doing?" she asked.

Rayna took Ben from her and kissed his fuzzy head, snuggling him to her chest. "Okay. Thanks for watching Ben."

"No problem," Angie said. She placed her hand on Rayna's arm and squeezed it gently. "If you guys need anything, please let me know."

Rayna nodded, trying to blink back the tears threatening to come again. She spotted Carol, Ethan and Chloe standing on the far side of the room. They were shaking hands and hugging people who stood in line to talk to them. Rayna knew she should join them, but she didn't have the energy. She didn't want to be touched or listen to condolences and act like she had strength that she didn't. She looked around the room at all the people talking and eating. It seemed too loud for a funeral. They should talk in whispers, or not at all. Didn't they see how much pain was in the room?

"How can people carry on like normal?" Rayna said as someone laughed loudly next to her. "How can they be crying in the sanctuary then come out here and eat brownies and visit..."

"People grieve differently, Rayna," Angie said gently. "I think everyone is still in shock. They are coping the best they can. Besides, hard as it is, today should also be a celebration of Jim's life."

"A celebration." The words were bitter on her tongue. "What's there to celebrate? Carol is alone. Ethan and Chloe lost their dad. My children lost their grandpa. Ben won't even remember him, the girls barely will..."

"I know. But you know, Jim didn't believe death was the end. He had hope. That's what we celebrate. He lived a good life, even if it was shorter than what we would have wanted." Angie squeezed her arm again. "It's going to be okay."

Rayna resisted the urge to shake loose of Angie's touch. Her words made her angry, though she wasn't sure why.

It was a few hours before they finally got to go home. Rayna was exhausted by the time she laid Ben down for a nap. She put a movie on for the girls in her bedroom and closed the door, then rested her head against the wood for a minute. With a heavy sigh she pushed off it and walked slowly down the hallway. She was thinking she would make a cup of tea, when she saw Ethan still standing in the doorway with his coat dangling from his hand.

"Ethan?" she walked up to him. "You okay?"

Ethan nodded slowly, his eyes fixed on something on the floor in the living room. He moved forward and bent to pick it up. It was the toy airplane they had gotten Emma for her birthday. He twirled it slowly in his hand. "Did you know he wanted to be a pilot?"

Rayna nodded. "He told me that once."

"I just found out," Ethan said. "I didn't know. There's so much I don't know." His voice caught as his shoulders began to shake and tears splashed from his eyes.

Rayna felt sick watching her big, strong husband look so broken. She wrapped her arms around his waist, almost staggering as he leaned down on her, completely overcome. There was nothing to say, nothing she could do. So, they just stood like that for a long time, trying to keep each other from falling apart.

CHAPTER TWENTY-FOUR: CHLOE

Chloe lay on her bed, looking at all the familiar items that made up her childhood memories. Her walls were covered with different posters of bands, mostly the Backstreet Boys and U2. In the corner she had her toy box; plastic horses and other animals lay piled and forgotten, untouched since her elementary school days. On a bulletin board hanging over her desk she had pictures tacked up of her high school friends, mostly of Craig goofing around. There were also a few of Ethan and herself, and a family picture taken at her graduation. She went over, pulled it from the board and took it back to her bed. As she stretched out again on the covers, she studied it carefully. Her dad looked so relaxed and happy, his arm slung over Chloe as they smiled at the camera. She ran her finger over his face, wishing she could feel his warmth instead of the cool photograph paper.

It had been a month since she'd gotten the call from Ethan. One month since they'd buried him. She could hardly believe it had been that long already. After the funeral it felt as if normal everyday life should have stopped, but that wasn't the case. Their lives had been shattered, but the days moved relentlessly forward. It was almost insulting the way they had to keep going in normal routines when they would never feel normal again. They still ate and slept, Ethan still needed to work on the ranch and soon Chloe needed to return to her job.

When was the last time she had talked to her dad? A week before he had died? Her dad wasn't much of a talker when she called, so it was probably only for a few minutes or so and about nothing important. Did she say she loved him before she hung up? Chloe put the picture down and hugged her pillow to her chest, trying to contain her emotion. Why hadn't she come out more? Why hadn't she visited? She had been so wrapped up in her own life; she hadn't spared her family much thought these last few years. Because they were supposed to always be *here*. Whenever she came back, there they were, living the same lives they always did. If there was one thing she could count on, it was that. She felt angry. Betrayed even. How dare he leave her like this? Didn't he know she still needed him? It may not have seemed that way, but she did.

Chloe wiped her face and sat up. She could hear her mom out in the hallway, cleaning or something. She supposed she should help. That was why she was in Silver Heights still, to be there for her mom. But her mom was like a rock–she hadn't even cried yet as far as Chloe had seen. They had barely exchanged two words since the funeral. They just moved around the house in silence with the ghost of Dad between them. Chloe stood, opened her bedroom door, stepped out into the hall and nearly tripped over a cardboard box. She looked around and saw several boxes littering the hallway.

Her mom came out of her room holding one taped shut and labeled 'bedroom stuff.' She looked at Chloe as she set it down. "I could use some help this afternoon."

"What are you doing?" Chloe said, looking around. "Are you... are you packing?"

"I am," Mom said.

"*Why?*"

"I'm moving to Ethan's, and they're coming here. It makes more sense for it to be that way," Mom stated, setting the box down.

Chloe stared at her. "When did you guys decide this?"

"Today."

"Today? Wait... Does Ethan even know you're doing this?"

"Not yet."

"Mom!"

"What?" Mom turned to grab another box.

"You can't do this."

"Of course I can." She went to the kitchen with Chloe on her heels.

Chloe felt hysteria rise in her. "Are you insane? You can't just decide to switch houses."

"Don't talk to me like that, Chloe. I'm still your mother," Mom snapped.

"So, I lose my dad and now I'm losing my home?"

Mom stilled, turned and faced her. "You have made it perfectly clear this isn't your home anymore."

Chloe glared at her, rage making her hands shake. "Don't you put that on me now. Don't try to make me feel guilty."

"I'm not trying to make you feel guilty. Don't be dramatic, I can't handle it, not today."

"*Dramatic?* Dad is gone, just because you seem ready to move on doesn't mean the rest of us are there yet. It's only been a month."

Mom's face twisted. "Get out."

"What?"

"Get. Out. I will not be spoken to like that. Do you hear me? Get out!"

Chloe turned and fled to her room. She slammed the door and slumped to the floor with her face in her hands, sobbing. She pushed herself up and started to pack frantically, shoving things in her suitcase. She grabbed the photos off her bulletin board and looked around for anything else of value. This time when she left she wouldn't be coming back. Silver Heights had nothing for her now. She changed quickly out of her sweats and into one of her work outfits. She would go straight to the office and catch up on what she had missed, even though she technically didn't need to start work till next week. It would be good to do something that felt normal.

She shouldered her bag, pushed the door open and came face to face with her mom.

"Chloe..."

Chloe shoved past. "I'm leaving, as you wished."

"Chloe wait, please."

Something in her mom's voice made her stop, there was a weakness in it she had never in her life heard before. Chloe turned slowly. "What?"

"I'm sorry," Mom said. "I don't want you to leave like this."

Chloe clutched her bags. "I don't think my staying here is helping you any."

Mom stared at the ground, looking suddenly fragile and older than her years. Chloe's anger slipped as she softened. She dropped her bags and moved to hug her. They wrapped their arms around each other. "I'm sorry too," Chloe said, pulling back. "Are you really going to move?"

Her mom straightened. "Yes."

"There's nothing I can say to stop it?"

"No, there's not."

Chloe sighed. She wasn't the one to deal with this. Maybe Ethan would have better luck.

"You don't have to go," Mom said.

Chloe looked at her bags. "I need to." As she said the words, she knew they were right. "I think I need some time doing normal things for a bit. I'll come back though, I won't wait so long to visit." Her voice caught. "Will you be okay?"

Her mom nodded.

Chloe grabbed her bags and headed for the door.

"Chloe?"

Chloe turned to look at her mom.

"You won't lose your home, you know. You always have one with me... wherever I am."

Chloe bit her lip and then nodded. "Love you, Mom. I'll call, okay?"

"Okay."

Chloe left the house and loaded up her stuff. She got in the driver's seat, adjusted the mirror and pulled out of the driveway. Leaving now felt different from the times she'd left before. Her earlier conviction that she was done with this place melted away as her house faded from view. In fact, for maybe the first time Chloe wasn't sure she wanted to leave. Her heart had always been elsewhere growing up, but now it seemed like it was here. Or maybe it always had been in Silver Heights and she had never realized it. It was with her family and friends and the people who had known her since she was born. She had always been so determined to get away she had missed what was important: being with the people she loved and who loved her. Well, Chloe was done making that mistake. Life was too short to miss out on what was important. She knew for now that she needed to go back to the city, and she wasn't exactly sure what she was going to change, but it would be something. Something that brought her closer to home.

She was about to pass by Ethan's place when she hit the brakes and turned down his driveway. She might not be able to talk sense into their mom, but maybe Ethan could. Chloe parked beside Rayna's minivan and got out, feeling a little out of place in her city clothes and brand-new car next to the farmhouse and dirt-stained van. She saw Rayna sitting on a spread-out blanket, watching her girls run around the yard. Ben was on his belly beside her, playing with some Tupperware containers.

"What are you dressed up for?" Rayna called as Chloe walked gingerly across the lawn trying not to trip as her high heel shoes sunk into the soft earth.

"I'm going back to Calgary today," Chloe said, sitting down beside her.

"Really?"

Chloe nodded. "It's been a month, I need to get back. I can't stay here any longer doing nothing." Her eyelashes fluttered as she beat back the tears gathering. "Oh, for heaven's sake. These damn tears won't stop coming."

"It's okay," Rayna said, rubbing her back.

Chloe blew out a lungful of air, collecting herself. "Do you think I'm a terrible person for leaving?"

"No, not at all. You need to do what's best for you. If that's going back to your life in Calgary then that's what you should do. How's your mom today?"

"Not great. I think she's starting to lose it. She's been so strange since it all happened, very... stone-like. Not that I blame her. But she's literally going crazy now. Actually, I was wondering if you knew where Ethan was?"

"Out working on something," Rayna said. "Why?"

"I was hoping he could go talk to Mom." Then an idea occurred to her. "Actually, you might be better."

"Me?" Rayna said. "Why? Talk to her about what? And what do you mean going crazy? I can't picture her in any other state than poised and put together. 'Get tough and do what needs to be done,' that's pretty much her motto."

Chloe nodded. "I know, but, well... she's packing up the house."

"Packing? Is she planning on moving?"

"Apparently. She said it makes more sense for you and Ethan to live there now. Can you go talk to her? Please? I'll watch the kids."

Rayna shook her head, "Why on earth do you think she would talk to me?"

"She's not listening to me. Someone's got to get through to her."

Rayna just might do the trick. There was some weird connection between them. Chloe had noticed it before, but it was more pronounced now. Like they shared some secret or something.

"And you think I can?" Rayna lifted her eyebrows. "To be honest Chloe, I have enough trouble handling Carol in her normal state. I don't think I want to know what Crazy Carol is like."

"Come on, Rayna," Chloe said. "Ethan's got enough on his plate and I can't do it. Please?"

Rayna sighed and got to her feet, "Fine, I'll go. But if I'm not back in an hour, come looking." Then she hollered at her girls, "I'll be back in a bit, okay? Listen to your Aunt Chloe."

Chloe watched Rayna get in her van, then she turned her attention to her nephew. She moved him so he was in front of her and studied his features. He was so much bigger than when she had seen him last. All the kids were. *No more,* Chloe thought firmly. She wouldn't miss out on their lives anymore. A while ago she had decided what was important, and she had made the wrong choice. She wouldn't make that mistake again.

CHAPTER TWENTY-FIVE: CAROL

Carol stood there long after the sound of her daughter's car faded away. A fierce feeling of loneliness swept over her. The only sound echoing in the house was the steady ticking of the clock. This was how it was now, so she supposed she better get used to it. She had to get used to a lot of things, like the bed being too big and cold at night, no coffee ready and waiting for her when she got up, no one to talk to or fight with over which television channel to watch. Having no one to hold her, no one to talk sense into her. How was she to do this? How could she get used to all of it?

The dam inside was breaking, so Carol quickly distracted herself. She went into the living room, grabbing an empty box on her way and set it by her feet. She began slowly plucking the pictures and décor from the wall and place them carefully inside. She had to keep busy, keep from dwelling in the sorrow threatening to overcome her. Because if she let it, she would be finished. She would collapse and not be able to rise again, so it was best to keep it tamed and controlled deep inside her. Carol had practice doing this. It wasn't the first time she'd had to deal with death's cold, unforgiving grip in her life.

There was a knock on the door. Carol jumped and dropped the picture she was holding. *Please don't be another person from church.* She couldn't handle their soft-spoken words and broken eyes right now. It felt like Carol did most the comforting when visitors came, and she didn't have the strength for it today.

"Hello? Carol?"

She relaxed a little hearing it was only Rayna. "In the living room," Carol called. Chloe must have told her what was going on. That was good, she could help finish the packing then they could get her place ready for the switch.

Rayna cautiously made her way in, looking around at all the boxes half-packed around her. "Hey, Carol..." she started, but Carol cut her off.

"It's good you're here. You can help me load some boxes into the truck, the ones taped shut are good to go."

Rayna sat on the edge of the couch, "Do you mind if we sit for a sec?"

"I'm busy, I don't have time to sit."

"Just for a quick second."

Carol huffed a sigh. "Fine." She sat beside Rayna and looked at her, "What do you want?"

"What's going on? What's all this?" Rayna gestured to the boxes.

"We're switching houses," Carol said, her tone one of impatience.

"Are we?"

"Yes, it doesn't make sense for me to live in the Big House. Ethan should be on the main farm yard now since he's the one working every day. And why do I need such a big house? You need more space than I do, it's just me now and..." she faltered for a second, then shook her head. "It's just me so it makes sense to downsize."

"Don't you think it's a little too soon?" Rayna asked.

"Too soon?" Carol's voice shook.

Here was another person telling her how heartless she was. They just didn't get it, how could they? She was tired of seeing the judgment on their faces. "You think I'm... what? I'm unsentimental? That I just want to erase every trace of my husband? Who I've been married to for almost thirty years? I'm not some heartless widow. I'm being practical. Which, by the way is something you have never been. You... you just come over here and try to tell me I can't do what's best for the family. You and Chloe both think you know better."

"That's not what I meant," Rayna said. "It's just, you're going through a tough time and I think we should slow down before we make any big decisions."

"A tough time," Carol laughed bitterly. "It sure is a tough fucking time."

Rayna's jaw dropped open.

Carol clapped her hand over her mouth.

"Goodness," she said, lowering it. "You must be rubbing off on me."

Rayna snorted, then a laugh bubbled out.

"It's not funny," said Carol.

"No... no sorry." Rayna tried to keep her face straight, but she succumbed again and had to bury her head in the couch pillow to muffle the sounds.

"Are you quite done?" Carol frowned when Rayna emerged red-faced with tears in her eyes.

"Yes, sorry." Rayna wiped her face. "Sorry, it just sounded so funny coming from you."

"Yes, well, I haven't had much practice," Carol said dryly.

Rayna nodded, fighting a smile, "It was good for the first time."

Carol shot her a look then got up from the couch. She went over to the wall and gently removed a framed photo. It was a black and white family photo from when Ethan and Chloe were young. They sat on straw bales wearing coveralls while she and Jim stood behind them smiling at the camera. Carol lightly touched Jim's face.

"He was so handsome," she said. "I loved him since we were kids. We grew up together here in Silver Heights, you know."

"I know," Rayna said softly.

Carol set that one down and picked up another. It was only the two of them in this one, right after they first got married. They were smiling, standing with the Big House behind them, having just finished moving in. They were so young, kids really. It was a lifetime ago.

"This is one of my favourites." Carol said more to herself than to Rayna. "It was our first year farming together, and we almost didn't make it. We were so unprepared... Jim's father never mentored him the way Jim has trained Ethan. We really had no clue what we were doing. Then one night in the summer it hailed so badly all the crops were ruined. The hail came down, some the sizes of softballs. I've never seen anything like it. Jim was so downhearted; we couldn't catch a break with anything that year. So, that night while the storm raged on outside we sat together on the couch and watched a bunch of old western movies. We cranked the volume up as high as it would go to drown out the sound of the hail destroying everything we had tried to build that year. For a few moments we just forgot and were us..."

"That was one of the worst times, but it turned out to be one of the best as well. Even though the world was falling apart, we had each other. I thought we always would." She turned and looked at Rayna. "I'm fine with a lot of this, you know. Well, not fine. That's not the right word. I can *accept it.* What I struggle with though, is the thought that I could live longer without him than the time I spent married to him. I'm only in my fifties. Life is still so bloody long, and I have to do it without him now."

"I know," Rayna said. Then she flushed, clearly feeling foolish for trying to identify with what Carol was going through. She got up and moved so she was next to Carol and looked down at the photograph in her hands. "He was a really good man. He always made me feel welcome."

"And I don't," Carol stated.

"Well... no. You don't."

Carol smiled a little. "He used to get so mad at me for that. He really liked you." She placed the picture in the box next to the others. "Strange, isn't it? Last month I would have said 'he likes' now it's 'he liked.'" Carol gasped suddenly, her hand flying to her mouth as she tried to suppress her sudden burst of emotion.

"It's all right," Rayna said. "It's good to cry."

Carol waved her words away and shook her head. She gulped a few times and breathed deeply. "It hits me now and then. Like someone is standing on my chest. I forget they're gone and then it hits." She started to shake.

Rayna hesitated, then put her arms around her. Carol rested her head on her shoulder and finally let herself cry.

"It's okay." Rayna patted her awkwardly on the back.

"Sorry," Carol sniffed noisily and pulled back.

"Don't be." Rayna gently guided her back to the couch. "It's fine."

"No, not that. I'm sorry for how awful I've been to you. I've been such a terrible person."

Rayna looked at her, surprised.

"I know," Carol said. "Shocking to hear me admit it. I wanted to talk to you about it for a while but, well, I'm not good at admitting when I'm wrong. We are family though, you know? I need all the family I can get right now."

Rayna's cheeks turned pink. "It's fine." They were quiet for a moment, then Rayna tentatively asked, "Who... who is they?"

"What?"

"You said it hits you that 'they' are gone."

"Oh," Carol said. "I guess I mean Jim and... my mom."

"When did your mom pass?"

"When I was young, twelve I think," Carol said. "She... well. She took her own life."

"I'm so sorry," Rayna said. "I had no idea."

"I don't talk about it much. I'm not even sure the kids know. She was a good mom, but she struggled with depression. It broke my dad. He was the one who found her..."

Carol remembered it like it had happened yesterday, coming home from school to find her dad sobbing at the kitchen table. It hadn't even been a bad day. Her mom had been normal that morning, smiling and singing as she made breakfast. Jim was all she really had after that.

"All these years later, it still haunts me," Carol said. "I loved my mom, more than anyone. I felt like I didn't have a family after that, not for a long time. But Jim and I built a family together, and they were all that mattered to me."

"You felt like I threatened that," Rayna said, more as a statement than a question.

"A little bit, yes. You will understand one day, when your Ben finds a woman he loves. It's hard for a mother and a son to adjusted to that." She paused. "While we are having this heart to heart, I might as well add that I... I feel quite lost. I don't know who I am anymore without Jim." Carol blinked and brushed away another tear.

"Do you remember what you said to me when I lost the baby? You said 'I wish to God this didn't happen, but it did and we can't change it. But you can't let it ruin you.'"

"What a self-important arse I was."

Rayna's lip twitched, "Yes, a little. I can't imagine how you're feeling Carol. I know it hurts for us, Ethan's barely functioning, but I know it's worse for you. I don't know what I would do if something happened to Ethan... but I know you will be okay. If anyone can be after something like this, it's you. You're the strongest person I know."

"I'm not."

"You are. You've taught me a lot about being a mom and a wife. And about faith..."

"I feel so resentful of God." Carol looked down at her lap. It felt wrong to admit it out loud, but there it was. "He could have stopped it. He could have saved him. Why didn't He?"

"I don't know. But I think... I think it's okay to feel angry," Rayna said slowly. "From everything I've learned about Him, I think He would understand. I think... He may even be fine if you want to say fuck a little more."

"Don't swear," Carol said automatically.

They looked at each other, then broke out laughing.

"Oh my goodness, it feels good to laugh," Carol said. "It's good to know I still can."

"It's good to know you could in the first place." Rayna grinned.

Carol snorted. She stood up and looked around. "We should get going. You better head home and start packing too."

"Carol, we really don't have to switch houses."

"No, it's what's best. Besides, I... I don't feel right being here without Jim. It hurts too much."

Rayna nodded. "Okay. I'll tell Ethan then."

A wave of gratitude washed over her. As Rayna got up to leave she blurted out a little impulsively, "Oh, and Rayna?"

"Yes?"

"If it's not too weird, maybe you would like to call me Mom?" She held her breath, waiting.

Rayna looked at her, her eyes wet. "I'd like that. I'd like that a lot, Mom."

CHAPTER TWENTY-SIX: RAYNA

"It's not that hard."

Rayna attempted to keep the look of skepticism off her face as she stared at the many switches and dials of the feed truck Ethan had just painstakingly explained.

Ethan sighed. "Do I need to go over it again?"

"No, I got it." Rayna tried to sound more confident than she felt. It wasn't just learning how to run the feed truck, it was the learning how to drive a standard on top of it all. She had done fairly well when Ethan was sitting in the passenger seat guiding her, but as soon as he left it was like everything he had taught her went out of her head and she stared dumbly around, feeling like an idiot.

"I can go over it again."

"I got it, Ethan."

He gave her the same look that he had when he first heard her and Carol's plan. They had both agreed Ethan could not keep up the pace he was going. Running a ranch this large was not a one-man job–it had barely been a two-man job. Dan had been trying to lend a hand since the accident, but he had his own farm to run.

"You need help," Carol stated to Ethan last night after they had finished unpacking their last box of kitchen things. "Rayna and I have come up with a plan. She will work with you and I will watch the kids."

The expression that took over Ethan's face was what Rayna imagined the unathletic kid received when captains were picking teams.

"Why don't you come help?" Ethan asked his mom. "You know what you're doing."

Rayna hadn't taken offense; it was the question she had poised to Carol right before Ethan got home. Carol explained to him what she had to her. "I will sometimes, but this is your and Rayna's operation now. You two are partners, and you need to learn how to work together."

So that was how Rayna ended up behind the wheel of a vehicle bigger than she had ever driven before. It was the lesser of two evils; the tractor was a whole other level she wasn't ready to tackle yet. She had tried once in their early years of marriage and had nearly destroyed a fence.

"Are you sure..." Ethan said.

"*Yes*, Ethan. I'll radio if I need to." *Like if I'm dying*, Rayna privately added. It wasn't that she was too proud to ask for help, it was that she hated the way Ethan treated her like a child playing with a breakable toy whenever she did.

"All right," Ethan sighed. He flicked on the switch that would mix the silage as he loaded. "Remember, flick this off before you drive. You know where you're going right?"

"Yes." Rayna waited until Ethan got out and clicked the passenger door shut before mentally going over all the instructions. *Clutch, shift, gas... ease off the clutch, not too fast. Flick that switch off, then lower the spout, open the door so the silage spilled out, ease forward....* no problemo.

"All right, you're good to go." Ethan's voice came over the radio. "Remember..."

"Flick the switch off," Rayna muttered along with him. She stared at the tractor ominously watching her, wishing he would drive away and not sit there, judging her. Slowly she put the truck in gear, eased off the clutch and pressed the gas. The truck jolted forward and her heart lurched in her throat. She was off, rumbling down the road, bumping painfully in the seat.

Ethan's voice came over the radio. "Go a bit slower. This road is pretty rough."

Rayna made a face at the black radio and tried to press the gas lighter. She pulled out onto the road and then turned to go into the field.

Okay, Rayna, you can do this...

Her thought was cut off by a loud smash and the truck banged to a stop. Rayna's feet flew off the pedals and the truck stalled. She looked in her rearview mirror and saw she had driven too close to the fence and the spout of the feed truck had caught a post going into the field.

"Shit, damn it all to hell!"

Rayna opened her door and dropped to the ground. She ran to look at the side of the truck, feeling as if she might puke. It was dented, but other than that it looked like it should still work... Rayna slumped against the side of the truck. What was she doing? She couldn't run machinery, she wasn't some tough farmer woman. Rayna sat on the ground with her back resting on the wheel, feeling so overwhelmed she had to fight not to cry like a child. How was she to do this? She was going to let everyone down. Ethan wouldn't be able to manage by himself, they would have to sell and move to the city. He would hate it there and sink into depression. Her kids would resent her because it would be all her fault...

No, Rayna, pull it together. You got this. You need to do this. Rayna gave herself a mental shake. She needed to calm down. The world would not end because of a dent. She needed to think positively, that's what Angie would tell her to do. So maybe she wasn't a natural farmer, but she wasn't the same wuss who had moved out here all those years ago either. She had pushed three babies into the world, written a book due to hit the shelves soon, and had almost successfully kept chickens alive. So, she could bloody well drive a truck! She would do it, for Jim and for Ethan.

Filled with a new sort of manic, determined hope, Rayna went around and got back in. She slowly backed up and twisted the wheel, then cautiously inched forward across the Texas gate into the field. She probably should have gone a little further out, but she was too nervous. Quickly, she flicked the switches, lowered the spout and opened the door to let the silage spill out. She inched forward, leaving behind her a long line of cattle eating with their heads down. She let out a breath she hadn't known she was holding when everything worked correctly, no damage done. After the truck was empty, she reversed her steps and twisted the wheel to bring the truck home. Only three more loads left to do.

Rayna parked beside the silage pit and radioed to Ethan, letting him know she was back and ready for the next load. She leaned back, feeling like she passed some sort of test. She felt a little foolish for her little breakdown- one little dent wasn't bad for her first time going solo. Ethan probably wouldn't even notice it. Besides, he shouldn't expect her to be an expert on her first go around. It took time. She was slowly getting better at all the farmhand stuff.

For example, this morning she had helped Ethan tag a few calves. Ethan would pin down the newborn calf to tag it, while Rayna held a cattle stick and kept the mother at bay. She had only run away a few times, leaving Ethan to bat away the huge cow's face and yell at her. But she was getting braver. It was easier for Ethan than it was for her; he was a good few feet taller and much stronger than her. Surely those things were important when it came to staring down an angry cow wanting her calf. If Rayna was honest, part of the problem was she couldn't quite shake the image of Jim being trampled under those hooves... it was hard not to think of it. She wasn't sure how Ethan could carry on around the beasts with the confidence he did. She supposed it was a man thing, not to dwell in fear but to march forward. Still, if someone as experienced as Jim had found himself in that situation... the fact that Rayna could be in a field full of cows at all was quite the accomplishment.

Steadily, Rayna did get more confident and her fears began slowly melting away. There was just too much work to be done to dwell on her own insecurities. As May came, Ethan started to get busier with seeding and more of the cattle workload fell onto Rayna. Even though it hadn't rained yet and the seeds would be wasted on the dry ground, they had to start. They had waited long enough and needed to seed in order to qualify for insurance. Rayna knew Ethan was stressed over the dry weather. Everyone was on edge about it as whispers of a drought were filling the farmers' ears. Rayna tried to reassure him it would rain. Of course, she had no idea if it would, but lately it was her job to be supportive and try to keep him upbeat.

With Ethan in the fields seeding, checking the cows came down on Rayna's shoulders. She was given clear instructions: if there was a problem she was to call Ethan. If she couldn't get a hold of him, she had Daniel's number, and he promised to come if he could. Most the cattle had given birth by now, though there was still a few who ambled through the field with their pregnant bellies bulging and swaying as they walked. Rayna had gotten quite good at tagging and castrating the calves. She found it was best to ignore the mother cows as they pawed and snorted while she handled their newborns. Mostly they were all about intimidation and no action. That was what she told herself anyway.

She was out in the field now, slowly driving the quad through the herd, making sure all was well, when she spotted a cow lying down a little ways away. Rayna drove up to it, careful to keep her distance and recognized it immediately. It was a cow she had seen starting labour this morning. Rayna checked the watch on her wrist. It was a quarter to twelve.

"Shit," she said as she fished out her cellphone. The cow had been working on it way too long; the calf would need to be pulled. She dialed Ethan's number, but it went straight to voicemail. He must have been in a field with no reception.

She tried Daniel, but he didn't answer either so she left him a quick voicemail. "Dan, it's Rayna. I've got a calf that needs pulled and I can't get a hold of Ethan. Can you call me back? I might need you to come over."

Rayna hung up and stared at the cow who was labouring hard. Any longer and they would lose them both. Rayna gripped the quad's handles. She could at least move her to the barn so they would be ready when help came. Hopefully Daniel would get her voicemail and hurry over.

"Okay, girl. Easy does it." Rayna edged the quad up and the cow got to her feet. The calf's front hooves were barely peeking out. Rayna tried to not rush the cow as she gently guided her in the barn's direction. She imagined being chased by a loud machine was the last thing the cow wanted in the midst of labour, but there was no helping it. Rayna got her to the barn and got off the quad. She walked behind her down the alleyway and into the shoot, which clanged shut around the cow's neck. The cow bawled with fright as she tried to escape the metal bars by jolting forward, then pulling back. Her legs splayed out on the wooden floor as her belly rose and fell rapidly, her eyes darting wildly around.

"Hey, it's okay girl. You're going to get help." Rayna pulled out her cellphone again and tried to reach Ethan and Daniel, but there was still no answer.

"Well, we've come this far," Rayna muttered.

She had seen Ethan do it a million times... It seemed like a straightforward operation. With shaking hands, Rayna went over to the wall where they kept all the supplies. She grabbed a long heavy chain and two hooks that looked like miniature coat hangers. Next, she grabbed the calf jack. Ethan didn't use it often, but he was a lot stronger than her and she would need the extra support. Rayna wrapped the chains behind the hooves and secured the hooks. She grunted as she lifted the calf jack up and placed it on the cow's hips. She hooked the chain to the jack, then she rolled her shoulders back and planted her feet.

"Let's do this girl. On the count of three, okay?" Rayna breathed. "One, two, three." With the contraction Rayna pulled the jack down and cranked it a few times, her muscles quivering with the strain. The calf edged out a little more, its nose making its way out to the world. Encouraged by seeing progress was being made, she repeated the process. She pulled down hard, helping the cow push the calf's shoulders out. Then with a sound like a plunger, the rest of the calf slid out and landed hard in a splash of blood and afterbirth. Rayna fell on her backside with the calf between her legs, its head lolling as it lay there, stunned by its rather abrupt entrance.

"Hey, there!" Rayna laughed. She instinctively put her fingers into the calf's nostrils and pulled out the junk plugging them. "Hey, little guy, we did it!"

"Rayna!"

Rayna turned to see Daniel hurrying towards her. "I got here as soon as I could, are you okay? You're crying! Are you hurt?"

Rayna hadn't even realized her face was wet. She got shakily to her feet. "No, I'm good." She laughed again. She had never felt like this before. It was like she was on some sort of high.

"I can't believe I did it," Rayna said, trying to explain the tears falling onto her wide smile. "I just can't believe it."

"Yeah... you did good." Daniel eyed her suspiciously.

Together they released the cow into a pen bedded down with straw and put the calf in with her. The mother immediately began to lick her calf and guide it on to its shaking legs. Slowly, the calf edged its way down to the mother's udder and began sucking.

"It's quite something." Rayna leaned against the fence. The blood and afterbirth was drying on her arms and clothes, making her feel stiff and itchy, but she didn't mind.

"Yup, it is." Daniel nodded. "Are you good if I get going?"

"Yes, of course, thanks Dan."

Daniel nodded and hurried towards the barn door. All the men were on edge with the weather. Rayna was too, but in this moment she wasn't worried about anything. She had never felt so... useful. Was that it? For maybe the first time in her life, she felt like she was actually a capable person. She could drive a big standard truck, tag and castrate calves, help cows give birth, as well as raise her kids and take care of her family. Against all odds, Rayna had turned out to be a real pioneer woman. The thought made her smile.

CHAPTER TWENTY-SEVEN: ETHAN

They needed rain.

It was that simple. They needed the clouds to open up and water to gush down and satisfy the dry, thirsty land.

In March, Ethan had thought about it in passing. The snow had disappeared by then and it was starting to get a little dry, so rain would have been welcome. No worries though, it would come.

Then April came and still the rain did not. Ethan started to get a little worried. He and the other farmers remarked on the dry weather at church, murmuring their concerns to each other and the prayer times started to include a request for rain. Still, it was okay. He had feed to give the cows, and they didn't need to go to grass till June anyway. They had time.

Then May hit.

Still no rain.

The murmured concerns had developed a slight panicky edge to them. They should have seeded weeks ago, but with no rain nothing would grow from their efforts. Ethan talked with the crop insurance guys who advised him to seed anyway. So, Ethan had got in the tractor and drove back and forth across the sunbaked fields, spilling the seeds into the dusty ground, praying it would rain.

Now, they were at the end of June and it was obvious to everyone it wasn't just dry; it was a drought. Last year it had been dry and other areas of Alberta had suffered badly with drought; now it seemed it was their turn.

By now, Ethan had run out of winter feed to give the cows so he was forced to move them to grass, where they methodically ate through every living plant they could find. No rain meant no crops, no crops meant no feed for the cows in the winter, and no grass to replace what they ate now. Ethan had been rotating them through the fields, letting them eat whatever they could find in each. Soon though, he wouldn't have anywhere left to move them.

The fields weren't the only things suffering, without rain and the usual runoff from the snow all the dugouts that weren't spring fed were slowly drying up. They were being reduced to little ponds in the middle of a muddy hole which rapidly decreased every day. The cows had to wander in so they could reach the water to drink, and Ethan ended up pulling out a couple each week who got stuck in the mud.

He was doing this now, having secured the strap around the cow and chained it to the front loader of the tractor. The sun beat down overhead, making his skin slick with sweat. A fine layer of dust clung to him, making his lips taste of salt and grime. The miniscule dirt particles were everywhere. His scalp itched and his eyes permanently stung with it. Vehicles travelling down the gravel roads kicked up dense clouds behind them that lingered for several minutes, making it impossible to see a few feet ahead. Ethan had a feeling if he cut himself, all that would come out would be a puff of dust.

He gave the cow a reassuring pat as she bawled and swayed, unable to move with her knees glued in place by the mud. He got in the tractor and slowly backed up while simultaneously lifting the header. He continued to move backwards until she was on the edge of the dugout, where she instantly collapsed. Ethan stopped and got out, undid the strap and set a small pail of oats beside her head. He grabbed a bucket from the tractor and wandered into the dugout towards the water in the center. The thick mud caused each step to strain his legs. He carefully filled the bucket then made his way back to the cow and set it beside the oats. She gave another bawl and lapped at the water greedily.

Ethan patted her again. "There you go girl, you'll be all right."

He hoped he wasn't lying to her. He straightened and looked around at the herd ambling slowly along, their heads bent as they tried to scrape more from the ground than it could give. Nutrient-wise, they were getting what they needed, but it wasn't enough to fill their bellies, so they wandered all day in a vain attempt to feel full.

Things might have been fine if his dad was here. He would know what to do. He would have told Ethan to save some winter feed instead of going through it all so quickly. He probably would've seen this drought on the horizon when the months continued to stretch without a drop of rain. They would have sat down and made a plan. Instead of trying to make all the decisions himself, Ethan could have followed whatever his dad decided, as he had done his whole farming career.

But that wasn't possible. His dad was gone.

Ethan heaved a sigh and got back into the tractor and drove slowly to the farmyard. He had to admit, his mom had been right about the move. It was way more convenient living on the home quarter, once he got over the strangeness of moving back into his childhood home. He parked just as the van pulled up and Rayna and the kids piled out. Emma and Grace were still wearing their matching bright pink swimsuits from their time at the pool.

He walked over to them, the prickly brown grass crunching beneath his boots. Brown was everywhere; the trees, the fields, the lawn... he'd never hated a colour so much.

"Hey," Ethan said, taking the stack of towels from Rayna so she could unbuckle Ben. "How was swimming?"

"Terrible," Rayna said, lifting Ben up.

"Was it crowded?"

"It was, but not with humans. The grasshoppers were unbelievable." Rayna shook her head. "Honestly, it was like a horror movie, you should have seen it. The lifeguards spent the whole time fishing them out with a net and literally filling garbage bags full with them. I couldn't even get Grace to go in the water."

"As long as they stay there and don't come this way," said Ethan.

The grasshoppers had so far been staying about thirty miles south of them, having recently taken over the town. When Ethan drove through it, it was like his vehicle was being pummeled with bullets. His windshield was constantly covered in thick yellow splotches from where the bugs slammed into the glass. Just last week his truck was getting hot, so he took it to the shop and they emptied two-thirds of a five-gallon pail of grasshoppers out of his radiator. It really was like a horror movie.

"Are you coming in?" Rayna asked.

"No, I should..." Ethan paused.

Should what? What should he do? Keep re-checking the fields to see if anything miraculously sprung from the ground for the cows to eat? He'd never been so bloody useless in his entire life.

Ethan ran his hand through his hair, feeling the dirt scrape against his scalp. "The cows have pretty much finished with that field. I've got to move them tomorrow for sure."

"Where will you put them?"

"I still have that oat field. It's about three inches high. I was hoping to save it for some bales if it rained, but no way are we going to get any out of it now. I guess we'll move them there tomorrow." It was his last option. "I don't know where they will go after that."

The words came out heavily, weighed down by the failure he felt rubbing him raw. He knew it wasn't his fault; he wasn't in charge of the blasted weather. Still, he couldn't shake the feeling he should be doing better; he shouldn't be so bloody unsure of himself. Like he was stumbling through a maze with his hands out in front and his vision gone.

"Don't worry about after right now. We'll figure it out as it comes, we just have to take it one day at a time," said Rayna.

Her words caused a stir of annoyance in him. He clenched his fists to keep from throwing a sharp retort at her. These past few months it was like their roles had switched; suddenly Rayna was the leveled-headed, reasonable one, and he was the emotional wreck.

It was clear early on Ethan wouldn't be able to manage the workload by himself. He had tried his best to stay on top of it, but he was working ridiculous hours and barely sleeping at night. He stayed up late, sick with worry over the list of things needing to get done. He'd never talked about it with Rayna, but one evening he had come in from working to find his mom and Rayna ready to ambush him. Apparently, they had conspired together to create a plan so Rayna could come help him. Now she worked steadily with him each day without complaint and fell exhausted into bed with him each night.

Their new system should have been a good thing. Ethan knew he should be grateful for all Rayna was doing, but he couldn't help but feel like it was another area he was failing in. It bugged him to see Rayna working so hard. She had enough going on with the kids and her book, which was supposed to be coming out soon. Both had been put on the back burner so she could help keep the ranch functioning. Ethan had intended on finding a hired hand so he could ease some responsibility off her, but with the drought and uncertainty about feed, he wouldn't be able to afford it.

He looked at her now with her confident lift in her chin, as if she knew everything would be fine. Where she got this burst of faith, he had no idea.

She eyed him cautiously, watching his emotions flicker across his face. "You okay?"

He forced his shoulders to relax; it wasn't her fault he was so uptight. She was just trying to help. "Yeah, fine."

"Why don't you come inside? It's almost time for supper anyway. You can hang out with the kids before bedtime."

Ethan rocked on his heels then nodded. He went in and sat on the couch with a glass of lemonade clutched absently in his hand, watching the kids bring out every toy they could find. They played with them for two seconds before trying to steal what their siblings had. Their shrieking voices filled the house as they scrambled around the carpet, lost in their own little world.

Thirty-some years ago, it was Ethan who would have been kneeling on this very floor, taking toys from Chloe, who would then run screaming to their mom. He didn't have the greatest memory, mostly he could only recall little flashes of his childhood, but he remembered his father always looking old and tough. He would come in at supper and sit at the head of the table with his hands marked with dirt that wouldn't wash off. His face looked tired from a long day of work, but he would always ask Ethan and Chloe questions about what they did or what they had learned at school.

During harvest, Ethan would spend as much time as he could in the combine with his dad. He would sit on the dusty floor and watch as the header of the combine sucked the crops in and spat them out in the hopper as grain. The large front windows made him feel like he was hovering right above the swaths, almost able to reach out and touch the crop before it disappeared into the sharp rotating teeth of the combine. He would sit there for hours with his head resting on the window and bumping against the glass as the machine vibrated beneath them. They never talked much on those occasions; both of them were content listening to the radio and sitting in companionable silence.

Ethan would stay with his dad until the sun disappeared and the only thing visible was the light from the headlights illuminating a few feet ahead of them. Bugs would dash across the yellow beams and now and then Ethan spotted a mouse scrambling out of the way. He could remember thinking his dad must be lost–the field went on forever and everything looked the same.

But when he looked at his dad, Ethan saw his eyes were alert as he sang along to the radio and twisted the wheel with expert confidence. Ethan knew then that they would be fine. Even with the darkness of night draping over everything around them, his dad knew exactly what he was doing.

Ethan felt like that now, lost in a sea of darkness with a clear path only a few feet ahead, but this time his dad wasn't there to guide him along. He was the one who was supposed to know what to do now. He should be the one his kids looked at and saw a tough, old farmer. Ethan didn't feel tough. He didn't even feel that old. He still felt like an inexperienced child needing a hand to guide him.

He felt stupid thinking this and took an impatient swig of his lemonade, letting the sour, sugary taste dance across his tongue and burn his throat. He pushed himself off the couch and wandered into the kitchen where Rayna was stirring a pot full of meat sauce.

She looked up as he came in, "Spaghetti tonight. That okay? We're low on groceries."

"You didn't get any in town?" Ethan asked, resting against the counter.

"I forgot."

Ethan watched the steam swirl from the bubbling water as Rayna cracked noodles in half and put them in. "We'll have to put up a temporary fence tomorrow in that oat field." He drummed his fingers against the counter. "Should last a couple days, maybe."

"Okay." Rayna's eyebrows pulled together in concern. "You doing okay?"

"Fine, why?"

"Just checking in." She turned back to the stove.

Ethan watched her for a few minutes then went back to the living room.

That night he lay in bed, feeling Rayna's warmth beside him as her soft breathing filled their bedroom. He checked the clock again; only an hour had passed since he had last looked. He flipped over on his side and closed his eyes, willing sleep to come, but it stayed stubbornly at bay. Finally, when the sun was beginning to peek across the sky, Ethan swung his legs over the edge of the bed and pulled his jeans on.

Rayna's sleepy voice rose behind him. "You're getting up? What time is it?"

"I'm going to go check the oat field, see what we'll need for a fence." He grabbed the first shirt he could find and pulled it over his head. He drove down the dirt road, turning the radio on out of habit. They would move the cows this morning, he decided. The oat field would last for a while and give him some time to figure out his next move. He needed to calm down. This wasn't the first drought to hit Alberta. He needed to stop panicking.

Ethan pulled up to the approach of the field and stopped the truck. He opened the door and got out, a crunch sounded beneath his boot. He lifted his foot to see the crushed remains of a grasshopper. He stared at it for a minute, then looked around him. The ground looked as if it was moving there were so many grasshoppers hopping back and forth with their wings clipping together. Ethan stumbled into the field and stared at the scene before him.

Gone.

It was all gone.

The entire quarter was chewed down to nothing, as if it had never been there at all.

Ethan stood there for a long time, his hands resting uselessly by his sides. The sun was up properly by the time he forced his legs to move and get back in the truck. He twisted the key. A Paul Brandt song burst through the speakers as it rumbled to life. Ethan slammed his fist into the stereo, cutting it off.

He pulled up to the Big House and went inside, the clatter of breakfast filling his ringing ears.

"Ethan?" Rayna came from the kitchen holding a box of cereal. "Hey you want some eggs..." she stopped when she saw his face. "What is it? What's wrong?"

"It's gone." Ethan blinked. "We've got nothing left."

"What do you mean?"

Frustration rose inside him, like a beast trying to burst from his skin. "The bloody oat field. The grasshoppers came last night and ate the whole bloody quarter. We have no more feed, I have nowhere left to move the cows to."

"I'm sure we can figure..."

"Figure something out?" Ethan finished for her. "Tell me Rayna, what do you suggest? Please, I'd love to hear your thoughts."

"Calm down, Ethan." Rayna looked over her shoulder to where the kids sat at the kitchen table.

"How am I supposed to calm down? We've got nothing, Rayna."

Rayna grabbed his arm and pulled him down the hall to their bedroom. She shut the door and turned to face him. "I know things are difficult," she began. "But you've got to keep it together. You're going to scare the kids."

Ethan sat down on the bed and rubbed his hand over his face.

Rayna sat next to him and gently put her hand on his arm. "We are going to get through this."

Ethan felt his anger melt away, along with his energy. He pushed a breath out. "I don't know what to do."

He hadn't said those words out loud yet. Hearing them made him burn with shame.

"I know," Rayna said quietly.

She put her arms around him and pulled him to her. He rested his head against her chest; it felt so good to be held and surrounded by her warmth and softness. Her familiar scent filled him and he felt himself stir. He moved his head up and kissed her gently. He sighed against her lips then kissed her again, pressing his mouth against hers and forcing it open, searching with his tongue for hers. He needed a few moments to forget, to not have this weight slung around his neck. He pushed Rayna down on the bed and leaned over her.

"Ethan, the kids." Rayna said pulling away from him.

"It's fine."

He clumsily pulled at her ponytail, releasing her curls and he buried his hands in them, kissing her harder. She squirmed underneath him, pushing her hips against him and filling him with heat. He broke off their kiss, impatiently undoing his jeans and shoving them down. Rayna mirrored him. Then they came together. Ethan moved hard, gasping and sweating, letting his senses completely take over and forget for a moment how out of control he felt. He collapsed on top of her when he finished, breathing her in.

She stroked his back and kissed his neck. "I love you, Ethan."

Her words made a rush of emotion almost choke him. He closed his eyes and tried to push it back down.

The phone started ringing in the hallway. Rayna gently pushed Ethan off and hurried to do up her jeans. She went out in the hallway just as Grace answered the phone.

"Hi, this is Grace speaking. How can I help you?" Grace said in her best grown-up voice. Then she bellowed at the top of her lungs, "Dad it's for you!"

Ethan zipped his jeans and went out, "Thanks Gracie," he said, taking the phone. "Hello?" He listened for a few minutes, his shoulders started to relax.

"That would be amazing. Honestly. I really appreciate it.... Okay, yes. Sounds good." He hung up and looked at Rayna. "That was Craig's dad. He said their crop field has a bit of growth and he can't do anything with it, so he's offering to let us graze the herd on it."

"Thank God." Rayna quickly put her hair back in a bun. "Let me call your mom to take the kids and we can go."

****

A couple weeks later, Ethan twisted the valve to shut the hose off that was emptying water from the five-thousand-gallon trailer into the trough by his feet. Several cows were already drinking from it before putting their heads back down to continue tearing the plants from their short roots. To the left of him, Rayna was checking the power of the temporary electric fence that stretched for two miles around the herd. Not that the cows would wander far if they got out–the only source of water in this field was the trough Ethan had just set up. All the dugouts were completely dry now, so Ethan had to fill the trailer from the spring-fed one and haul water out to whatever field they had set the cows up in.

He leaned over and cupped a handful of water and splashed it over his face. The temporary relief from the continuous heat felt nice. They had been working for five hours straight getting everything set up. In a couple days they would do it all over again, assuming another neighbour would have a field they could go to. It was how they were surviving the past two weeks. Day by day on the grace of the other farmers who had no animals they needed to feed.

Rayna walked over to him, her hair stuffed under a baseball cap and dirt clinging to the sweat on her face and arms. She looked around at the herd and said, "Good enough for today."

"You know Bill from church?" Ethan said, kicking at the dust. "He's sold over fifty per cent of his herd now."

Rayna looked at him, "Are we going to have to sell more?"

Ethan gave a half-hearted shrug. He wasn't sure what was best. Every week he had to decide how many he would keep and how many to sell. A few of his neighbours had sold everything at this point, but Ethan was sure it wouldn't come to that for them. If he could hold on till it rained, they would survive. That was his hope anyway. The truth was, they had no feed for winter and it would be insanely expensive to get enough for the number of cows he had now. Not only would they make no money from the farm this year, they would have to spend a great deal of money just to maintain what they had.

"Well," Ethan said, looking around. "The cows are eating today. I don't know what they will eat tomorrow."

"You say that every day."

"It's true every day."

Rayna snorted. "Right. Well, let's head home. My back is killing me and I need to drink something."

"I'll be right behind you," Ethan said. He watched Rayna get on the quad and steer it out of the field, leaving a strip of dust behind.

Ethan got in the semi-truck hauling the trailer and sat for a minute with the air conditioning blasting. "They're eating today," he said to himself, then turned the steering wheel and headed towards home.

CHAPTER TWENTY-EIGHT: RAYNA

Rayna shifted in the saddle, trying to stretch out her legs. She tugged at her t-shirt, it made an unpleasant sucking sound as it detached from her damp skin. She felt sticky and sore... and dirty. Her cracked lips tasted like dirt when she tried to wet them with her tongue, and her legs and back hurt. Beneath her, Roman snorted and shook out his mane, as if in sympathy for her discomfort. Rayna gave him a little pat then adjusted her baseball cap as they continued their slow meander forward.

Ahead of them the cowherd stretched for a mile down the ditch line. Their noses were constantly to the ground as they munched determinedly on the grass and their tails swished back and forth as they tried to shake off the flies plaguing them.

The hundreds of cattle backsides facing her were a familiar sight by now. They had moved the herd to the ditches a week ago, after the county had sent out a bulletin giving permission. The news came in the nick of time; the ditches were basically the only food left now for the animals to graze. Ethan usually took the front of the procession on the quad and Rayna followed behind on Roman. She enjoyed the horse's company, and it was good for him to graze alongside the cattle. They started as soon as daylight began and stayed out until the brink of evening before moving them back into the field for the night.

It made for long days and sore nights. Rayna could barely move by the time she dismounted. She tried to walk alongside Roman some of the time to help with the aching in her legs, but it didn't seem to make much of a difference. She didn't mind it though, even with her muscles protesting, the sun burning her skin and sweat sliding down her back. She enjoyed the peacefulness of the task and the feeling of Roman's powerful muscles moving beneath her.

Riding had become like all things on the farm; not only doable, but enjoyable. She had come a long way from the ignorant, fearful girl she had been when she first moved out. In fact, she had become quite competent if she said so herself. The roar of the quad approaching made Rayna jerk upright out of her thoughts. The cows around her didn't bother to look up at the familiar sound as they kept to the task of trying to fill their bellies.

"How's it going back here?" Ethan asked, killing the engine.

Rayna shrugged, "Fine."

"Want some water?"

"Sure."

Ethan got off the quad and reached up, handing her the water bottle. She tipped it back and gulped down the liquid, then crunched the plastic in her hand. The lukewarm water hit her stomach too fast, making her feel a little sick.

"Thanks." She wiped her mouth and handed it back to him.

"Craig is on his way. He should be here in ten minutes."

"Oh, my God. I forgot."

Ethan laughed. "How could you forget? You barely slept last night."

"I know! I just did," Rayna said.

It was the only thing on her mind for the past few months–she had no idea how she could have forgotten in the last few hours. Well, to be more accurate, yesterday had been the day she had been looking forward to, but today was big as well. Yesterday was the day her novel, *In the Sirens of the Night*, had officially hit the shelves. Angie and Mila had thrown a little dinner party for her yesterday to celebrate, with a pyramid of her books on the table as the centerpiece. The day Rayna had received her copies of the book she had sat with them in the living room floor, caressing each cover in an amazed awe. This was her work, her words between the covers. It was an actual, real book. Her name glinted in gold writing on the dark blue cover, and on the dedication page she had written with careful consideration: *To my grandma, who taught me how.*

The whole process had seemed long to Rayna, though everyone assured her it was one of the fastest publications they'd seen. She had taken the time waiting for her book to come out to outline her next novel, which her agent seemed enthusiastic about. But finally, after months of waiting, it had happened–she was published.

And today, the day after the big launch, was the day her agent Maggie had told her she could expect some reviews to go up online. There were a few magazines Maggie had confirmed would do a review, and she said Amazon would have some too. Rayna had been more nervous for this day than the actual launch. It was one thing to have friends and family proclaim they liked it. And a completely different thing for strangers, who didn't care one bit about her, to say they did.

Rayna hadn't wanted to sit around the house refreshing the webpages all day, so she decided the best thing to do was to keep her mind off it until later this afternoon. Craig had agreed to come help with the cows so she could leave early.

"How long till he comes?" Rayna asked.

"About ten minutes. You can go now if you want, he can use his truck when he gets here," Ethan said.

"Are you sure?" Rayna asked, already tightening the reins in her hand.

"Yeah, go. I'll see you tonight."

Rayna pulled Roman's head around and headed for home. She resisted the urge to push him into a gallop. He had been out in the sun all day without water too, and she knew it wouldn't be fair of her. Finally, she got to the barn and quickly peeled the saddle and blankets off Roman, then gave him a fast comb down. She released him into the pen beside the barn where he headed for the water trough. Then she hobbled as fast as her legs could go to the house. It always felt odd walking after riding for so long, like she was a sailor swaying on the ground, trying to get her land-legs back.

Rayna kicked her boots off on the porch and headed straight for the computer. There were a few missed messages blinking on the answering machine. She ignored them as she pulled up a chair and impatiently clicked the mouse, waking the screen up. She opened up a new webpage and was typing in the title of her book when she paused.

This was a big moment; she should make it somewhat special. She would only read the reviews of her first novel for the first time once. Did she really want to do it covered in dirt and stinking of her own sweat? Rayna made up her mind, pushed away from the computer and headed for the bathroom. She had a quick shower and changed into a clean shirt and jean shorts. Then she grabbed a wine glass and filled it halfway with her favourite merlot. She took one of her grandma's novels from the shelf and carefully set it beside the computer screen. Rayna didn't have any pictures of her grandma, a fact she regretted terribly. But the novels were the next best thing. Whenever she read the words her grandma had written, she got a glimpse of the woman she had loved so much. She could hear her voice in the dialogue, her laugh in the humour. Rayna secretly hoped one day when she was gone, her children would feel the same about her own work.

"Okay, Grandma, here we go," Rayna said as she hit enter and waited for the search results to flood the screen.

The first one to pop up was a link to her book on Amazon, she would look there later. The second was a review written by a rather prestigious magazine in the States. The phone rang but Rayna ignored it and with shaking fingers she clicked the article open.

She read it quickly, paused, and read it again slower.

Then one more time.

Rayna stared at the screen for a moment, then clicked back and scrolled to the third link from a review blog. She opened it and scanned it quickly. Then she went to the Amazon page. Her eyes skipped the four-star ratings and went to the two and one-star ones.

The phone rang again.

Rayna picked it up. Before she could say anything, Maggie's voice spoke fast.

"Rayna, finally! Have you got any of my messages? I have been trying to reach you. Listen, don't read the reviews yet okay? Just hold off..."

"I read them." Rayna's voice sounded high and tight.

"Okay, well, don't panic. Not everyone will like it, that's a given. You shouldn't pay any attention to reviews anyway. It's a fantastic book, I wouldn't have asked to represent you if I didn't think so, okay? Don't worry. Besides, there are more reviews coming out later this week, and I know for a fact some of them are positive. So, don't let these ones get in your head."

"Okay," Rayna said.

She hung up.

The phone rang again.

"Rayna, it's Mila, have you got my message? Have you looked at the reviews?"

"Yes."

"I know it's not what you wanted to see, but don't worry. It's not that big of deal. My second novel had some terrible reviews, and it sold fine. These really don't mean anything. It's a great book."

"Okay."

Slowly, she placed the phone down on the receiver. Numbness spread through her body. The glass of wine sat forgotten by her hand. Rayna looked at her grandma's novel staring at her beside the computer screen. Her gut twisted with shame. She reached over and knocked the book down so she could escape from its disappointed cover.

Rayna got to her feet and followed them outside to her van. She backed out of the driveway and twisted the wheel towards town. The words from the reviews danced in front of her eyes *'weak characters,' 'hard to follow,' 'inaccurate facts.'* God, what had she been thinking? How could she have put her words out there like that? Everyone saw right through her. They saw she was an uneducated wannabe who had no business writing a book. *What had she been thinking?*

It seemed like Rayna had barely blinked and suddenly she was parked outside Angie's house. She didn't even remember deciding to go there. She got out and knocked on the front door, her hands shaking as she waited.

Angie opened it and smiled when she saw her. "Hey! What are you doing here? Did I forget we were meeting or something?"

Rayna burst into tears.

"Oh, honey. What is it? What's wrong?" Angie guided her inside to the kitchen table. "Is it Ethan? The kids? The cows?"

Rayna shook her head, snorting unattractively. She wiped her nose on her sleeve, trying to contain the flow.

"Okay, well... here have some iced tea." Angie got up and poured Rayna a glass and set it in front of her.

Rayna tried to give her a shaky smile, took a swig and immediately gagged.

"Sorry, I should have warned you. It's real unsweetened tea. Tastes bitter as hell, but it's supposed to be healthy."

Rayna hiccupped. "That's... disgusting."

"It is, I'm going to add some sugar," Angie said, rubbing Rayna's back. "What's up sweetie? What happened?"

"My book... the reviews were terrible." Shame burned through her again. It was just so embarrassing. She had an image of the reviewer sitting behind his desk, snorting with derision as he clapped her book shut, unable to finish it. Then he hunched over his computer with a cigar hanging from his lips and glasses perched on his nose as he typed out his review, shaking his head with laughter.

"I'm sure they weren't that bad."

"They were," Rayna said miserably. "I can't believe I thought I was a writer."

"Ray, you are a writer. I read your book, remember? And I loved it."

Rayna ignored her. "This was supposed to be it, you know? The thing I was always meant to do, and I failed. What am I supposed to do now?"

"What do you mean 'do now?' You're doing a ton of stuff."

"Like what."

"You're a mom. And a rancher. And a wife. And a writer. What more do you want to do?"

"That doesn't count though," Rayna said, her eyes filling again. It just didn't... yes, she was enjoying having a bigger role on the ranch, but writing was *her thing*. It was her life calling. What she had been doing since she was a child. It was what she had always been good at. Or it was supposed to be, anyway.

The words spilled out of her. "What's my purpose? What am I supposed to do with my life if I'm not successful at writing? I'm going to wake up one day, old and grey and realize I've accomplished nothing."

"Oh, give it a rest."

Rayna's mouth fell open.

"I get you're upset. Your dream has been attacked, and that is a hard pill to swallow. But Ray, the truth is as long as I've known you, you've been searching for this magical thing that will make you happy and filled with purpose. I hate to break it to you, but life doesn't work that way."

"I haven't been..."

"Yes, you have," Angie said impatiently. "You keep thinking all these things will finally make you happy. Like getting away from your parents, moving out here, having kids, having a career, working on the ranch, publishing your book, etc. Then when you get all those things, you're still unhappy. You know what? If you're not happy where you are, no matter what the circumstances may be, you're not going to be happy somewhere else. Happiness is a damn choice."

"I don't..."

"And, you know what else? You have to stop wrapping up your identity in what you do. Whether you're a stay-at-home mom or working or successful or whatever. That's not what makes you who you are." Angie leaned back satisfied. "Now, drink your disgusting tea and for goodness' sake stop complaining. Then go home and work on your next book, because you're talented and it would be a waste to quit."

Rayna stared at her, a million retorts ready on her tongue, but she let them die away. She took another small sip of the tea and grimaced. "This really is terrible, you know," she said quietly.

"I know."

Rayna stood up. "Well... thanks, I guess."

"You're welcome. See you Sunday?"

Rayna nodded and let herself out.

She pulled out of the driveway, feeling slightly stung by Angie's lack of empathy. In fact, this was the first time Rayna had left Angie's feeling even worse than when she had arrived. Although, Angie had been listening to Rayna's problems for a few years now—she supposed she was bound to crack at some point.

God, was she really the type of person who was always battling unhappiness? A new thought hit her with cold horror. Was Rayna like her *mother* after all? What terrible irony that would be. The one person Rayna always swore she wouldn't end up like, and it turned out to be who she'd been resembling her whole life.

No, her mom was a drunk. That was her problem, and Rayna had never let alcohol control her like that. And yet... that wasn't her mom's only issue, was it? No, her mom was a pessimist on steroids. Her mom was never happy. Her mom was everything Angie had accused Rayna of being.

How depressing.

Rayna gripped the steering wheel so hard her hands hurt. That wouldn't be her, not anymore. That would not be Rayna's life. She would be happy and content even if it damn well killed her. She needed to be more like Angie, carefree and letting life roll off her back. What did Angie have that Rayna lacked? Probably a better childhood, but how long could Rayna pin all her problems on that? No, that was too simple of an answer. Tons of people had shitty childhoods, and they'd turned out fine, even if they were a little damaged.

Maybe it was the faith thing. Rayna could see that, how believing in something bigger than herself could help take the pressure off a bit. It wasn't like she didn't have any faith. She wrote prayer letters now and then as she had done when she had lost the baby. But she reflected now; it was usually in times of crisis or when she needed something. She didn't have that easy friendship with God that Angie had.

Rayna finally pulled up to the house and parked the van. She went in and caught sight of the glass of wine waiting by the computer. It would not be a celebratory drink anymore, but wine could have other purposes. She took it to the living room and sat on the couch, sipping it slowly, letting the rich flavor fill her mouth. She swallowed and grimaced, the taste not sitting right in her stomach. Maybe she should eat something first. She should probably start supper. Carol would be by with the kids anytime now and Ethan would probably invite Craig in. Rayna grimaced, thinking how Ethan would ask how the reviews were. She shouldn't have made such a big deal out of it.

Tears sprung in her eyes again and she shook her head. Crying again! Why was she such a mess? *Get a grip already,* Rayna told herself firmly.

This morning life couldn't have been better and now it felt like the entire world was one giant dump. Okay, that wasn't exactly true. The drought was terrible, Ethan was stressed, and they literally would not be making any money this year (any daydream of sales from her book, complete with a movie deal, saving the day were firmly squashed). So yeah, a few things could have been better. But still. She had at least felt, maybe not happy, but peaceful. Angie was right though, she shouldn't let some tiny little incident like some bad reviews get her down. Onward and upward, as they say.

Rayna forced herself up and went into the kitchen. She opened the fridge and scanned the contents, trying to find some inspiration for supper. She would get something cooking then spend some time working on the first draft of her next book. Things would be fine, she would *choose* for them to be fine.

She wasn't her mother.

She wasn't.

CHAPTER TWENTY-NINE: ETHAN

A few days later, Ethan pulled up to the driveway to see Daniel waiting for him. He was leaning against his truck with a six-pack dangling in one hand.

Ethan parked and got out. "Hey, Dan. How's it going?"

Daniel shrugged. "Want a beer?"

"Sure."

They stepped up onto the porch and sat on the bench. Ethan cracked open a beer can and took a sip. He didn't drink beer all that often; it used to be just now and then on a lunch break with his dad. He enjoyed the cool bubbly sensation running down his throat; the taste bringing to mind slow summer afternoons and golden fields.

"Rayna home?" Daniel asked.

Ethan shook his head. "She's over at my mom's picking the kids up."

They had put the cows away early today, as it was Sunday and under normal circumstances they would have taken the day off. But the cows needed to eat no matter what day it was, so they had skipped church to let them feed. Rayna had been over at his mom's for most the evening. Lately, they had been spending a lot of time together. They had softened towards each other over the years, but ever since his dad died it was like a switch was flicked and suddenly they weren't just being friendly, but friends. It was a nice change. Ethan had been tired of all the drama.

"How are you guys managing?" Daniel asked.

"We're running out of ditches to graze. Would have been nice to win those twenty bales."

Daniel grunted in agreement. The Ontario farmers had more bales than they needed this year and had donated some to the desperate farmers in Alberta. The CN Rail line had given free freight to get them over here and a lotto was held to see who would get them. Of course, Ethan hadn't won.

That would have been too easy, it would've been like getting a break for once. Obviously, that wasn't in the cards for him.

He took another swig from the can then said, "I got a cousin in Saskatchewan I might buy some bales from." It would cost an arm and a leg, which he didn't really have to give, but there weren't many options left. He was considering selling more cows, though their price wouldn't do much to cover the cost of all the winter feed they would need. He would have to get a second job somewhere.

Ethan sighed and leaned back against the bench. "Living the dream, aren't we?"

"Living the dream." Daniel raised his beer and took a sip, then laughed bitterly. "I was, anyway."

Ethan waited, suspecting with a sick twist in his gut what he was going to say next.

Daniel let out a heavy sigh. "We're selling the rest of them Thursday. Dad and I decided. We can't do it anymore. Even if it rains." He shook his head. "We just can't make it work."

Ethan stared at the can in his hands. "I'm sorry Dan."

Daniel shrugged. "It is what it is. Dad's excited to do something other than farming, I think. They might sell the farmhouse and move into town."

"What are you going to do?"

"I got a job on the rigs." He tried to sound nonchalant about it, but his hands tightened around the beer can, making it crunch beneath his grip.

"Oh."

"We need the money. It's only for a bit until I can figure something else out."

"I might be joining you. I don't know what we're going to do."

They sat in silence, drinking, until Daniel crushed his last can and stood up. "I should get going. Keep the rest." He nodded to the remaining beer and hopped off the deck.

"I'll come to the sale Thursday," Ethan called after him.

Daniel paused at his truck and nodded, unable to speak.

Ethan watched him drive away, feeling sick. Dan was the third rancher around here to sell everything. Maybe he should consider it. Find a job with less stress, normal working hours, a dependable wage... the sick feeling grew. He wasn't that kind of guy. He needed to be outside, working with his hands, and go to bed bone-tired at the end of the day. He needed the diversity of ranching, the freedom it gave. Where else could he get a job like this?

This was what he loved, even if he had to work hard, long hours through the bitter cold and blazing sunlight. Even if it was stressful and barely paid the bills most years. It was important work. People needed to eat, they needed farmers. It was a privilege to be a vital part of what made the world go around. It was also a part of his legacy; he couldn't give up all that the generations before him had built.

But there was still the fact the cows needed to eat this winter, and he had nothing to give them. He couldn't blame Daniel for deciding to let it go, even though it must be killing him. He knew Dan had the same passion for farming that he did. What would Dan do? He would hate being on the rigs. Ethan couldn't see how that would last.

Maybe they would move to Toronto, where Mila had lived. He hoped not, he could barely imagine life without Dan around. They had been together since childhood, going through school side by side and then to college in the same agriculture and livestock program. He thought of watching them drive away, leaving him here alone in Silver Heights. He could picture Mila sitting in the passenger seat with her golden hair blowing in the wind. The image in his mind shifted to the last time he had watched Mila leave Silver Heights, how he had stood with his hands dangling by his sides as her car pulled further from view.

Ethan reached down and grabbed another beer. He took a few swallows, then before he changed his mind, he pulled out his cellphone. He scanned through the contacts until he landed on her name, pressed dial and waited. After a few rings, she picked up.

"Hello?"

"Hey Mila, it's Ethan."

There was a pause. "Hey, Ethan."

"Danny was just here. He told me you guys are selling."

He could hear her sigh as she answered. "Yeah, we are. It was a tough decision. Dan's pretty heartbroken over it."

"I'm sorry. I wish there was something I could do."

"We'll be all right."

An awkward silence followed. Ethan pressed the phone hard against his ear. "Well... I guess I'll let you go," he said, feeling foolish.

"Thanks for calling, Ethan."

"Yeah, course," he said brusquely, suddenly wanting to hang up. "Take care."

"Wait, Ethan?"

"Yeah?"

"I just... I wanted to say, I guess, sorry. For all the stuff that happened between us. I know its ancient history and everything worked out in the end. But I never apologized and, well... I guess I'm just sorry. I didn't treat you well back then."

"It's fine," Ethan said, his face heating. "It was a long time ago."

"I know. I just felt like it should be said."

"It doesn't. You did nothing wrong, we just... it's fine."

"I hope one day, maybe, it can be less awkward between us."

"It is, it's fine," he said again. "Have a good night, Mila."

"You too, Ethan."

He flipped his phone shut and stared at it. Why did he do that? Why did he call her? Ethan shook his head and leaned back with the beer resting on his knee. She was right, everything had worked out in the end. They really didn't need to hash out what had happened between them again. He meant it when he said she had done nothing wrong. If anything, he should be thanking her. If she hadn't turned him down and walked away, he never would have married Rayna. Never would have had Emma, Grace and Ben.

He had loved her once, and maybe a part of him always would. But it was a small part, like the fondness for an old childhood memory. Sometimes, something reminded him of her, of when they were together and it stopped him for a moment. He could remember so clearly what it was like to be there and feel and think the way he once did. But it was easier to let go as time went on, easier to snap back to the present and forget it all.

Ethan chugged the rest of his drink and threw the empty can in the box just as Rayna pulled up in the van. He got up, a little unsteadily, and went over to help unbuckle the kids from their car seats.

"Drinking?" Rayna asked. She raised her eyebrows at the empty cans on the porch.

"Daniel was over." Ethan carried Grace into the house, her long limbs dangling as her head rested against his shoulder. "You took a while coming home."

"We were visiting." Rayna hitched Ben up on her hip and held Emma's hand, taking them to the bedroom. Bedtime went smoother than usual, since the kids were exhausted from staying up past their bedtime. They moved like zombies as he and Rayna gently forced them through the motions of changing and brushing their teeth before putting them to bed. Ethan watched from the doorway as Rayna tucked the bedding tightly around each of them. He went to their bedroom and laid back on the bed, feeling suddenly exhausted.

Rayna came in a few minutes later and sat down heavily beside him. "Mom wants to know if we'll go over for dinner tomorrow. I said sure."

"Okay."

"Oh, and you will never guess what she told me."

"What?"

"Apparently, Chloe is moving back."

Ethan's eyebrows rose. "Really?"

"She hasn't told me yet, but I guess she took a job at the newspaper. Apparently, she's been talking to Craig a lot. Mom thinks as soon as she moves Craig will ask her out. I'm going to call her tomorrow and get the details."

"Huh."

Daniel quitting farming, Chloe moving back and getting together with Craig again... it was as if Silver Heights was descending into chaos.

"So, what did he want?" Rayna asked, leaning back.

"Who?"

"Danny. When he came over."

"They're selling," Ethan said.

"Everything?" Rayna's eyes widened. "That's terrible. What are they going to do?"

"I don't know. They'll figure something out."

Rayna shook her head. "That's really too bad. I should call Mila."

"I called her." The words slipped out of him. He glanced at Rayna and saw her eyebrows raise slightly.

"Oh? How was that?"

Definitely an icy tone. He shouldn't have told her.

"Fine, I just wanted to see how she was," Ethan said.

"Very considerate of you."

"I thought you guys were friends."

"We are, doesn't mean you two need to be."

"We're not."

"Why did you call her then?"

"I don't know."

Rayna didn't respond.

Ethan sighed and tried to change the subject. "Dan might go work on the rigs for a bit. Sucks for him, he won't like it at all. But who knows, maybe that will be me soon." The words tasted bitter in his mouth. He knew a few guys who worked in oil for a living. They didn't seem to mind it, but they were gone for months at a time to the far remote places of Alberta, doing work no one liked, covered in grime and freezing in the cold. While they made more money than Ethan ever would, he never envied them and he really didn't want to join them.

"Don't say that. It's going to be fine," Rayna said.

Ethan didn't want her empty optimism right now. He wanted to complain, for her to be as worried as he was.

"I don't think you get how bad things are," he said testily.

Rayna abruptly sat up and looked down at him. "Of course I do, Ethan. I've been right here beside you this entire time. I know what's going on."

"Then you should know that it's not guaranteed everything will be okay," Ethan said, his body rigid.

"Pouting about it won't fix anything."

Ethan got off the bed and started towards the door.

"Where are you going?"

"To check the fence."

"It's fine Ethan, it doesn't need to be checked. Can you sit down? I need to talk to you about something."

Ethan turned. "What?"

What now?

"Can you sit?"

"Just tell me, Ray."

"Fine," Rayna said. "I'm pregnant."

Ethan blinked. "What?"

"I'm pregnant. I took the test this morning."

"You're pregnant."

Rayna nodded. "I know it's not the best timing but..."

"Not the best timing? Rayna, we can't have a baby right now. I can't do all this work by myself."

"I can still help for a while. It's going to be fine."

Ethan clenched his hands into fists. If he heard *'it's going to be fine'* one more time, he was going to hit something.

"I'm not having my pregnant wife out working on the ranch. Don't be stupid," he snapped.

"Don't call me names. This isn't my fault, you know."

"Oh, and I suppose it's mine?"

"Well," said Rayna. "You're the one who wanted a quickie with the kids outside the door."

"This is just perfect," Ethan spat. "This is exactly what I needed."

"Calm down!"

"Don't tell me to calm down, Rayna. How is this supposed to work? I'm going to have to get a second job. I can't do it all on my own, and I can't afford to hire someone to help."

"I don't know, Ethan. It's not like I planned this. I don't know how it will work. What do you want me to do?"

"I want you to be helpful!"

"*Helpful?*" Rayna stood up, her frame shaking. "All I have done is help you. How dare you suggest that I haven't been..."

"Well, you sure won't be now."

"I *told* you, I can still do a lot for a few months."

"And risk losing another baby? Maybe you're willing to take that risk, but I'm not."

Rayna froze.

Ethan sighed. "I didn't mean..."

"Don't," Rayna said in a deadly whisper. "You selfish, self-centered bastard. Just don't."

Rayna pushed past him and left the room. Ethan heard the front door slam shut. He said a word that usually came from Rayna's mouth, and aimed a frustrated kick to the night table, sending it crashing. The lamp broke as it hit the ground and Rayna's books scattered across the carpet.

"Daddy?"

Ethan started. Emma was standing wide-eyed in the doorway.

"Emma, honey, go back to bed." He went over to her, she took a step backwards and his chest tightened. "It's okay. I'm sorry, honey." He knelt and gently pulled her in for a hug. She stood stiff as a board in his arms. "Go back to bed, okay?" He led her to her bedroom and tucked her back under the covers.

"Are you okay?" Emma whispered.

"Of course. Have a goodnight sweetie." He kissed her forehead and backed out of the room, gently closing the door.

Ethan sighed, resting his head against the frame. What was wrong with him? He'd just yelled at his wife for being pregnant with his child. What kind of man did that? Ethan pushed off the doorway and went back into the bedroom. He bent and set the nightstand back upright and carefully set the broken lamp on top, then started picking up all the fallen books.

He had overreacted.

He knew that.

He was just so bloody tired. Tired of trying to solve one crisis after another. There was constantly something to worry about, some event outside of his control which made him feel like he was running backwards instead of forward. They would find a way through though. They always did. He should go find Rayna and apologize. Maybe drink a glass of water to lift the buzzing feeling in his head... His thoughts froze as his fingers rested on Rayna's writing notebook that had landed open when it fell. His eyes fastened on the words at the top of the page.

I can't help but feel it's all been a mistake.

He picked it up.

CHAPTER THIRTY: RAYNA

Rayna took long, angry strides down the driveway, not paying any attention to the direction she was going.

How dare he.

What gave him the right to say such things and react like that? Yes, he was stressed, she could give him some leeway because of that. But it didn't excuse everything. Actually, scratch that, he didn't deserve that excuse. She was stressed too and did she go around biting people's heads off? No, she didn't.

Not today, anyway.

Rayna followed her feet and turned off the road into a field. A trail of dust swirled behind her. In every direction grasshoppers flitted around, some crunching beneath her steps. She was sick of them. She was sick of this drought, of the worries and nothing ever being easy.

"Go away!" Rayna yelled, stomping down on a few unlucky ones, the sickening crack of their bodies leaving a smear of yellow on her sneaker. The others ignored her and kept hopping along in search of any food left in the bare field. She huffed a sigh and plunked down. The dry ground scraped at her arms as she leaned back on her elbows. The sun was just peeking through dense grey clouds as it began its descent into the horizon. The air around her felt heavy, but maybe it was her imagination. Maybe it was her anger that made her chest feel like it was pushing against a weight.

Rayna looked down at her stomach, imagining the tiny grain of a baby in there. She hadn't been the least bit surprised when the test read positive this morning. After being pregnant four times, she had gotten to know her body well enough to notice when it was being shared. Even though she knew it wasn't the best timing for them, she couldn't help but feel a little thrill of excitement when the test confirmed her suspicion.

Another baby.

Another addition to their family. What would this one be like? Wild and crazy like the first two, or soft and gentle like her precious Ben? It was a good thing. Of course, it was a good thing. She pressed her hand delicately on the curve of her stomach. It had grown soft over the years of childbearing, and the slight pouch of her belly sat ready and waiting to expand yet again with new life.

"There're some things you should know," she said, patting where she imagined the baby rested. "First off, life can really suck sometimes. Things don't always go how you want them to. And Mom and Dad will fight now and then, but don't worry. We do love each other. For better or for worse."

It was a different kind of love than when they'd first started out, back when she was aimless and lost, needing an escape. Now she felt a little surer of herself, more capable and independent than before. It was strange thinking back to how it all began. To all the steps she had taken and the numerous twists in the road, which had led her here, to this moment, sitting in the dust in a field in the middle of nowhere.

What was it Angie had practically yelled at her? Happiness is a choice, and no matter what she did or where she ended up, she wouldn't be happy unless she chose to be. It probably made sense. The more Rayna thought about it, the more she realized she didn't know if she believed in fate necessarily. She didn't know if everyone's lives were perfectly mapped out and all one had to do was follow the signs and they would fulfill their life's purpose. She wasn't even sure if she believed God had a set plan for everyone. Maybe he had a path he wished people would take, but was she here because she was meant to be? Or was it simply because of the choices she had made?

That's what it really came down to: choices. Most people seemed to think there was a right or a wrong one to make, but Rayna wasn't sure about that. Maybe everything would have been fine if she'd never married Ethan and she went off on a different path. It could have been. But despite all the difficulties over the past years, this place was her home. She never wanted to lose what she and Ethan had. She wanted to hold tightly to it, to her family, to the land and the people here.

"You're going to like it here," Rayna said to the little fetus. "And your daddy is going to love you, don't worry about that. He's just stressed right now. But as soon as you come out, you will see what a great dad he is."

Ethan was an amazing dad. Rayna knew it the moment he held Emma for the first time. She understood the bond between a mother and a baby. They shared the same body for nine long months, and then the baby fed from the mom's breast for the better part of a year. Her babies were extensions of herself, pulled to her by the scent on her skin. But the bond between a father and a baby was something else, something special. Every time a new baby had been born, Ethan took to them like they had always been a part of him. Rayna felt a wave of affection whenever she thought of him cradling their soft newborn in his thick, callused hands. She knew it would be the same for this new baby.

The sun had properly begun to set now, the light around her beginning to fade into a light grey, but the heat from the day still lingered on her skin. She should head back. Ethan hated when she stormed out in the middle of an argument, but sometimes she needed some space to think and calm down.

Rayna sighed and forced herself to stand. "All right, let's go. Thanks for the chat, little guy." She gave her stomach another pat then made her way out of the field and down the road towards home. She walked slowly, enjoying the peace before heading back into the storm. She hoped he had calmed down by now too. She hated when they went to bed angry and laid stiffly on opposite sides of the bed, both of them determined not to touch. She preferred being able to move next to him and curl against his warmth as she drifted to sleep.

Rayna reached the house and cautiously entered. Seeing he wasn't in the living room, she plodded down the hall to their bedroom. She opened the door and squared her shoulders.

"Hey, Ethan. I'm sorry for leaving, I just..." She stopped at the sight of him sitting on the edge of their bed, holding her writing notebook in his hand. "What are you doing with that?"

Please, don't say reading it.

"I hoped this would be it, the place I was searching for, but it's not at all how I imagined." Ethan read from the page. He looked at her. "That was the nicest part."

"Ethan..." Rayna clutched the doorknob so hard her hand hurt. She remembered writing that, the hurt and the heartache she had been battling. Her frustration had spilled forth in ink on the page.

Her cheeks flushed.

"Is this how you really feel?" He held up the journal.

"No, Ethan, that wasn't ever meant to be read."

"But you did write it," Ethan said evenly. There was no fight in his voice; he sat slumped on the edge of the bed, clutching her notebook. Rayna had never seen him like this, so defeated. Not even after his dad had died.

"I did write that, but it was a long time ago." She was desperate to explain.

"What am I doing all this for, Rayna?" He asked looking at her. "What are we fighting so hard to keep? If this is how you feel?"

"It's not." Rayna came into the room and sat beside him. "It's not, Ethan. I wrote this when I was in a terrible place, after we lost the baby. It was a long time ago."

"There are others like it."

"I know." She gently took the notebook from him. "Writing is how I process things. It helps me get my feelings out so they aren't bouncing around in my head all the time. I don't mean half the things I say."

"Didn't seem like that."

"It's true. Ethan, I love you. I don't regret a single thing about us. I know these past few months have been hard, but for me, they've been some of the best. For us, like, I just feel like we are in this thing together you know? With all the stressful and hard things, I feel so peaceful, and I know I don't feel that way a lot... I don't know if I'm making sense. I do love you, Ethan. I love you and Silver Heights and the life we built together. I really didn't mean..."

Ethan moved forward and cut her off by pressing his lips against hers. She jerked back in surprise, and then she leaned into it, trying to communicate how much she meant what she had just said. He cupped his hand against the side of her face and moved his lips slowly, lingering over her own. He pulled back, so they were nose-to-nose and stared right into her eyes. "I don't want to fight anymore, Ray."

"I don't either."

"You know, I knew when I saw you for the first time that I'd love you forever. With your dark curls and chocolate eyes, wearing that green dress. I knew then."

"You remember the colour of the dress?"

"Of course, it was a very sexy dress."

"It was your sister's."

"Don't ruin it for me."

Rayna grinned. "You're lying anyway. You couldn't have known then."

"I did," Ethan vowed. He rested his forehead against hers, his whispered breath hot on her face. "I'm sorry for what I said. It's amazing that you're pregnant."

"I'm sorry too."

Ethan froze then tilted his head, his eyebrows furrowing. "Do you hear that?"

"Hear what?" Rayna twisted, listening. A light tapping noise was slowly getting louder, dancing across the roof and hitting the window.

"Is it...?" Ethan peered out the window.

"Raining," Rayna breathed.

They both jolted up and raced out to the door, pausing breathlessly on the porch. Rain fell down in a steady stream, getting heavier and heavier as they watched. Ethan let out a loud whoop and grabbed Rayna's hand, pulling her with him out onto the yard. Within seconds they were soaked, their hair plastered to their faces and their clothes weighed down against their skin. Ethan spun her clumsily around in a circle, his feet unsteady in the increasingly muddy yard. The tense moments of before melted away as their laughter rang out louder than normal with long-awaited relief. Rayna lifted her face upwards to the sky, letting the droplets hit her face and slide down her chin, washing away the dust and the grime, the worries and the doubts. Letting it wash everything clean and make it new again.

****

The rain didn't last very long, pouring only a couple inches into the thirsty ground that gratefully accepted it. It was enough though; in one night Silver Heights was transformed. The dust settled, so the roads were no longer like driving through a desert storm, and the plants lifted a little as a bit of life was soaked into them. Rayna took the kids for a walk the next day, drinking in the clear, light breeze. It was as if the land had given a loud sigh—the birds seemed to chirp a little louder and there was a bright, clean scent filling the air with irrepressible optimism.

Rayna smiled as she walked, watching Emma and Grace race ahead as she pushed Ben in a stroller. It was a beautiful day, and she was full of energy and life. She even felt lighter; while there were still challenges needing to be faced, they seemed a little more manageable today. It wasn't just the rain. It was her, finally feeling a little bit settled. Today everything felt right–things between her and Ethan were better than they had in a while, refreshed like the mushy ground beneath her rubber boots. Not only that, but despite her earlier disappointment she found she wasn't quite done with writing. As she walked, little tidbits of sentences were starting to form, and she itched to write them down. If the crowds and critics didn't love her writing, she would learn to be okay with that. It always was more for herself anyway.

Today she was content.

Happy.

It felt good to be happy.

Rayna walked on, slowly savouring the joy that filled her insides. One thing she realized was feelings were temporary, and there probably was a part of her which would always battle restlessness. She might always have to fight the unhappiness, which had stuck to her since her childhood. But right now, she didn't have to fight anything, and she was going to drink her fill of it. She stopped as her eye caught something and she bent down, her fingers grazing the earth below.

There, buried in the dead, brown grass; a little green stem. New life pushing its way through, as it always seemed to do. A little sign of hope.

Rayna straightened, feeling satisfied, and looked around, soaking in the beauty of the place she had come to love as her home. The wide-open skies, endless fields and sounds of nature were more welcoming than any city street she had ever lived on. This was where she belonged. This was home. With Ethan, the kids, Angie, Tom and her new mom, Carol. Even with Danny and Mila. With all of Silver Heights standing beside her, and Jim and her grandma keeping each other company while they looked down from above. It really was all she had been searching for; she'd just never realized she had already found it.

"Thanks," she whispered to the heavens, and then she turned and hurried after her children, feeling ready for all that would come next.

ACKNOWLEDGMENTS

First off, I need to thank my mom and my sister, Paige, for their never-ending encouragement and support. They read all my first drafts of everything (even when they don't want to) and are the first people I bounce ideas off of. Thank you so much for the hours spent editing, listening, consoling and believing in me. Thank you also to my dad for answering all my ranching questions and giving details about how he survived the drought of 2002. Also, to my sister, Raelyn, for all your hard work designing my beautiful website and cover. I would be lost without you! And to my other sisters, Brooke and Mya, (yes, I have a lot of sisters) thank you for being so excited and supporting me every step of the way.

Thank you to the Red Deer Writer's Ink group for inspiring me to take my writing seriously and for being the first non-family members that I shared my writing with, and for clapping after I did! And to my first beta readers, Margo and Laura, thank you guys for being willing to read my manuscript and for not laughing at me. Also, to the Women's Fiction Writing Association, I can't tell you how valuable being a member has been for me. Thank you for answering all my questions, providing so many learning opportunities and for all your support. I wouldn't be published if it wasn't for you.

A special thanks to my husband Matt, even though you never finish reading a thing I write you are always telling me what a great writer I am and believe in me more than I do. Also, I won our bet. And to my girls Eden and Hazel, thanks for teaching me to operate through sleep deprivation and limited alone time. Very valuable stuff. And of course, a big thank you to Black Rose Writing for taking me on and making my dreams come true.

Last but certainly not least, thank you to you, Reader, for picking up this book and taking a chance on a new author. I hope you enjoyed it and that we can travel many places together over the years.

ABOUT THE AUTHOR

J.L. Cole resides on an acreage in the beautiful Brownfield, AB area with her husband and two young daughters. When she isn't busy chasing her children, she can be found helping on the family ranch or writing at her kitchen table. *Silver Heights* is her first novel but certainly not her last.

To keep up-to-date with the latest news check out her website; www.jl-cole.com or follow her on social media.

NOTE FROM THE AUTHOR

Word-of-mouth is crucial for any author to succeed. If you enjoyed *Silver Heights*, please leave a review online—anywhere you are able. Even if it's just a sentence or two. It would make all the difference and would be very much appreciated.

Thanks!
J.L. Cole

Thank you so much for reading one of our **Women's Fiction** novels. If you enjoyed the experience, please check out our recommendation for your next great read!

City in a Forest by Ginger Pinholster

Finalist for a *Santa Fe Writers Project Literary Award*

"Ginger Pinholster, a master of significant detail, weaves her struggling characters' pasts, present, and futures into a breathtaking, beautiful novel in *City in a Forest*. –*IndieReader Approved*